Praise for the Books of Linda Reilly

"A very fun cat-centric novel, along with strong writing, fun characters, and a crowd-pleasing finale." —*Kings River Life Magazine*

"I thoroughly enjoyed this puzzler of a mystery. Reilly cooks up a perfect recipe of murder and mayhem in this charming cozy." —Jenn McKinlay, *New York Times* bestselling author

"Smart, sassy, and a little bit scary. Everything a good cozy should be!" —Laura Childs, *New York Times* bestselling author

"Foodies and mystery lovers will come for the red herrings and stay for the cheese." —*Kirkus Reviews*

"Masterful misdirection coupled with a pace that can't be beat, Linda Reilly has grilled up a winner for sure!" —J. C. Eaton, author of the Sophie Kimball Mysteries, The Wine Trail Mysteries, and The Marcie Rayner Mysteries

"A well-crafted and fun start to a new series! Carly and her crew serve mouth-watering grilled cheese sandwiches while solving crime in a quaint Vermont town. Plenty of twists and turns to keep you turning the pages and guessing the killer to the very end." —Tina Kashian, author of the Kebab Kitchen Mysteries

"A delightful and determined heroine, idyllic small town, and buffet of worthy suspects make this hearty whodunnit an enticing start to a decidedly delectable new series! This sandwich-centric cozy will leave readers drooling for more!" —Bree Baker, author of the Seaside Café Mysteries

Books by Linda Reilly

Grilled Cheese Mysteries

Up to No Gouda
No Parm No Foul
Cheddar Late Than Dead
Brie Careful What You Wish For
You Feta Watch Out
Edam and Weep

Cat Lady Mysteries

Escape Claws
Claws of Death
Claws for Celebration
Claws of Action
The Girl with the Kitten Tattoo

Deep Fried Mysteries

Fillet of Murder
Out of the Dying Pan
A Frying Shame

Apple Mariani Mysteries

Some Enchanted Murder

Edam
and
Weep

A Grilled Cheese Mystery

Linda Reilly

BEYOND THE PAGE
PUBLISHING

Edam and Weep
Linda Reilly
Copyright © 2025 by Linda Reilly
Cover design and illustration by Dar Albert, Wicked Smart Designs

Beyond the Page Books
are published by
Beyond the Page Publishing
www.beyondthepagepub.com

ISBN: 978-1-966322-21-4

This book is for all those who devote their time, energy, and resources to saving and rescuing animals. In my personal book, you're all heroes.

ACKNOWLEDGMENTS

I have so many people to thank for helping me pull this book together. To my editor, Bill Harris, I can't imagine where the Grilled Cheese series would be without your guidance, encouragement, and spot-on editing. To Dar Albert of Wicked Smart Designs, thank you for bringing Balsam Dell to life in your gorgeous cover designs. You consistently nail all the details that make the town so special. To my friends and fellow authors, Debra Sennefelder and Jenny Kales, a heartfelt thanks for brainstorming with me, and for always boosting my morale. I value your friendship more than you know. To Wendi Murphy, my friend and culinary advisor, thank you for bringing the book's recipes to fruition—and for making the taste testing so much fun! A huge hug to my friend Judy Jones, for cheering me on when I needed it most and for always listening to my convoluted plot ideas. Your input is forever invaluable. A shout-out to Stephanie Moussa, my social media diva, who keeps my postings current when I would rather write! And to Susie Shepardson, my lifelong friend, for always being there.

CHAPTER 1

CARLY HALE GRINNED AT HER MOM, THEN GAVE HER A QUICK SQUEEZE. "Well, if you aren't the spitting image of *I Love Lucy*, I don't know who is."

Rhonda Hale Clark patted the carroty curls poking out from beneath her lime green head scarf. "I told you I was going all out for this gig, didn't I?" She did a fast little twirl, sending her full skirt swirling around her knees like an open umbrella. "Oops." Her curls tilted slightly, and she reached up to adjust them. "This silly wig keeps shifting. I'll be right back." She dashed off into the corridor that led to the restroom area.

The "gig" was the local high school's fundraiser for a new gymnasium floor. Twice during the past winter, the aging floor had been damaged by water pipe breaks. Since classes had ended for the school year the week before, the gym was available for the "Nifty Fifties Diner Bash" the school was sponsoring.

Moving her gaze slowly around the gym, Carly smiled at the stunning transformation. The kids who'd volunteered for the event had created a replica of a 1950s diner, complete with movie posters from the era. In the center of the gym, makeshift dining booths had been set up, each of which could seat four people. One of the kids' dads had lent his prized vintage jukebox—a working marvel of lights and color stocked with old records.

Carly had volunteered, along with at least two dozen other vendors, to serve food reminiscent of the era. In keeping with the theme, she was making simple grilled cheese sandwiches using American cheese and white bread—a staple of 1950s diners. And because she was absorbing the cost of the bread and the cheese, every penny she made on the sales would be donated to the fundraiser.

Carly was the owner of Carly's Grilled Cheese Eatery, a popular restaurant in Balsam Dell, Vermont. She'd opened the eatery nearly three years earlier, after her husband's untimely death had sent her back to her hometown to heal. As her grief subsided, her dream of owning a grilled cheese restaurant grew. She took over the lease of a failing ice cream parlor and the rest was cheesy history.

Her assigned table, at one corner of the gym, was near the entrance to the hallway that led to the school's vending machines and restrooms. Several other vendors were setting up their tables, all of which were graced with red-and-white-checkered tablecloths. Carly was anxious to sample some of the offerings, if she could get a quick break during the event.

At the table next to Carly, a late twentyish woman garbed in a white, sailor-style halter dress was busy setting up her "Pie by the Slice" display. Behind the woman was a wheeled cooler. Her lips coated in candy pink gloss, she smiled at Carly. "Hi, I'm Tillie Lloyd. I think this will be great fun, don't you?"

Carly returned her smile. "Hi, Tillie. I'm Carly, and it's nice to meet you. And yes, I do think it'll be fun. A blast from the past, as my mom likes to say."

Tillie's blue eyes, which came close to matching the streak in her blond hair, sparkled like sapphires. "You're the grilled cheese gal, right?"

"That's me, but I also love pie. What kinds will you be selling?"

"I'm keeping it simple. Apple pies and lemon chiffon pies. What do you think?"

"Perfect for the era," Carly enthused, though she was sure people ate other types of pie in the fifties as well.

"By the way," Tillie said, "you look adorbs in that poodle skirt. And your hair! How did you do that?"

After washing her hair the night before, Carly had used bobby pins to secure circular curls in her short, chestnut-colored hair. When she brushed them out in the morning, she had the old-style bob she'd hoped for.

"I slept in bobby pins," Carly said with a laugh. "And I bought the poodle skirt online." She imitated her mom's twirl, making Tillie giggle.

Carly reached beneath her table and pulled out her sign. On it was a chalk sketch of a grilled cheese and two pickle chips resting on a blue plate. The words *Grilled Cheese 50 cents* were written in script along the bottom. Her bestie, Gina Tomasso, a greeting card designer, had made the sign for her.

"Hey, that's cool," Tillie praised, then sighed. "Darn it. I should've made a sign, too."

On the table perpendicular to Carly's, a scowling man who looked to be in his late thirties had set up a large cardboard display of the beverages he'd be selling. His straight dark hair was receding from his forehead, and his brown eyes flashed with anger. He shot a glare at Carly, then stalked off toward the restrooms.

Tillie wrinkled her nose. "What's his problem?"

Carly shrugged. "I don't have a clue. I've never seen him before."

Her heart skipped when she saw another man coming toward her. Her fiancé, Ari Mitchell, was lugging the portable griddle she'd be using for the event. The sight of his dreamy smile and warm brown eyes always made her insides flutter.

"Hey." He set the griddle on a corner of the table, then gave her a quick kiss. His cheeks flushed when he saw Carly's neighbor gawking at them.

"Ari, this is Tillie," Carly introduced. "She'll be selling pie by the slice."

Ari grinned and shook Tillie's hand. "Oh, man, I love pie. Nice to meet you."

Tillie beamed. "I'll make sure I save an extra-large slice for you."

Ari located the floor outlet beneath Carly's table and plugged in the griddle. "The parking lot is already filling up," he said. "I lucked out and found a spot near the rear entrance to the gym. They're keeping the door unlocked during the event to make it easier for vendors to get in and out. I'll be right back with the cooler." He dashed off.

"He's a real cutie," Tillie commented. "Your hubby?"

"My almost hubby," Carly clarified. "Our wedding is a little over a month away, and I still have about a thousand tasks left on my to-do list."

Rhonda emerged from the restroom corridor, this time sporting a crimson scarf.

"Why did you change your scarf?" Carly asked. "I loved the green one."

"Well, the green one didn't love me," Rhonda huffed. "The more I toyed with it, the worse it looked. This one's longer, so I had better luck with it. Do you know I had to watch an online video to figure out how to make all the knots and twists? I don't know how those gals in the fifties did it with such ease."

"Rhonda!" Tillie went over and hugged Carly's mom. "I'm so glad to see you."

"Tillie! I didn't know you'd be here." Rhonda took the woman's hand.

"Are you . . . Carly's mom?" Tillie asked her, bouncing her gaze from one to the other.

"I sure am," Rhonda said proudly. "Carly, Tillie is one of the library's volunteers. She reads to the little ones every other Saturday morning. They adore the way she does the voices of the animals."

"I enjoy it," Tillie said, blushing at the compliment.

Rhonda rubbed her hands together. "Okay, what can I do to help?"

"You could set out paper plates and napkins," Carly said. "Maybe open that big jar of pickle chips? Once I start grilling, I'll have my hands full."

"I'm on it."

At that moment, the scowling man who'd stormed out earlier returned, this time wheeling a portable fridge on a dolly. He rested the dolly behind his table and plopped a power strip on top of it. He pointed beneath Carly's table. "I need access to an outlet, and that's the only one within fifteen feet of my table. Why don't you switch tables with me?"

"I'm sorry," Carly said evenly. "But this table was assigned to me. I can show you the chart—"

"I don't need the chart. I need that outlet. You need to switch spots with me."

Carly felt her temper bubble. Was he totally clueless? Did he not notice that she had an electric griddle? Forcing herself not to react to his rudeness, she said, "I'm afraid I can't do that. I have a portable grill, and it needs to be plugged in."

"Is that so? Well, I have a fridge, and *that* needs to be plugged in."

"Did you write that on your form?" Carly asked him. "That you'll need access to an outlet?"

3

Each participating vendor had been given a form to complete, describing their product and their requirements for setup.

He averted his gaze. "No one gave me a form. If they did, I never got it."

Carly doubted that. His expression had all the telltale signs of a big fat lie.

She decided to try a different approach. Her hand extended, she smiled and went over to him. "I'm Carly Hale. I'm sorry if we got off on the wrong foot. And you are?"

Ignoring her hand, he said, "Brice Keaton. Then I guess you and me will have to share that floor outlet. I brought a power strip. I have another one in my SUV if I need it. I might have to hook two together."

Carly knew that wouldn't fly with Andy Fields, the event coordinator. Andy was an earth science teacher at the high school who doubled as assistant basketball coach. The few times she'd spoken to him, he'd emphasized safety. In several areas, the gym floor had buckled from water damage. A power strip would only increase the risk of someone tripping and falling. Not to mention the electrical hazard.

"Excuse me," Brice said brusquely. His power strip in hand, he brushed past Carly so roughly that she had to step backward to keep her balance.

Fury blazing in her eyes, Rhonda started toward him, but Ari was already there. Ari had walked up behind Brice so quietly Carly had barely noticed him.

"What are you doing?"

Brice jerked his head up. "Oh, um, I'm plugging in my power strip." He aimed his chin in the direction of his display. "I don't have an outlet near my table, so I'll have to share this one."

Ari bent down on one knee and lifted the power strip. He turned it over, then rose to his feet and handed it to Brice. "You can't use this for our griddle. For starters, it doesn't have a high enough wattage capacity. Even if it did, plugging in a second appliance would create a safety hazard."

"Oh, really?" Brice shot him a dark look. "And I suppose you're an expert?"

Carly stifled a smile. She didn't usually approve of having Ari, or anyone, speak for her. In this case, however, she was glad to let Ari run with it.

"I guess you could call me an expert," Ari said. "I'm a licensed electrician with seventeen years' experience. Does that qualify?"

Brice's face turned tomato red. "This whole stupid thing isn't fair," he sputtered, throwing his power strip on his own table. "First off, they stick me in this corner with no outlet. Then I find out I'm barely ten feet away from the soda machine in the hallway. How can I make money for the school if the soda machine is cheaper?"

Ari was quiet for a moment, then he walked over and examined Brice's display. "You know, you've got a really cool sign here. I like the way you made a collage of old-time soda bottles."

"My girlfriend made that," he said flatly.

"Well, it looks great. Personally, I don't think you'll have any trouble selling beverages. Everyone attending knows this is a fundraiser." He smiled and stuck out his hand. "I'm Ari, by the way."

Brice ignored Ari's hand. "Brice, and a cool sign doesn't solve my problem, does it? I need to keep my drinks cool."

Ari cupped his chin with his hand. "Okay, here's a thought. I have another large cooler in my truck. If you want to use that instead of the fridge, I'll be happy to pick up some ice for you at the gas station. It's only a minute drive from here."

At that point, Carly stepped up next to Ari and spoke directly to Brice. "Just my two cents, but I think having an open cooler with the soda bottles stuck into the ice will be way more enticing than you having to remove them from a fridge where people can't see them. Customers like to see what they're buying, right?"

Brice started to respond when a thirtyish man came striding toward them, clipboard in hand. Garbed in a blue and white bowling shirt and pleated trousers, Andy Fields grinned at everyone and said, "Hey, everyone. How's everything going over here?" His eyes widened when he spotted Rhonda. "Rhonda! How nice to see you. I didn't know you'd be here."

Rhonda gave him a faint nod. "Hi, Andy."

"We're doing great," Carly said, "but I'm afraid we're having an issue with an electrical outlet."

"Listen." Brice shook his finger in Andy's face, then pointed it at Ari. "This dude tells me I can't use my power strip in *her* outlet. So where do I plug in my fridge?"

His face reddening, Andy began shuffling through his clipboard pages. "Mr. Keaton, please calm down. Let me check your form. I don't recall you mentioning a fridge—"

"So what if I didn't? You obviously didn't use your brain, did you? How else did you expect me to keep my soda cold?"

Ari made a calming gesture with his palms. "Keep it respectful, okay?"

"Ah, here it is." Andy unclipped the form Brice had filled out. Carly was sure it was the form he claimed he never received.

Carly sidled closer to Andy and sneaked a peek over his arm. Andy was right. Brice had left the "requirements" section blank. In spiky handwriting, he'd filled in only the bare minimum.

His mouth twitching nervously, Andy showed the form to Brice. "You wrote 'soda,' that's all. I'm afraid—"

"I don't care what I wrote," Brice said, moving closer to Andy. "You need to fix this, okay?"

Andy's face blanched. By that time, a few curious onlookers had gathered. One of them, a young man with muscled arms garbed in a white T-shirt and dungarees, stepped forward. "Everything okay here?" His hair slicked back à la

James Dean, he flashed a winning smile at Brice. "Hey, man, that sign is a gas. I'll come by later for a Moxie." He turned and tapped Andy's shoulder. "Let me know if you need any help, Andy. I'll be hanging around all day. Stay cool, everyone!"

Carly wished he hadn't used that particular phrase, but somehow it seemed to diffuse the tension. Or maybe Brice didn't want to take his chances with a man who looked in such excellent shape.

Looking defeated, Brice went behind his own table. He motioned Ari over. They spoke briefly, then Ari said to Carly, "I'll be right back. I'm going to head out for some ice and bring my other cooler in."

She shook her head and smiled. Even after Brice had treated him so rudely, Ari still wanted to help him. "You are the kindest man on earth, you know that?"

He winked at her and strode off.

Andy tucked his clipboard under his arm, then rocked back on his heels. "Well, um, okey dokey then. I'll leave all you people to set up. Rest assured, I'll be back later for a grilled cheese and a nice slice of pie!"

He hurried off, clearly anxious to get away.

Carly glanced up at the gym's wall clock. The event would be starting in twenty minutes. She wasn't sure if anyone would want a grilled cheese at ten in the morning, but she was ready to serve if they did.

Rhonda, who'd held her tongue during Brice's tirade, plopped a stack of napkins on Carly's table. "It was all I could do not to sock that guy," she muttered in Carly's ear. "If he pulls another stunt like that, he'll have me to answer to. And it won't be pretty."

Uh-oh. Rhonda was in mama lion mode.

"Mom, it's okay," Carly soothed. "It all worked out, right?"

Rhonda huffed out a breath, then gave a tight smile as she fanned out the napkins. "Is Ari sticking around to help you make grilled cheese?"

"No. He has a project at home he wants to finish. Which is fine, because Grant will be here in an hour or so," she said with a grin. "I'm so glad he's home for the summer. It'll feel like old times."

Grant Robinson had been Carly's original grill cook. To her chagrin, he'd left Balsam Dell for Boston the previous September to begin his first semester at culinary school. Carly was happy that he was fulfilling his dream, but she missed him terribly. His unique grilled cheese creations were still popular at the eatery. Even more important, he'd become a close and supportive friend. She still thought of him as part of her team.

Because he was staying in town with his folks for the summer, he'd landed a coveted job assisting the head chef at the Balsam Dell Inn, where Carly and Ari's summer wedding would be held.

"It'll be nice to see Grant again." Rhonda tied an apron around her waist.

"You miss him, don't you?"

"A lot," Carly said, reaching into her cooler for a tub of butter. "I haven't seen him since his spring break. By the way, how do you know Andy Fields?"

Rhonda averted her gaze. "If you must know, miss nosy pants, I used to visit the high school classes every month with reading recommendations. Some of the books weren't available in the school library, so I would encourage the kids to visit our beautiful town library."

"Do you still do that?" Carly asked her.

"No, I um, got too busy with other things. Our senior librarian took over for me. A bit grudgingly, I have to admit. She's not great with teenagers."

Carly shook her head and laughed. "Wow. The things I don't know about you. Are you also an undercover spy?" she teased.

"Possibly." Rhonda wiggled her eyebrows.

Carly glanced up to see Ari walking toward them, his arms laden with his spare cooler and a large bag of ice. Carly grabbed the ice from him so he could set down the cooler on Brice's table.

Brice mumbled a thank-you and took the ice from Carly. Still unsmiling, he opened the bag and dumped the ice into the cooler. After that he began tucking soda bottles into the ice, arranging them in a way that was visually appealing. Carly suspected he'd actually liked Ari's idea but was too pigheaded to admit it.

"Hey, I'll give you a buzz later to see how things are going," Ari said, popping a kiss on Carly's cheek. "Text if you need anything, okay?"

"I will."

Watching him leave, she marveled at how lucky she was to be marrying Ari.

Shortly after that, a scratchy sound erupted from the overhead speakers, followed by Andy's cheery voice. "Testing. testing. Good morning, guys and gals! We're about to open the doors to the public, so you can start preparing your food. Let's all make a stash of cash for the new gymnasium floor!"

The vendors clapped and hooted, then went to work.

Soon, the scent of grilled hot dogs, along with the whirring sounds from a frappe machine, filled the air. Carly found the combined aromas of sweet and savory irresistible. She was anxious to make the rounds and test some of the offerings. First, she had to serve grilled cheese.

The folks waiting at the door had entered en masse. They went in all directions, wherever their noses and taste buds led them. The man who'd lent his jukebox for the day played a number, an old Elvis tune. An elderly couple began dancing to the song, attracting some mild applause.

Carly and her mom had formed a two-person assembly line. Carly buttered the bread, plunked the cheese in between, and set each sandwich on the grill. When golden brown, she plated them and gave them to Rhonda, who sliced each one into two triangles and added pickle chips. Instead of collecting fifty cents from everyone, Carly had set up a large can for payments. Some folks tossed in a couple quarters, but most paid extra. Best of all, everyone walked away with a smile.

"This really is fun," Rhonda quipped. "Thank goodness you brought vinyl gloves. My hands would be a greasy mess without them."

Next to Carly, Tillie was carving pie slices as fast as she could.

A sudden break in Carly's line of customers made her squeal. "Grant!" She scooted around the table and wrapped him in a hug, then stepped back and stared at him. "You look wonderful. And you cut your hair!"

No longer did he have the dreads he once sported. His hair was short and neatly trimmed.

"Yeah, I thought it was time," he said, his dark brown eyes twinkling. "They were a pain, anyway, and my dad is ecstatic. He never did like the dreads. And you look so *nifty* in that ensemble!" He grinned and ruffled her hair, then went over to greet Rhonda. She kissed his cheek soundly.

"When either of you wants a break," Rhonda said, "just flick me a text and I'll take over for you." She waved her goodbyes and toddled off to join some friends in one of the booths.

More customers began lining up. With a knowing smile, Carly held up her spatula. Grant instantly took over for her. *Old times,* she thought wistfully.

"I start work at four today," Grant said, flipping over a sandwich. "Which means I can stay here till you pack up."

Carly handed a plate to a customer. "So, you like working at the inn?"

"Aw, man. Totally. The work is fast-paced and I'm learning so much. The head chef is such a pro."

Carly's heart swelled. She loved seeing Grant this happy, living his dream.

It had taken some persuading to get his folks to agree to culinary school. Grant was also a gifted cellist. His mom and dad, both music professors at the local college, had envisioned him having a glorious career as a classical musician. But when his dad realized how much his son loved to feed people, he gave his blessing to Grant's chosen profession.

The gym was brimming with hungry customers, while the jukebox pumped out a steady stream of oldies. Carly and Grant worked in harmony for an hour or so, watching coins and dollar bills fill up the can.

Brice, meanwhile, wasn't getting a lot of takers. Carly couldn't help wondering if the permanent scowl etched on his face was turning away business. When she slid a glance over at his table, she saw him barking into his cell phone. "Where are you? I thought you were coming over?" Then, after a pause, "Okay, just hurry up." He disconnected to wait on a little boy, who'd asked for a grape soda.

Brice handed him the bottle and waited for the mom to pay.

"Eww," the little boy grumbled. "This bottle is wet."

"Yeah, well, that's the nature of ice, kid. It melts. Take it or leave it."

The child's mom, poised to pay for the soda, gawked at Brice. "Put it back, honey. We'll get a drink somewhere else." She grabbed her son's hand and tugged him away.

Carly and Grant exchanged glances, and Grant shook his head. *Wow,* he mouthed.

"Okay, this isn't working," Brice sputtered. He waited until Carly had served her last customer, then picked up his power strip and went in front of her table. "Like it or not, you're gonna have to share this outlet with me so I can plug in my fridge. Can you turn off your grill while I plug this in? I don't want to get a shock."

Incensed at his demand, and his rudeness, Carly said, "No, Brice. I will *not* unplug my grill, and you will *not* plug in that extension. Now, please go back to your—"

"That does it." The sharp voice came from behind Brice.

No one had noticed Rhonda storming over, but suddenly her manicured finger was inches from Brice's thin nose. "Listen to me, you bully," she said between clenched teeth. "You were told it would be hazardous to double up on that outlet. Now I'm here to tell you that if you say one more word to my daughter, or even come close to her, it will be *hazardous* to your health. Do you understand me? Now go back to your own table before I drag you there myself."

CHAPTER 2

IF A TOOTHPICK HAD FALLEN, CARLY WOULD HAVE HEARD IT.

Stunned into silence, Brice froze in place. A few customers had lined up behind Rhonda, presumably to buy grilled cheese. From their expressions, it was obvious they'd been witness to her harsh words to Brice.

Still clutching his power strip, Brice scanned the faces of the gathering onlookers. Not one looked sympathetic. His shoulders dropped, then he dashed off toward the hallway that led to the restrooms.

With a groan, Rhonda pressed her hands together and squeezed her eyes shut. "Please forgive me, everyone. I'm *so, so* sorry for losing my cool like that."

Carly rushed over to Rhonda and cupped her shoulder. "It's okay, Mom. There's nothing to feel bad about."

Tillie joined Carly and rubbed Rhonda's arm. "That's right," she said, "you stood up to a bully. That was the right thing to do."

A few of the bystanders murmured in agreement. "You told him off good," an elderly woman declared, and her companion gave a vigorous nod of his head.

Grant, who'd remained silent until then, held up his spatula with a cheery smile. "Anyone for grilled cheese?"

The waiting customers moved forward in a wave.

"I'll see you later, honey," Rhonda murmured to Carly. "My gal pals will wonder where I disappeared to." She gave her daughter a quick hug and hurried off.

After that, Carly's table got even busier. Several people paused at Brice's table, apparently hoping to buy soda. When no one materialized to help them, they walked away.

It was nearly eleven thirty when a mid-thirtyish woman carrying a large bag of ice approached Brice's table. Looking baffled by his absence, she set the ice on the floor and went over to Carly and Grant. "Hey, do you guys know where Brice Keaton went? I'm supposed to be meeting him here." She pushed a strand of her straight brown hair behind one ear.

"We haven't seen him in a while," Grant replied, "but I'm guessing he's still in the building. He left all his soda here."

"Thanks." She flashed a brief smile, then pulled her cell phone out from her denim cross-body purse. After thumbing a text, she set her phone on Brice's table and began removing the soda bottles still in the cooler. Then she peered into the cooler and frowned.

Seeing her dilemma, Grant smiled at her. "I see you brought more ice. Need some help pouring out the melted ice?"

Her eyes widened. "Oh, that would be great. I wasn't sure where to dump it. I'm Yvette, by the way."

"I'm Grant. Happy to help out."

Carly waved a greeting to the woman as Grant carried the cooler out through the nearest exit. "I'm Carly. Nice to meet you, Yvette."

"Yeah, likewise. This place is really rocking, isn't it?"

Before Carly could respond, Grant returned and set the empty cooler on Brice's table. Yvette thanked him and set the ice bag next to it, and Grant returned to the griddle.

As if he'd timed it, Brice emerged from the hallway and came up beside Yvette. "What took you so long?" he snapped at her.

Yvette's face flushed. "I'm sorry, but I couldn't get off work earlier. Believe me, I tried." In a quieter tone she said, "He's here, Brice. I saw him skulking outside the school when I came inside."

Brice's face blanched. "He? You mean—"

Yvette nodded.

Brice darted his glance nervously over the crowd. "Did he see you?"

"I'm not sure. I don't think so."

"Okay, then keep your eyes peeled. If you see him coming our way, give me a heads-up. I don't want that creep coming near you."

After overhearing the exchange between the two, Carly's curiosity shifted into high gear.

Was Yvette Brice's girlfriend? Her friendly demeanor was a far cry from his crabby one. He also hadn't shown her much gratitude for delivering a heavy bag of ice to his table on a hot summer day. And who was the man Brice was worried about?

The noon hour was approaching, and the gym was getting packed. The sounds of music and laughter floated over the air, enhanced by the tantalizing aromas from the various food tables.

The line at Carly's table was growing longer. She wanted Grant to take a break, but she was sure he'd refuse. She was slicing a golden-brown sandwich in half when a familiar voice in front of her said, "There you are. I've been looking all over for you."

Carly looked up to see Don Frasco holding up his cell phone in front of her. Don was the sole proprietor and editor of the *Balsam Dell Weekly*, a free newspaper that was mostly ads sprinkled with stories of local interest.

These days he was wearing his ginger-colored hair in a stylish fade with longer hair on top and a side part. The early stages of a beard were visible over his freckles, giving him a more mature look. Carly thought it suited him.

"I figured you'd show up eventually," she said, adding a pickle beside the sandwich. "Getting some good photos for the paper?"

"Yeah, I took a ton of pics, and I interviewed Andy Fields, the guy who's running this whole thing." He looked over at Grant and grinned. "Hey, man. Great to see you."

"Likewise," Grant said, waving his spatula.

"Want a grilled cheese?" Carly teased. She knew Don despised anything with cheese.

"Yeah, right." He rolled his eyes. "Actually, I can't stay much longer. Can I get a picture of you two making those sandwiches?"

Carly and Grant obligingly struck a pose with a plated grilled cheese.

Don made a face. "Carly, I need a bigger smile."

Resisting a snappy retort, she stretched her lips. Don snapped a few pics with his cell. "Perfect." He dipped his chin toward Brice's table. "I'll grab a root beer from that guy, and then I'm bailing."

"Busy day?" she asked.

Don shrugged. "Yeah, you know. Places to go, people to see. Later, guys!" With that he was off to Brice's table, where he purchased a root beer and left.

"He was sure in a hurry," Grant noted. "Hey, Carly, why don't you take a break? Check out the other tables."

"I was about to tell you the same."

"I'm happy flipping grilled cheese. You go ahead. I think I saw a cotton candy machine," he said with a grin.

"My weakness," she admitted with a groan. "Okay, but I won't be long." She removed her vinyl gloves, stuck some cash in her poodle skirt pocket, and went off to check out the other vendors.

Along the back wall, people were lining up for a selection of foods that were mind-boggling. Meat loaf slathered with gravy, slabs of cherry angel food cake, and hot dogs with every imaginable topping. And those were only a few of the choices. After scanning the offerings, Carly bought a hot dog with mustard and relish, and then a paper cup stuffed with purple cotton candy. She spotted her mom and friends and wove her way over to the booth where they were seated. Empty paper plates in front of them, they were sipping the last dregs of their pink lemonades.

"Carly!" the women all greeted her at once.

"Hey, ladies. Nice to see all of you. Mom, where's your wig?"

"Oh, the silly thing was starting to feel too tight, so I took it off and stuffed it in one of the gym lockers."

"They told us we could use the girls' lockers, but at our own risk unless we brought our own padlock," one of the women explained. "But you knew that, right? You must've gotten the same email."

Carly remembered something about using the lockers in Andy Fields's most recent email to the participants. But because she didn't intend to use one, she'd forgotten all about it.

Rhonda scootched over on her bench. "Come on, honey. Squish in next to me and eat your hot dog. You must be starving by now."

Carly did as her mom instructed. In between bites of her hot dog, she fielded questions from the women about her upcoming wedding. She was gobbling her last bite when a teenaged boy wearing baggy shorts and sneakers sauntered up beside their table. With a smirk, he aimed his cell phone at Rhonda and snapped a picture, then laughed and strode away.

Rhonda laughed. "He must think I'm a movie star."

Carly wiped her lips with a napkin and excused herself. "Duty calls," she said. "Talk to you later, Mom. Bye, ladies!"

After dumping her trash, Carly was heading back to her table when she noticed a dark-bearded man wearing mirrored sunglasses standing near the center of the gym. Garbed in jeans and a short-sleeved pullover, he was turning slowly in a circle. He appeared to be looking for something—or someone. Although she couldn't see his eyes, the expression he wore was fierce. He reminded her of an owl scanning the landscape for a tasty meal.

When the man's mirrored gaze landed on her, a shiver raced up her arms. She hurried back to her table and let out a relieved breath. Not that the man looked dangerous. But there was an intensity about him that made her want to flee in the other direction.

Grant was sipping on a cola. "Here, I got one for you." He handed Carly the bottle and she twisted off the cap.

"Thanks. I just scarfed down a hot dog and I need something cold." She took several sips from the bottle. "Things quieted down, I see."

"They did," Grant said. "I think the bulk of the crowd has left. It's already after two. At most we'll get a few stragglers."

Carly looked over at Brice's table. Save for the checkered tablecloth and Ari's cooler, it was empty.

Grant caught her glance. "Yeah, he packed up a few minutes ago and left. Some scary-looking dude was walking in this direction, and Brice bolted. He couldn't get out of here fast enough."

"What about Yvette?"

"She went with him."

Odd, Carly thought. "At least he left Ari's cooler here. "Strange guy, wasn't he?"

"An angry one, for sure." Grant secured a twist tie around a loaf of white bread. "I don't think he did very well, sales-wise."

"Given his attitude," Carly said dryly, "I'm not surprised."

By two forty-five, the crowd had trickled to a handful of people. Carly's mom and gal pals had vacated their booth and left. Vendors were packing up their tables. Some were already wheeling dollies out through the side exit. Tillie had sold out of pie half an hour earlier and left with a cheery wave.

"We may as well pack up," Carly told Grant. She transferred the contents of the payment can to a canvas envelope and zipped it. "I'll count it later, but I think we did well."

She hadn't heard from Ari, which Carly found odd. Maybe he'd gotten so involved in his project, whatever it was, that he lost track of time. She turned and smiled at Grant. "Hey, thanks for helping out today. Once again, you're a lifesaver."

"Hardly," he quipped. "Besides, it was fun."

"What are your hours at the inn?" She tucked the remaining paper plates into her cooler.

"From four until closing, every Thursday, Friday, and Saturday. Those are the busiest times during the summer. But that means I'm free to fill in for you during my off days, if you need me."

"I might take you up on that," Carly said. "Val and the chief have a vacation coming up, and Suzanne and Jake plan to take Josh camping."

Grant started to say something when Carly's cell phone rang. She excused herself and dug it out of her tote, smiling when she saw Ari's face. "Hey, sweetie. How's your project going?"

"Carly, we have a situation here," Ari said in a quiet tone.

Carly's stomach lurched. "Are you okay?"

"Havarti and I are both fine. It's just, well . . . an unexpected visitor arrived today. You and I need to talk."

"You're scaring me, Ari." Carly's voice rattled. "Who is it?"

He paused and then said, "My sister, Leslie. I haven't seen her in a few years. And wait till you hear what she wants."

"Is it bad?" Carly choked out.

"It isn't good. Are you almost ready to leave?"

"Grant and I are packing up now. I'll be home as soon as I can."

A lump of fear blossoming in her gut, Carly steeled herself for the worst.

CHAPTER 3

CARLY HAD ORIGINALLY PLANNED TO STOP BY THE EATERY TO SEE HOW HER team was doing before heading home. Ari's call had derailed her plan, so before she left the school, she gave Nina Cyr, her assistant manager, a quick call.

"Hey, how was the fundraiser?" Nina chirped.

"It was good. Grant was a huge help. Everything okay there?"

"Of course it is. A little quieter than usual. Probably because everyone was at the high school scarfing down diner food!"

"Probably," Carly said. "If you're okay without me, I'll leave you and Val to close up. Isn't this the weekend you're moving?" Nina was giving up her cramped apartment and moving into the second story of a two-family home in Balsam Dell. Carly had seen the photos. The neighborhood was lovely, the street tree-lined and quiet—at least in the pictures.

"Yup. Someone's helping me pack today, but tomorrow's the actual move. You sound odd. Is something wrong?"

"Everything's fine," Carly assured her, though she knew it was a fib. Whatever news awaited her at home, she knew from Ari's voice that it wasn't good. She pulled in a breath. "Good luck tomorrow, Nina." She disconnected before Nina could ask any more questions.

The ride home took fewer than ten minutes, but Carly's heart pounded like a jackhammer all the way. When she reached her and Ari's newly renovated home, she swung into the driveway and parked behind his truck. A car she'd never seen before—a white Ford sedan with a Rhode Island plate—sat next to the truck.

Her legs shaky, she climbed the front steps and entered the narrow foyer. The AC felt good, almost chilly. She dropped her tote on the hallway table and rubbed her arms.

The first sign that something was off was Havarti, or rather, his absence. Where was the little Morkie? He usually rushed over to greet her as if she'd been away for a year.

Voices drifted from the kitchen. Carly started to head that way when she saw a little girl with braided, carrot-colored hair and pink eyeglasses sitting on the patterned sofa. Nestled in the child's lap was Havarti's furry head, his eyes closed in a blissful snooze. The little girl's eyes widened as Carly approached.

"Hi there," Carly said in a cheery voice.

"Hi," the girl said softly, her hand buried in the fur of Havarti's neck.

"I'm Carly. What's your name?"

"Quinne," the child replied.

"I see you made a friend," Carly said, going over to sit on the edge of the sofa. "Wow, he sure likes you."

The dog glanced at Carly and thumped his tail, but didn't move from his comfortable spot. His furry face rested against the child's short-sleeved jersey top, which was emblazoned with tiny pink poodles.

A gap-toothed smile spread across Quinne's face. "I like him, too. Do you speak French?"

Surprised at the question, Carly replied, "Well, I did, a little, back in high school. I think I've forgotten most of it."

It was then Carly realized that Quinne had a tablet resting beside her. Without dislodging Havarti, the child lifted the tablet with her free hand and showed it to Carly. "I can already count to ten. Un, deux, trois, quatre . . ." She began reciting the numbers until she reached ten. "Dix!"

"Quinne, that's amazing," Carly said with a tiny laugh. "I can barely remember one and two."

"Hey, sweetie." Ari came out from the kitchen and went over to the sofa, his expression unreadable. Definitely not his jaunty self. "I thought I heard you come in. I see you've met Quinne." He smiled at the little girl.

A petite brunette garbed in summery green shorts and a flowered blouse trailed behind Ari, then came over and stood beside him. "Hello, I'm Leslie Mitchell, Ari's sister." She extended her hand, a hint of anxiety in her dark brown eyes.

Instead of taking her hand, Carly rose from the arm of the sofa and gave Leslie a light hug. "It's so great to finally meet you, Leslie."

"You, too." Leslie stepped back awkwardly and folded her hands. "I see you've met my niece, Quinne."

"I have." Carly smiled at the girl. "In fact, she gave me a French lesson."

This was the first Carly had ever heard of a niece in the Mitchell family. She wondered if the child was Ari's niece, too. He'd never mentioned having one.

"It'll be the first of many, I'm sure," Leslie quipped, gazing warmly at Quinne.

"Hey, why don't we all go outside and sit under the umbrella table?" Ari suggested. "I made a jug of lemonade, and we still have some sugar cookies."

Quinne's hazel eyes brightened at the mention of cookies. "Come on, Havarti. We're having cookies!" She shifted off the sofa, leaving her tablet on the cushion. Havarti trotted behind her, his tail wagging like a flag in the wind.

Talk about instant bonding, Carly thought.

Ari and Leslie carried the sugar cookies, lemonade pitcher, and drinking glasses out to the backyard patio, while Carly grabbed a box of Havarti's dog cookies.

A mild breeze rustled the lush green leaves of the maple tree that dominated the small yard. Along the rear property line was a row of neatly trimmed juniper hedges. Stockade fencing ran along each side of the yard. Not only did it provide privacy, but it made for a safe play area for Havarti.

Quinne's brow furrowed. "Can't he have a people cookie?"

"Sorry, honey, but those aren't good for dogs." Carly removed a bone-shaped cookie from the box and handed it to Quinne. "Give him this. He'll love it. It tastes like peanut butter."

Quinne sniffed the cookie, then held it out to Havarti. The dog took it gently from her fingers, then chomped it and swallowed it within seconds.

Quinne squealed with delight. "He loves it!"

Carly grinned. "See?"

Ari poured lemonade for each of them, and Quinne helped herself to a daisy-shaped sugar cookie. For a while they all made small talk—chatting about the weather, and the traffic on the trip from Rhode Island. Carly was feeling antsy. Whatever message Leslie had driven all this way to deliver, she was anxious to know what it was.

"Quinne," Ari said to the little girl, "Havarti loves to play fetch with his tennis balls. They're out there by the tree, if you want to toss some to him."

Quinne gulped her last swallow of lemonade, then swerved off the bench. "Come on, Havarti. Let's play fetch!"

As Leslie watched her niece bounce away with the dog, her eyes filled with unshed tears. Her features were so like Ari's, with her dark eyes and strong jaw. Something was troubling her deeply.

His voice taut, Ari plunged right in. "Carly, Leslie plans to spend a few days in town. She came here to ask for a portion of the proceeds from the sale of my house."

Carly was stunned. Not only at Leslie's plea for money, but at Ari's harsh tone.

Ari and Leslie's mom had died several years earlier. When Ari decided to stay in the house they inherited from her, he had the property appraised and paid Leslie half the amount. According to his attorney, that was the fair way to buy out her share.

"I . . . I'm sorry," Carly stammered, "but I thought that was all settled after your mom died."

Leslie folded her hands on the table. "It was, but my situation has changed." She glanced nervously at her brother, then back down at the table.

Ari picked up the thread. "It turns out that Leslie's ex, who divorced her almost four years ago, had drained nearly all their joint savings. Part of that was her portion of the house proceeds from when our mom passed. He claimed it was for a medical emergency—gall bladder removal—but it turned out his health insurance paid most of it. Suddenly, he had a new wife with a baby on the way. The little boy is almost two now."

"Leslie, I'm so sorry," Carly murmured. "Did you have a lawyer representing you?"

Leslie's voice trembled as she continued the story. "I did, but he said that when my ex withdrew money from our joint savings, we were still married, so he had a right to it. The judge agreed, so there was nothing I could do."

That didn't sound right to Carly. And she still didn't understand how Quinne figured into the equation.

"Leslie, forgive me," Carly said softly, "but you said Quinne is your niece. How is she related to you?"

Leslie blinked and took a sip of her lemonade, then pulled in a deep breath. "My ex has an older brother, Perry, who's always been a ne'er-do-well. Had a real wild side. Anyway, Perry had a girlfriend, Bonnie, and together they had a little girl. Bonnie adored the child, but to Perry she was just an afterthought. Five summers ago, before my divorce, Perry "borrowed" a friend's motorboat and took Bonnie out on the lake where the friend lived. Perry had been drinking heavily. He lost control of the boat and hit someone's dock, head-on. The boat upended and they were both thrown backward into the water. Bonnie's neck snapped, killing her instantly. Perry lived, but he's paralyzed from the chest down. The police charged him with reckless operation, plus a host of other things. Not that it mattered. He's in a state-run care facility now, living in his own private hell, which he richly deserves." Her lips twisted. "I don't have an ounce of pity for him."

Carly felt her insides roll over. "What about the little girl?" She was so gripped by the sadness of the story, she barely got the words out.

Leslie wrapped her small hands around her glass. "Bonnie's mother, the child's grandmother, was given custody of her. The grandmother wasn't the nurturing type, but she put on a good act. Her main concern was the money she got from the state for the child's care. But fate got her, too. She developed lung cancer and couldn't care for the child any longer. The little girl ended up in a group home for children, until . . ." Leslie's eyes welled with tears.

Carly reached for Leslie's hand. "Until you took her, right? The little girl is Quinne, isn't she?"

Leslie squeezed Carly's fingers. "Yes. Even though she's technically my niece, I'd never even met her until after the accident. But when my ex told me what was happening, I was heartsick. I visited Quinne at the children's home. She looked so lost, so sad. She'd been an only child with an indifferent grandmother for so long, she was having trouble making friends. I made the decision right then that I wanted to adopt her. The social worker at the children's home is helping to facilitate it, and we've made substantial progress. At the moment, I'm Quinne's foster mom. But I want to be her real mom," she added softly.

Carly glanced toward the backyard, where Quinne and Havarti were having a grand time playing together. "Does Quinne have any memory of her parents?"

Leslie shook her head. "No, she was only about three when the boating accident happened. Quinne and I have both been to counseling, and Quinne is adamant that she wants to live with me. And I desperately want to adopt her."

Ari broke in. "Even though Quinne's father gave up his parental rights," he explained to Carly, "Leslie is worried that she can't provide for her financially."

"I'm . . . a dental hygienist," Leslie quickly explained, her face flushing slightly. "I mean, the job pays well and all, but I've never had to provide for a kid." She twisted her hands. "The thing is, I want to buy either a house or a condo for me and Quinne. Right now, we're living in a one-bedroom apartment. I've been sleeping on the pullout sofa so she can have the bedroom."

Something didn't make sense to Carly. If Leslie was earning decent money, why couldn't she get a loan? That's what most people did when they wanted to buy a house. She sensed Leslie wasn't telling the whole truth. Was she in debt? Had her ex drained her of her savings?

Ari still hadn't spoken much, but Carly could see the wheels of his mind spinning. He loved his sister dearly, that much she knew. Did he sense Leslie was leaving out a chunk of the story?

A squeal erupted from Quinne, followed by a peal of laughter. She was having a blast playing fetch with Havarti. The two were rolling on the ground like a pair of rambunctious puppies.

"I'll cut to the chase," Leslie said, sitting up straighter. "I, um, looked online at the property records for Balsam Dell. I saw that Ari recently sold our mom's house for way more than it was worth when he bought me out. I feel"—she swallowed—"that Ari should pay me the difference. You know, half of what he made on the sale, minus what he already paid me after Mom died. That seems only fair, right?" She looked directly at Carly, no doubt hoping for an ally.

"And I explained," Ari said tightly, "that I sold the house at its current value. That's how it works. I used the proceeds toward the purchase of *this* house. And might I add, Carly and I have a wedding coming up in a little over a month."

Carly saw that Ari was struggling to keep his cool. As for herself, she felt tongue-tied. She had no idea how to respond. Was Leslie's way of thinking valid? Carly didn't think so, but then, she knew almost nothing about real estate.

"I know," Leslie said, tearful now. "And I'm sorry about the timing. It's just . . . I'm worried that if I can't show adequate housing for Quinne and me, the court might deny the adoption."

A heavy silence fell over them, like a weighted blanket making the summer heat feel even more stifling.

"Carly and I need to talk privately about this," Ari finally said. "We're not going to decide anything today."

"That's fine," Leslie said weakly. "I didn't expect an instant answer. I'll take Quinne back to our motel now and we can grab an early dinner. It's over by the highway, not far from here. Maybe we can talk again tomorrow?"

Ari rubbed a hand over his face. "Fine. I'll call you in the morning."

Carly reached over and touched Ari's arm. "Before Leslie leaves, I need your help with something." She smiled at Leslie. "We'll be right back."

Once they were inside the house, Carly said, "Ari, I have perishables in the car, butter and cheese. They're in a cooler, but they need to be refrigerated."

Ari kissed her cheek. "I'll bring them inside."

"Wait." She squeezed his arm. "Your sister and Quinne have had a long day. I know you're not thrilled with Leslie right now, but she's really in a tough spot. I was thinking—maybe I could whip up a mac and cheese dinner for all of us. It's easy, and most kids love it. We have watermelon sherbet in the freezer. It's a perfect dessert for a warm evening."

Ari sighed, then shook his head and smiled. "I had a feeling you'd want to feed them. Quinne is a sweet kid, isn't she?"

"She is, and she adores Havarti. At least let's do that much. You and I can talk later, after they're gone."

Ari wrapped her in a hug. "Okay, I'm fine with that. Why don't you go outside and tell Leslie, while I get the stuff out of your car?"

• • •

After a satisfying meal of mac and cheese, salad, and warm breadsticks, Quinne's eyes were beginning to droop. Carly was relieved to see that the child was a good eater, not the least bit picky about the veggies in her salad. At her age, Carly would never have eaten cucumber slices or raw tomatoes.

They all enjoyed a scoop of watermelon sherbet, then Quinne gave Havarti a squishy hug and kissed him on the snout. "I'll see you tomorrow, Havarti," she promised, with a hopeful look at her aunt.

"Yes, we will," Leslie said, taking Carly's hand. "Thank you for a lovely meal. Tomorrow's another day. Maybe we can work something out."

Ari bristled at his sister's words, but then he walked her and Quinne to the door. "I'll be in touch early tomorrow." He bent toward Quinne and smiled. "Bye, sweetheart."

"Bye, Uncle Ari! Bye, Auntie Carly!"

The urge to hug Quinne was overpowering, but Carly resisted. "Bye, Quinne. I loved meeting you. Thank you for taking good care of Havarti."

Tablet in hand, Quinne skipped off toward the car. After the door closed, a pang gripped Carly's stomach. A day that had started out so enjoyable had ended in a colossal dilemma.

"She's hiding something," Ari quipped. "I feel it in my bones."

"I tend to agree," Carly said, "but I don't know her as well as you do. I don't really know her at all."

He touched Carly's cheek. "Now that we're alone, how about I bring two glasses of wine out to the umbrella table? Maybe we can figure out how to handle this."

Carly gave him a quick kiss. "I'm game. Havarti and I will wait for you outside."

The sky was still light, the sun dipping slowly toward the horizon. The breeze had picked up. Even with the temps still in the low eighties, it felt refreshingly cool.

Sitting at the umbrella table, Havarti at her feet, Carly smiled as she watched two squirrels chase each other around the big maple. Soon they'd hunker high in the tree, away from nighttime predators.

When Carly's cell rang, she was surprised to see her mom's face on the screen. Every Saturday evening at this time, Rhonda and Gary could be found dining at the Balsam Dell Inn. It was a weekly "date" to which they both looked forward.

"Hey, Mom, what's happening?"

In a shaky voice, Rhonda said, "Carly, I have disturbing news. Brice Keaton is dead. The custodian at the school found him in the locker room."

A wave of shock surged through Carly. "Wait a minute. Are you kidding me?"

"I only wish," Rhonda bleated.

"That's awful. Do you know what happened?"

A harsh sob erupted from Rhonda. "A . . . a scarf was tied around his neck—a dark red one. Someone strangled him with it. Carly, the scarf was exactly like mine. *Exactly*. I'm at the police station now, with Gary. They showed it to me." Rhonda's voice cracked. "They've been asking me questions for over an hour. They actually interrupted our dinner to make me come over here!"

Fear gripped Carly like a clamp to her heart. For a moment she couldn't breathe.

"But the scarf—it can't be yours, right? Didn't you wear yours home?" She tried to recall when she last saw her mom at the fundraiser.

Rhonda groaned. "No, remember I told you? That dumb wig was driving me crazy, so I took it off, and the scarf, before I left. I stuffed them in one of the lockers."

This can't be happening, Carly thought. *I've got to be dreaming.*

The back door closed abruptly, and Carly jumped at the sound. She turned to see Ari walking toward her holding two glasses of wine.

"Hold on a minute, Mom," Carly said. "Didn't you take them out of the locker before you left the school?"

"I tried to, but they weren't there. Someone had taken them. I checked several other lockers, but they weren't in any of them."

"Did you report it to anyone?"

"No, I didn't bother. The wig and the scarf were cheap. I only bought them for the event. I didn't think it was worth the trouble."

A cold shiver skittered down Carly's spine. A horrible feeling that the worst was yet to come fell over her like a shroud.

"Okay, Ari and I will be right down there. Stay put, okay?"

"Don't bother, honey. They're letting us go now. I'd invite you to the house, but I'm so exhausted I just want to fall into bed and sleep forever." Rhonda's voice wobbled. "See you in the morning?"

"Sure thing, Mom. And try not to worry, okay? It'll all get straightened out. Does Norah know yet?"

"No, I'm going to call her on the drive home," Rhonda said. "Right now, I just want to get out of this police station."

After the call ended, Carly looked up at Ari. His brow furrowed, he set down the wineglasses on the umbrella table. "What's wrong, honey? You're as white as a ghost."

Tears leaked down Carly's cheeks as she repeated Rhonda's story.

Ari's face fell. He wrapped Carly in his arms and whispered in her ear, "Not again. Please, not again."

CHAPTER 4

AFTER A NEARLY SLEEPLESS NIGHT, CARLY FORCED HERSELF INTO THE shower while Ari made them a quick breakfast of toast and oatmeal. Between her mom's unthinkable situation and the dilemma with Ari's sister, she couldn't make her mind focus. She managed to choke down only half the toast, and she barely touched her oatmeal.

Coffee. Today it would put her in survival mode—barely.

"What did Leslie say when you called her?" Carly took a long sip from her mug.

Ari sat down at the kitchen table. "She was horrified, for both of us. She insisted she and Quinne would be fine and not to worry about them. I told her I'd update her once we found out more information."

Carly broke off a corner of her toast and fed it to Havarti. He swallowed it happily and licked his lips.

"Violating the 'no people food' rule?" Ari teased.

"Seems like a good day for it," Carly said with a wan smile. "Ari, why don't you visit with Leslie and Quinne for a bit this morning, and then meet me at Mom's later?"

"I'm not sure that would accomplish anything." Ari dabbed his lips with a napkin. "You and I still need to talk about their money situation."

Carly sighed. "I know. Last night turned topsy-turvy so we never got to discuss it. The thing is, I feel so bad for Quinne. I think she loved visiting with us yesterday, and she sure got attached to Havarti."

Ari swallowed a mouthful of oatmeal. "I hear you, but it's not like Leslie gave us any notice before showing up yesterday," he said dryly.

Carly had to admit he was right. But something about that sweet little girl tore at her heart.

Seeing Carly's expression, Ari relented. "Okay, how about I treat them both to breakfast. I can text you later when I'm on my way to your mom's."

"Sounds good to me," Carly said, feeling relieved.

That decided, Ari called his sister. He arranged to meet her and Quinne at the coffee shop near the motel.

Carly hurriedly got dressed and headed to Sissy's Bakery, where she picked up a dozen of her mom's favorite almond croissants. The drive to her mom's felt surreal, as if she was floating in a dream. No, not a dream. More like a nightmare.

The sky was overcast, with dark clouds moving in swiftly. Just what Carly needed to worsen her already glum mood.

Someone had killed Brice Keaton, and it wasn't her mom. With only a little more than a month left until her and Ari's wedding, would she have to add solving a murder to her already overflowing to-do list?

• • •

The moment Carly stepped into her mom's cheery kitchen, Rhonda flew into her arms. Her normally made-up face was absent of color, and her eyelids were puffy. She clearly hadn't gotten much sleep the night before.

Rhonda's husband, Gary, wisely rescued the bakery bag before the contents got squished between the two women. A retired dermatologist, Gary was a kind man who doted on his wife. His disposition was as low-key as Rhonda's was buoyant.

After setting the croissants on the kitchen table, he motioned Carly to a chair and poured her a mugful of coffee.

"Thanks, Gary. Have you heard anything this morning?" Carly asked, almost afraid to hear the answer.

He sighed and sat down adjacent to his wife, who'd taken her normal place at the head of the table. "I spoke to the head investigator from the state police a short while ago. Forensics is still at the school, going over every square inch of the locker room where—" He dropped his head and rubbed his hands over his eyes.

Rhonda reached into the bag and pulled out a golden, almond-crusted croissant. She plunked it onto a napkin and tore off a flaky chunk. Crumbs flew all over the table.

Gary leaped off his chair. "I'm sorry, I'll get us some plates."

Rhonda waved a hand. "Don't bother. Napkins are good enough."

Napkins are good enough? Carly thought. Was this the same Rhonda Hale Clark who made her and Norah, as kids, eat cookies over the sink so that nary a crumb would reach the floor?

"Did you ever reach Norah last night?" Carly asked her mom.

"I did. She and Nate are coming over later. I'm surprised she hasn't called you."

Nate Carpenter was Norah's significant other. He was also part owner of the Flinthead Opera House on the outskirts of Balsam Dell, and had a singing voice that never failed to blow her mind.

"I'm surprised, too," Carly mused, although Norah was less of a worrier than Carly was.

"She thinks it will all blow over, and that the police have nothing. She also said that if history repeats itself, you'll find the killer anyway." Rhonda gave her an amused smile.

"That is not the least bit true, or funny," Carly fumed. Except that it was partly true.

"Mom, is there anything you can tell me about what happened at that school?" Carly asked wearily. "I didn't see you at all before Grant and I packed up."

Rhonda swallowed a mouthful of croissant. "My gal pals and I left a little after two. We were stuffed to the gills with all that so-called diner food."

"Where did you and the ladies go after that?"

"We went over to Debbie's house. She'd been begging us to come over and see her new furniture. Since we were all together, it seemed like a good time."

Rhonda rounded up some stray crumbs from the table and swiped them onto her napkin. "After we gushed over Debbie's furniture, she made some margaritas and we sat outside on her patio. I passed on the drink and had ginger ale instead, since Gary and I always eat out on Saturday night."

"How long did you stay?" Carly asked.

"I don't know. Maybe an hour and a half?"

"And after that?"

Rhonda averted her gaze. "After that I went home."

"You didn't make any more stops?"

After a pause, Rhonda gave an imperceptible shake of her head. "I got home a little after four. I wanted to shower and change before we left for dinner."

Carly knew the rest. Rhonda and Gary were dining at the inn when the police cut their dinner short and ordered her to come in for questioning.

"Mom, you had another scarf, a green one. Where did that end up?"

"In my purse," Rhonda said. "The fabric was flimsy, so I rolled it up and stuck it in a side pocket." Her eyes watered and she hitched in a breath. "Gary, you'd better show Carly the video."

Gary adjusted his rimless eyeglasses, then removed his cell phone from his shirt pocket. After a few taps, he held up the phone. "Someone posted this on a social media site yesterday. It apparently went viral."

Carly took the phone from Gary for a better view. The scene that unfolded on the screen made her stomach hurt. The video showed Rhonda ranting at Brice Keaton, her finger almost in his nose.

Listen to me, you bully. You were told it would be hazardous to double up on that outlet. Now I'm here to tell you that if you say one more word to my daughter, or even come close to her, it will be hazardous *to your health. Do you understand me? Now go back to your own table before I drag you there myself.*

Carly felt the coffee she'd swallowed gurgle up in her throat. She pushed it back hard, trying to keep it at bay. For at least half a minute, she couldn't speak.

She finally returned the phone to Gary, who was paler than she'd ever seen him.

"Who posted this?" Carly asked.

"Someone sent it to the police anonymously," Gary said soberly. "But since it's plastered all over social media, they should be able to track it to whoever posted it."

Even if they do, how would it help? Carly thought. The video spoke for itself. It clearly showed her mom issuing a threat to Brice Keaton. And now the man was dead.

Carly swallowed, then took a tiny sip of coffee. She managed to keep this one down.

"There were other people in that gym who weren't happy with Brice. A woman showed up before lunchtime. Brice berated her for not getting there sooner."

"His girlfriend?" Gary asked.

"I think so," Carly said. "Her name is Yvette, but I don't know her last name."

"So," Gary said, sounding animated now, "it seems our victim had a few potential enemies."

"Possibly," Carly said. "We don't know for sure. Although, there was a scary-looking guy wearing mirrored sunglasses who might have been looking for him." She described her brief encounter with the bearded man. "Right after that, Grant said Brice bolted as fast as he could and took off down the corridor toward the restrooms. His friend Yvette went with him."

Rhonda tapped her fingers on the table next to Carly. "Listen to me, Carly. I don't want you going after a murderer. I'd rather spend my life in prison for a crime I didn't commit than have anything happen to you. Is that clear?" She grabbed Carly's fingers and squeezed them.

Carly felt her throat clog. She knew her mom was serious. "Mom, you're not going to prison, and nothing will happen to me."

Rhonda nodded and reached for Gary's hand, and her gaze misted. "Gary has already retained a lawyer. He's driving down from Montpelier as we speak. Gary says he's a real bulldog when it comes to defending clients."

"He is," Gary confirmed. "He came highly recommended by an old friend of mine. I have every faith he'll straighten out this mess."

A wave of relief swept over Carly. "Oh, thank goodness. That makes me feel so much better. Then I'll stay so I can tell him everything I witnessed."

Gary and Rhonda exchanged glances. "Um, Carly," Gary said, "he's asked to speak with us alone for the first interview. He prefers to interview witnesses separately."

"But . . . I was there. I can tell him everything I saw!"

"I know, honey, but apparently this is how he works," Rhonda explained. "He's one of the top defense lawyers in the state, so we want to do what he says."

After hesitating for a moment, Carly agreed to do as they asked. "Okay, but be sure to give him my contact info. Tell him I'll be available twenty-four-seven, okay?"

"We will," Gary assured her.

Carly remembered that she hadn't told them about Ari's sister being in town. She gave her mom and Gary a brief recap of their visit.

"Well, good grief, Carly," Rhonda said, sounding more like the mom Carly knew. "You need to be sure Ari's sister, and that little girl, are okay. They need your help."

"But you need my help too," Carly insisted. "More so, in fact."

"Yes, but we have a crackerjack attorney who will shortly be advising us. Right now, Ari's sister and her niece need you. You have a good head on your shoulders. I'm confident you and Ari will figure out what to do. And remember, you're getting married next month." Rhonda smiled, but it looked more like a grimace of pain and fear.

Carly was at a loss. When she heard her cell ring in her tote, which she'd left near the door, she hurriedly dug it out. "Hey," she said, grateful to see Ari's face. "How's everything?"

"Everything's okay, but I'm more worried about you—and Rhonda." He sounded stressed. "Are you at their place?"

"Yes, but I'm leaving shortly. An attorney is on his way here, and he needs to speak to Mom and Gary alone."

Ari heaved out a breath. "Then please let them know we're both here for them. Are you heading home now?"

"I am. Leaving any minute."

"Good. Just so you know, Leslie and Quinne are going to meet us there."

"That's fine. I'll see you shortly."

Carly relayed Ari's message, which prompted a hug from both her mom and Gary.

"Call me after your attorney leaves, okay?" Carly pleaded.

"We will," Rhonda said, sniffling. "Knowing you and Ari are there for us, and that we have a good attorney, I'm feeling a whole lot better."

By the time Carly left, she was anxious to get home. Much as she hoped she and Ari could help Leslie, it was Quinne she was more concerned about.

Something else bothered her. Her mom claimed she'd gone directly home after she left Debbie's house that day. But when Carly asked if she was sure she hadn't made any other stops, she'd given a bare shake of her head and said she got home a little after four.

Maybe it was splitting hairs, but why hadn't her mom answered with a definitive *no* to the question?

CHAPTER 5

LESLIE AND QUINNE HAD ARRIVED AT THE HOUSE BEFORE CARLY. THEIR white Ford sat in the driveway behind Ari's pickup. As she got out of her own car, Carly couldn't help noticing that the Ford's backseat was piled with bags of clothing and personal items.

Before she'd even reached the front porch, Quinne had raced down the steps and wrapped her arms around Carly's waist.

"Wow! You must've had a good breakfast!" Carly hugged the child and then released her to Havarti, who was leaping into the air to reclaim Quinne's attention.

"Yup. French toast, blueberries, and strawberry milk. Auntie Leslie and Uncle Ari had pancakes. With *lots* of syrup. Like, whole *lakes* of syrup."

Ari did love his maple syrup. His sister apparently shared his maple passion.

Carly bent and rubbed Havarti's furry head. "That sounds like Uncle Ari. Where is he, by the way?"

"They're outside in the yard. C'mon." Quinne skipped inside and through the kitchen, and then out to the backyard, Havarti trotting at her heels.

Ari's face lit up when he saw Carly, not with joy but with relief. She suspected he'd had another difficult chat with his sister and was grateful for a break.

Quinne and Havarti immediately dashed to the back of the yard. They chased each other and rolled in the grass, Quinne squealing with glee.

Leslie rose from her chair, her expression worried. She hugged Carly. "Sorry you couldn't join us for breakfast this morning, Carly. Ari told me what happened to your mom. It's so . . . horrible. Are you okay? How's your mom handling it?"

Carly plunked down on the bench at the umbrella table. "I'm okay. Mom's holding up, but that's about all. A lawyer from Montpelier is on his way there. Gary, mom's hubby, is aware of his reputation and has a lot of faith in him."

Ari reached over and squeezed Carly's arm. "It's so frustrating. I wish we could do more."

"I do, too. But right now, we have to wait and see what happens with the lawyer. At least the police didn't detain Mom."

"Thank goodness," Ari agreed. "Unless there's something we don't know, the evidence sounds pretty circumstantial." He held up a glass carafe. "Iced tea?"

"Definitely," Carly said. "Are you playing cop now, Detective Mitchell?"

Ari filled a glass for Carly with the dark brown liquid. "By the way, Leslie made this. It's way better than the stuff I make. And no, I'm not playing detective. But I think your crime-solving tendencies might have rubbed off on me."

"Ari told me about your exploits with murder," Leslie put in. "I don't know whether to be impressed or terrified."

Carly laughed. "Neither. In each case, it was mostly happenstance." She took a sip from her glass. "Wow, Ari's right. This iced tea is fantastic!"

"Thanks." Leslie looked pleased, and the lines in her face relaxed.

"Carly," Ari said, lowering his voice, "Leslie and I talked at breakfast. As best we could in Quinne's presence."

"She had her earphones in and was listening to a French lesson on her tablet," Leslie clarified. "Normally I'd tell her that wasn't polite, but it gave Ari and me some privacy."

Ari leaned his tanned arms on the table and smiled at his sister. His voice grew soft. "You've done a wonderful job with her, Les. It looks to me like she's thriving in your care."

It was the first time Carly had heard him call her "Les."

Leslie smiled at her brother. "Yeah, well, the court is putting me through the wringer to approve the adoption. There are several reasons, but mainly I've had . . . well, issues of my own." She looked away, into the backyard, where Quinne was sitting on the grass beside Havarti. The child was chattering away to the little dog, who was listening with rapt attention.

Carly sensed that Leslie hadn't told the whole story. Did the clothing and other items piled into her car have anything to do with her troubles?

"Right now, I'm on vacation," Leslie explained, "but eventually I have to go back to work." She started to tear up, and then she swiped at her eyes with her fingertips. "Um, do you two mind watching Quinne for a bit? I have a raging headache, and I want to get some ibuprofen from my purse."

"Sure, take your time," Carly said.

Leslie swung her legs off the bench and hurried inside the house.

"She seems so forlorn," Carly said. "Did you talk about the money with her?"

"Briefly. She wants to get a bigger living space to encourage the court to speed up the adoption. And she wants to buy a two-bedroom condo so she can show stability. She's iffy about why she can't get a loan, though. I don't think she's telling me everything."

"I sensed that, too," Carly agreed.

Ari hesitated, then, "I saw the motel room she and Quinne are staying in. It's kind of a dumpy place. What would you think about them moving in to our upstairs, just temporarily? They'd have a full bath and a kitchen to themselves, and there's room for a second bed. I wouldn't be promising any money, just safe, clean housing for now."

A huge breath of relief left Carly's lungs. "Funny, but I had that same thought—even without seeing the motel. What about her apartment, though? Won't she still have to pay rent?"

"I'm not sure," Ari admitted. "But if necessary, I told her I'd talk to her landlord and see if I can get her a rental reprieve. She said he's a good guy, and she's been a model tenant."

Carly's brain was whirling. Between her and Ari's upcoming wedding and Rhonda's dicey situation, Leslie's timing couldn't be any worse. But she was family, and she needed help. That wasn't something they could ignore.

Ari leaned forward and kissed Carly on the cheek. "Thank you, honey. I knew you'd be on board. I'll give Leslie the news. This afternoon I'll fetch the rest of their things from the motel and help them settle upstairs."

Carly smiled. "Quinne will be ecstatic. She'll have Havarti all the time, at least for a while. You know, I wanted to ask you. Leslie said she's a dental hygienist. Do you know anything about her job?"

Ari topped off the iced tea in Carly's glass. "All she ever told me was that she works for a sole practitioner who has a long-standing practice. I never got a sense of whether she's happy there or not."

Carly found that strange. But then, maybe the job was just a means to earning a living. A lot of people stayed in jobs they hated because they couldn't afford to quit.

"Ari, before Leslie gets back, I want to show you something." Carly picked up her phone and punched in a few keys until she found the onerous video of her mom ranting at Brice Keaton at the fundraiser.

Ari's eyes widened as he watched Rhonda get angrier and angrier at the soda seller. "Uh, this doesn't bode well for your mom, does it?" he said quietly.

Carly shook her head. "No, and it scares me. I don't know where to go from here."

"On the other hand," he offered, "it's only a vague threat. Again, it's circumstantial. Not real evidence. At least that's my take on it."

"But that's not how people will see it," Carly said glumly, her heart scraping her rib cage. "Anyone who watches it will think it's a confession."

• • •

It was late in the afternoon before Leslie and Quinne were ensconced in their new digs. Quinne wanted to sleep in her aunt's room instead of in the spare room, so Ari set up a comfy cot for her, complete with Carly's flowered comforter.

For dinner they had take-out pizza, which put a huge smile on Quinne's face. Everyone was exhausted. Quinne conked out on the sofa, Havarti's furry head on her arm.

The next day was a workday for Carly and Ari, so they all went to bed right after nine. Carly missed her eatery and her team, as she thought of them. Valerie, her grill cook, had texted that morning to express her sadness over the events of Saturday. Her message was cautious, though—mostly she expressed her faith in Rhonda's innocence. But as the chief of police's wife, she had to remain neutral, at least outwardly.

Carly was surprised, and a bit disappointed, that she hadn't heard from Grant. He'd witnessed Brice's antics and the unpleasant exchange with Rhonda. Maybe he'd taken another shift at the inn and hadn't found the time to text or call.

Before "lights out," Quinne asked Carly if Havarti could sleep in her room. She looked so adorable in her pink pajamas and slippers that Carly's heart melted into a puddle.

"How about this?" Carly suggested. "I'll bring his bed up to your room and let him decide, okay?"

Quinne nodded uncertainly. Carly carried the dog bed upstairs and set it down beside the cot Ari had set up. Seconds later, Havarti raced upstairs and headed straight for his bed, putting a huge grin on Quinne's face.

In the morning, Leslie reported that the dog had forsaken his doggy bed and spent the night on the cot snoozing at Quinne's feet.

CHAPTER 6

NINA CYR NEARLY TRIPPED OVER HERSELF RUSHING OVER TO HUG CARLY. "Girl, are you okay? We heard about Saturday—it must have been horrible!"

Extricating herself from Nina's fierce hug, Carly smiled at her assistant manager. Always garbed in bright, occasionally clashing colors, Nina wore her emotions on her sleeve. Today her sleeves were part of a yellow tunic that topped off a pair of gauzy blue capris. Plastic lemon slices dangled from her earlobes like bursts of brilliant sunshine.

"Nina, I'm fine," Carly assured her. "You're here so early!"

Nina grabbed a mug from behind the counter and prepared Carly's coffee exactly the way she liked it. They sat on adjacent stools at the spotlessly clean counter.

"I came in extra early because, well . . . I wasn't sure if you'd have other things to do today. You know, with your mom," Nina said sheepishly.

Carly sipped her coffee, relishing that first intoxicating taste. The comforting sights and familiar aromas of her eatery lifted her slightly out of the doldrums. "When did you hear about it?" she asked Nina.

Nina's cheeks flushed pink. "Actually, Don heard about it first. He was helping me move yesterday. When we stopped for a break, he checked his phone and saw that awful video some idiot posted."

Carly had always viewed Don Frasco as a loner, but over the past several months she'd noticed a change. Nina had taken a shine to him, and Don had lowered his guard. The two had developed a kinship of sorts.

"I know," Carly groaned. "Taken out of context, it makes Mom look like a raging monster, doesn't it?"

Carly had spoken to her mom late the day before, and she'd sounded calmer than she had earlier. The attorney had met with them for over two hours, gathering information and devising a game plan. He'd set up interviews with both Carly and Grant for that afternoon, which would mean more time away from work for Carly.

"So Don helped you move? How did it go?"

"Pretty well," Nina said. "I had a mover take the big stuff, but Don and I lugged the boxes. Like, a *gazillion* of them. Not fun on a hot day." Her green eyes sparkled. "Anyway, we're both good at organizing, so we devised a system to have all the boxes unpacked by the end of the week. The apartment itself is so cool. I can't wait for you to see it." Her eyes misted and she leaned over and gave Carly another hug. "I'm so sorry. You've got more important things to think about."

"Don't be sorry. You, Val, and Suzanne are keeping me anchored. I can't imagine where I'd be without you all."

She debated whether to share her other news—that Ari's sister and niece had shown up unannounced on Saturday and would be bunking with them for a while.

The door swung open, interrupting her thoughts. Valerie Holloway came in and made a beeline for Carly, wrapping her in a hug that rivaled Nina's bearlike grasp. "I haven't stopped thinking about you since I heard," she said, her blond-streaked topknot bobbing a little. "Before you ask, Fred's been keeping things close to the vest, as they say. But I'm sure he'll want to talk to you before long."

I'm sure he will, Carly thought dismally.

In the past, Carly had been at odds with Chief Holloway, mainly over her involvement in murder investigations. His recent marriage to Valerie had softened his temperament. On occasion, he'd even shown grudging admiration for Carly's skills at nabbing killers.

This time would be different. Carly wasn't about to watch her mom go to prison for a murder she didn't commit. Whichever way the chief chose to handle it, Carly prepared herself for the battle.

The front door swung open again and Suzanne Rivers stepped inside. She was three hours earlier than her usual starting time of eleven o'clock. "The sky's the color of lead," she groused, dropping her purse onto the nearest table. "That big rainstorm's coming in fast. And look at you! You're pale as a marshmallow," she chided, marching over to Carly. "Have you eaten anything?"

Carly smiled at Suzanne's trademark bluntness. "Nice to see you, too, Suzanne. I had some oatmeal with blueberries at six thirty. And I've decided not to have any more morning biscuits until after my wedding."

When she first opened the eatery, Carly started off each morning with a cheesy grilled biscuit. It kept her going through the lunch crunch, which typically lasted until midafternoon. Over time it became a tradition.

Valerie went behind the counter and poured a coffee for herself and a second one for Suzanne. "Wait a minute. Didn't you say your dress fit perfectly?"

"Sure it does, right now." Carly snagged a napkin from the metal dispenser on the counter and dabbed her lips. "But I don't want to tempt fate."

A sudden crack of thunder made Carly jump. "Is that thunderstorm hitting us already?"

"Looks that way," Nina said, going over to look through the front window. "I see fat drops coming down already."

"I have extra umbrellas in my trunk, if anyone needs one," Carly offered.

With that, they launched into their normal routine. Food prep, wiping down tables and chairs, and the dreaded bathroom cleaning. Carly offered to do the bathroom, since she'd have to take time off later to meet her mom's attorney. And that was probably only the beginning.

• • •

Linda Reilly

Don Frasco was the first customer of the day. He closed his rain-soaked umbrella and tucked it into the corner near the coatracks, then headed to the refrigerated beverage case and pulled out a bottle of root beer.

"Hey." He dropped onto the stool closest to the grill.

Nina grinned at him, her green eyes lighting up. "Hey, you want your usual?"

Don's usual was a grilled bacon and tomato sandwich, sans the cheese.

Carly had known Don since her teenaged babysitting days, when his mom had asked her to sit with him one afternoon. When she'd tried making him a grilled cheese, he'd let out an ear-piercing scream, then stomped on the dining room table in his cowboy boots, leaving gouges in the wood. Carly was grateful his mom had never called her again. That was one babysitting gig she could do without.

"It's early, but okay." He smiled at Nina as he opened his root beer, and she slid a glass over to him.

"Nina tells me you helped her move," Carly said.

He lowered his gaze, his freckles deepening in color. "Yup. Hey, I saw that video of your mom that some jerk posted on the internet. I'm sorry that happened."

"You and me both," Carly said. "You were taking a lot of pictures that day. How did they come out?"

Don pulled his phone out of his shirt pocket and tapped at it. "See for yourself."

Carly scrolled through at least three dozen photos. Even with Don's photography skills, most were a jumble of faces all clustered together. She'd hoped to see if anyone had approached Brice Keaton or talked to him. Nothing helpful jumped out at her.

"Don, can you text these to me?" She gave him back his phone. "I want to look at them on my tablet and enlarge them."

"Don't I always?" He tapped at his cell and Carly's pinged with a text.

Carly had to admit, in the past Don had helped her pin down a few murderers, even risking his own safety at times. "By the way, do you know who the woman was that was with Brice? She told us her name was Yvette, but that's all."

He beamed at Nina as she set his sandwich in front of him. "Thanks, Nina. You know, she did look familiar." He took a huge bite of his sandwich and chewed slowly, then washed it down with a slug of root beer.

Carly's pulse sped up. "And?" she prodded.

"A couple of weeks ago, I got a flat tire. I went to the auto parts store to get a new one, and they put it on for me. I'm almost positive that's where I saw her. She was working behind the sales and service counter."

"Which store?"

34

"Panda Bear Auto Parts. Going south, it's right on the main drag. Big panda on the sign."

Carly was familiar with it. Ari sometimes shopped there for parts for his truck. She glanced outside through the front window. A steady rain was pounding the pavement.

Maybe it was time she treated her aging Corolla to a new pair of windshield wipers.

CHAPTER 7

After Don left, the eatery started to get busy. It was tourist season in the bucolic little town, and visitors loved to browse in the charming shops. With most outdoor activities curtailed during inclement weather, the tourists tended to flock indoors—a boon for local businesses. Gina's shop, a specialty stationery store called What a Card, was no doubt bustling with customers. Even so, Carly prayed Gina was staying laser-focused on finishing her wedding invitations so they could get mailed out on time.

Shortly after noon, Carly went into the kitchen and sat at the small table near the window. She wanted to take a quick break to call her mom.

Rhonda's voice was far from her usual cheery one. "Hi, honey," she said in a dreary tone.

Carly's heart dropped. "Mom, is there any news from your attorney, or the police?" she asked anxiously.

Rhonda let out a gusty breath. "Our attorney gave us strict orders not to talk to the police unless he's present. So far, we've heard nothing new." Her voice shook a little. "Poor Gary, his nervous stomach is acting up on him. He's gone through half a bottle of Pepto already."

Carly felt for him, but she was more worried about her mom. "I haven't heard from your attorney yet. Isn't he supposed to interview me?"

"I'm sorry, honey. I should have called you earlier. His name is Burt Oakley, and he's going to call you shortly. He's meeting Grant at his folks' house at two, and he wants to meet with you at the restaurant after that. Are you okay with that?"

If his timing was good, he'd catch her during the afternoon lull. They could sit in one of the rear booths, where they could talk out of everyone's earshot.

"Of course it's okay. Right now, you're my top priority."

After a pause, Rhonda said, "What about Ari's sister, and that little girl? What's her name?"

"Quinne, and don't worry. They'll be fine." Carly explained their current living situation.

"That's so kind of both of you to let them stay with you," Rhonda said jaggedly. "If only I weren't in this mess I could help you—"

"Mom, none of this is your fault. You did nothing wrong. Remember that."

Rhonda hitched in a shaky breath. "Yes, I did. I let that man goad me into threatening him. And now the whole world knows. Plus—oh, never mind."

After several moments of silence, Carly said, "What is it, Mom? Tell me what you were going to say."

Rhonda lowered her voice. "After Burt Oakley left last night, the police asked me if they had my permission to search my home and car. They said if I didn't give it, they'd obtain a search warrant anyway, so it would be simpler for everyone if I consented."

"So did you?"

"Yes, of course. I have nothing to hide. But when I told my attorney, he became quite annoyed with me. He told me I shouldn't have done that without getting him involved. He said that at the very least he'd have forced them to limit the extent of the search."

"Oh, Mom, I'm so sorry. With all the stress you're under, he shouldn't have reprimanded you. Did the police carry out the search?"

"Yes, late yesterday. Obviously, they found nothing. I'm sure they were hoping to find the wig hidden away somewhere, which would prove I was lying about it being stolen."

"And they didn't, which means no harm was done. In fact, it worked in your favor because you were so cooperative."

"Thank you, honey." Rhonda's voice grew tearful. "That makes me feel a little better."

They talked for a few minutes longer, Carly speaking in soothing tones until eventually Rhonda seemed calmer. Gary had picked up lobster rolls for lunch, and they were about to sit down and eat, so Rhonda ended the call.

One thing Carly was grateful for—no matter what dire situation Rhonda Hale Clark was facing, she never lost her appetite.

Suzanne came through the swinging door and hurried over to her. "Carly, you have visitors in the dining room."

Carly scraped back her chair. Burt Oakley wasn't due to stop by until after he interviewed Grant. "I think it's my mom's attorney," she said, wondering how they could talk privately in the busy dining room.

Suzanne looked baffled. "Uh, I don't think so. It's a woman and a little girl."

Carly swept past Suzanne and into the dining room. Seated in a booth near the front were Leslie and Quinne. The little girl spotted Carly immediately. Her face widened into a grin, and she waved at Carly. "Auntie Carly!" she trilled in her sweet voice.

Carly slid into the booth next to Quinne and gave her a one-armed hug.

"Hey," Leslie said, sounding contrite. "I hope you don't mind us coming in here. We were going to spend the morning in the park, but the bad weather botched that idea."

"Of course I don't mind," Carly said. "I'm happy to see you both."

"Auntie Leslie, can I take my raincoat off?" Quinne said, making a face. "It's getting the seat all wet."

"Sure." Leslie rose to help her, but Carly said, "You sit and relax, Leslie. I can help."

Quinne pulled her arms out of the sleeves of the flowered rain jacket, and

Carly tugged them off. She folded the jacket and set it on the bench. Suzanne rushed over with a dry towel, and Carly used it to wipe the seat.

"Who's this little princess?" Suzanne asked.

Carly introduced them, and Quinne asked her if she spoke French.

"*Oui, mon amie,*" Suzanne replied, then laughed. "That's about all I know. You look like a girl who would love some pink lemonade. Am I right?"

"Yesss!" Quinne clapped her hands. "And a plain grilled cheese with chips."

"I'll have the same," Leslie said, "but with a black coffee."

"Coming right up," Suzanne chirped. She went off to give the order to Valerie, and Nina scooted over to meet the newcomers.

Once again, Carly made introductions. Nina gushed over the two of them, then hurried away to seat a group of four teenaged girls.

Leslie looked down at the table, seemingly lost in thought. Carly's sixth sense told her that something else was troubling her, something she hadn't disclosed the night before. She remembered that the backseat of Leslie's Ford was jam-packed with clothes and sundries—far more than would be needed for a few days' visit. If Carly could find a way to chat with her alone, maybe she could coax her into revealing what was really going on.

"Carly," Leslie said quietly as their lunches were delivered, "Quinne and I are going to eat out tonight. We've imposed on you and Ari long enough."

Carly covered Leslie's hand with her own. "Listen to me. You're family, and you're not imposing." She winked at Quinne. "Besides, who's going to teach me more French if you don't have dinner with us tonight?"

"Auntie Leslie's favorite supper is hot dogs!" Quinne announced, then bit off a corner of her grilled cheese.

"Then hot dogs it is," Carly said. "You just made my evening easy breezy. Ari can do them on the grill, I have buns in the freezer, and I'll heat some frozen French fries. We can have vanilla ice cream for dessert."

"And Havarti can share my hot dog." Quinne took a noisy sip of her lemonade.

"He can have a tiny corner," Carly corrected gently. "Then you can give him dog treats for dessert."

That settled, Carly left them alone to eat. She instructed Suzanne not to charge for their meal.

By the time they'd eaten and were ready to leave, Quinne was eager to get back to Havarti. Carly had given her a thin slice of mild Swiss cheese for him. Quinne couldn't wait to surprise him with it.

• • •

By two thirty the rain had let up and the sky had brightened considerably. Carly was dashing toward the kitchen to have a quick bite of the eatery's signature salad when a familiar-looking woman strode into the eatery. She'd seen her recently, but where?

That blue streak in her hair . . . yes! It was Tillie, the pie seller from the fundraiser. She saw Tillie speak briefly to Nina, who smiled and waved an arm toward Carly.

Tillie rushed past Nina to greet Carly, giving her a light hug. "I'm so glad you're here. I was afraid you might not be in."

Carly stepped back and smiled at her. "It's good to see you, Tillie."

"You, too." Tillie held up a paper bag. "I remembered too late on Saturday that I wanted to save a slice of pie for your fiancé. Before I knew it, my pies were sold out! So . . ." She gave Carly the bag.

Carly peeked inside and saw a large container. "Tillie, this is so sweet of you. Thank you."

"I baked it fresh this morning. It's apple pie, made with Vermont apples. I cut a huge slice so you could each have a big helping. You can keep the container. I have a zillion of them."

Carly was impressed with her kind gesture. "You didn't have to do this, but Ari will be thrilled. Unless I eat it all before I get home," she joked.

Tillie wagged a finger at her. "Don't you dare," she said with a playful grin. She gazed all around the restaurant. "Wow, this place is wonderful. You really lucked out when you scored this location. The exposed brick walls, the pendant lighting. It's all so reminiscent of the old days."

Carly couldn't resist preening a bit. "Thank you. I chose the lights myself. Ari installed them. That's how we met, in fact."

"Like a storybook romance." Tillie clasped her hands together, then her smile faded. "Listen to me, babbling away when your mom must be crushed over what happened. How is she doing? I heard that the police interrogated her."

Nothing stays private in Balsam Dell, Carly thought wryly.

"Well, they questioned her," Carly revised, hating the word *interrogated*. "She's handling everything okay. She has a very supportive husband, and my sister and I are always there for her."

Tillie looked pained. "I was, um, interviewed by the police yesterday. They asked me if I witnessed the altercation between Rhonda and Brice Keaton at the school on Saturday." She lowered her voice to a near whisper. "You probably saw that dreadful video that's going around."

Carly swallowed. "Sadly, I did. What did you tell them?"

"Well, I explained exactly what happened, at least as I remembered it. I also told them how badly Brice Keaton had behaved toward Rhonda and everyone else." She bit down on one glossy pink lip.

Inwardly, Carly cringed. Would making Brice sound like a monster only fuel the idea that someone, namely Rhonda, might've wanted to do away with him?

Tillie touched Carly's wrist. "Carly, they don't seriously think Rhonda had anything to do with his death, do they?" Her voice quivered slightly.

Carly didn't know how to answer that. If she'd had a chance to talk to Chief Holloway, she might have some clue. As it stood now, all she knew was that the police questioned her mom for over two hours on Saturday before finally releasing her, and that a search of her home turned up nothing.

"I'm not sure what they think," Carly answered carefully. "I never like to assume anything where the police are concerned, so I'm trying to get more information. Did they ask you anything else?"

Tillie tilted her head and mulled the question. "Let's see. They asked how long I'd known your mom, did we ever work together, things like that. One thing I did tell them, in no uncertain terms, was that Rhonda Hale Clark wouldn't harm an ant, let alone a human." She crossed her arms over her chest to emphasize the point.

"I appreciate your faith in her," Carly said with a faint smile. "But I suspect that doesn't have much influence on the police."

"Yeah, you're probably right." Tillie sighed. "Hey, listen, I've gotta run. Let me know if you like the pie, okay? I stuck my business card in the bag."

"Will do, Tillie. Thanks again."

Tillie soared off like a bird in flight and went out the front door.

Carly headed into the kitchen. Nina had just prepared a new batch of salad, and Carly scooped some into a bowl. She poured herself a glass of spring water and sat at the small table.

"Who was that woman?" Nina asked. "If I'm not being too nosy."

Carly explained who Tillie was and why she'd stopped in.

"There are such good people in the world." Nina stuck one hand on her slim hip. "I wish there were more like her."

"Me too." Carly stabbed a forkful of field greens. "So, are you liking your new place so far?"

Nina's smile lit up her face. "Totally. It's sunny, has a big kitchen, and the walls are all freshly painted. My new landlord made sure it was spotless before I moved in. It made our job *so* much easier."

"Yours and Don's?" Carly said teasingly.

"Oh, all right," Nina said with a good-natured roll of her eyes. "I guess the whole world knows Don's been helping me. And before you ask, he's not moving in. Don and I are just friends." A blush touched her cheeks, making Carly wonder. Nina quickly changed the subject. "Hey, who was the darling little girl you were talking to earlier? She called you Auntie Carly, but I didn't know you had a niece."

"Her name's Quinne. She's visiting us with Ari's sister," Carly said vaguely. She didn't want to reveal the whole story, not until Leslie's situation was more settled.

After Nina returned to the dining room, Carly went back to finishing her salad. She rinsed her bowl and set it in the dishwasher, then freshened up her face in the restroom. The attorney would be arriving at any moment, and she wanted to look presentable. He'd texted that he expected to be there no later than four.

• • •

Burt Oakley came in at precisely four o'clock. Somewhere in his fifties, Carly guessed, he was tanned and clean-shaven with a full head of graying hair. His dress style was casual—a short-sleeved shirt and tan slacks. He gave Carly's hand a hearty shake and flashed a smile that failed to put her at ease. She led him to the rear booth, where they could talk privately.

"Would you like something to drink?" Carly offered.

"Any chance of getting an iced coffee?" He smiled.

"You bet."

Carly brought over an iced coffee for each of them. The attorney added three sugars to his, then removed his laptop from his leather briefcase.

"Let's get right to it, shall we?" he said brightly. "May I call you Carly?"

"Sure," Carly said, wishing she wasn't so nervous. Why did she suddenly have a case of the jitters?

Because my mom's freedom is at stake, that's why.

"Carly, I'd like you to relate the events that led up to the altercation between Ms. Hale Clark and Brice Keaton. Give me as much detail as you can recall."

Carly described everything as she remembered it, starting with Brice's complaint about the location of his booth. She explained Ari's offer to help by bringing a cooler and some ice, which Brice accepted.

The attorney's fingers flew over his keyboard. "Is that Ari Mitchell, your fiancé?

"It is. Anyway, after Brice set up his display with the ice-filled cooler, he still didn't seem to be getting a lot of customers. When a little boy buying a soda complained that his bottle was wet—the ice in the cooler had melted a little— Brice berated him and told him to 'take it or leave it.' The child's mom then refused to buy the soda, and that's when Brice expressed the opinion that he needed to plug in his portable fridge."

Oakley gave her a patient smile. "Carly, I sense you're trying to soft-pedal what happened because you don't want to sound angry. The truth is you have every right to be angry. Don't worry about speaking ill of the dead. Be blunt, be bold. Pound your fist if you want to! Focus on how he treated everyone. Tell me exactly how you saw it."

With that, Carly let her emotions fly. She told Oakley about the way Brice scowled at customers, how rudely he treated everyone around him, including the event director, Andy Fields. She heard her voice rising, growing shrill as she relived each scene.

"And then he committed the ultimate sin," Carly said, her teeth clenched. "He demanded that I unplug my grill so he could plug in his extension cord. He'd already been warned it would be dangerous, but he clearly didn't care. That's when Mom"—she swallowed—"kind of blew her stack at him. Not physically, only verbally," she hurried to add.

Oakley stared at her for several seconds, then nodded. "That was good, Carly. That's what I wanted to hear."

Carly's limbs felt numb, and a chill ran through her. A horrible thought occurred to her. "Mr. Oakley, were we just practicing for my testimony in court?"

"It's Burt, and I hope it won't come to that. We're still waiting for an official cause of death, and on forensic testing from the item allegedly used to strangle the victim."

"Do you mean the scarf?" Carly blurted.

"Exactly. Once the forensic results are available, and I've reviewed all the witness statements, we'll put together a strategy, should we need one. Keep in mind, the burden of proof will be on the prosecutor. We only need to establish reasonable doubt."

"But that's only if there's a trial, right?" Carly's voice squeaked.

"True, and as I said, I don't think it will come to that. In the event she's charged with the crime, my goal will be to get the case dismissed for lack of evidence. Anyone could have stolen Rhonda's scarf and used it to kill Brice Keaton. An argument, even a threat, does not a murder make."

Carly dropped her head in her hands. She'd never felt this helpless. She wished now she'd never participated in the fundraiser. She should have donated a check, which had been one of the options.

She removed her hands from her face and looked at the attorney. "Mr.—I mean Burt, Ari and I are getting married next month. Do you think we should postpone the wedding?"

Oakley reached over and touched her wrist in a soothing gesture. "Carly, I'll tell you what I would tell my own daughter if she were you. Absolutely not. I know how distressed you are, but it's far too soon to assume the worst."

That didn't make her feel any better, but she nodded her assent. "Okay."

Oakley sat back. He looked slightly troubled. "Carly, I . . . understand that in the past you've helped the police solve a few murders. At least that's the scuttlebutt. Is there any truth to it?"

Carly felt blindsided by the question. "There's some truth to it, yes. If you want details, you should speak to Chief Holloway. It's not something I feel comfortable talking about."

"That won't be necessary. All I ask is, whatever information you might learn, you bring directly to me, not to the police. Remember, our goal is to exonerate Rhonda, not to help the police. Do you see what I'm saying?"

Something about that statement rubbed Carly the wrong way. In her opinion, the police were not the enemy, yet that's how he seemed to view them.

Okay, there were times when the police had focused on the wrong suspect. That was the main reason she'd gotten involved in so many investigations. Ultimately, however, the information she'd supplied had helped them reach the truth. Justice was served and the innocent were exonerated.

"Yes, I see exactly what you're saying," Carly replied, a slight edge to her tone. "Which brings me to another question. My mom told me you were upset that she allowed her home to be searched without notifying you first. I don't understand that. She has absolutely nothing to hide, so why shouldn't she?"

Oakley pushed back his drink and folded his hands over the table. "Carly, let me explain something. It doesn't matter that she's innocent. It matters that if the police have carte blanche to search a home, or a car, they can do anything they like. While it's rare, there have been cases where evidence was planted by the police. Had I known, I'd have stepped in immediately to limit the scope of the search."

Carly had heard of such rare instances, mostly on TV crime shows. Even then, the accused were usually suspects well known to the police. It was inconceivable to her that the police would try to pin false evidence on a respected citizen like her mom.

"Thank you for the explanation," she said, her tone crisp. "I meant to ask you, was Grant Robinson helpful at all?"

"Yes, he was. He's a very observant, very intelligent young man. He thinks the world of you."

Carly noticed that he didn't smile. His 'tude, as Grant would call it, was seriously beginning to grate on her. "Thanks, that's great to hear."

Oakley nodded. "Let's continue."

For the next half hour or so, Oakley questioned her on every detail she could recall from the fundraiser. She was starting to feel like a suspect herself instead of a helpful, though biased, witness. She breathed a sigh of sheer relief after he packed up his laptop and left.

She carried their iced coffee glasses into the kitchen and rinsed them. Suzanne had already gone home—her shift ended at three—and customers were starting to come in for an early meal.

"You look tired," Valerie said with concern when Carly went behind the counter to help her.

She was tired, both physically and emotionally. She hadn't slept well, and it was catching up to her. And why hadn't she heard from Norah? By now they should be banding together like a two-woman Justice League in support of their mom.

Carly smiled weakly at Valerie. "I am a little tired. I'm going to take a minute to call Norah, okay? Then I'll come back for dining room duty."

Closing time during the warmer months was at seven. She and Ari were accustomed to having a later dinner. It worked with both their schedules. She was sure Leslie would be fine, but she was worried about Quinne. The little girl was probably used to eating an earlier dinner.

Carly called Ari to let him know about the "hot dog" night she promised Quinne. He assured her he'd have everything ready for grilling by the time she got home.

Norah was next.

"I knew you'd be calling," Norah fretted. "Carly, what are we going to do about Mom? You have some ideas, right?"

A fierce rush of love for her older sister washed over Carly. As strong and capable as Norah was, a family crisis could send her into fright mode.

Carly calmly explained that she'd met with the attorney, and that he was confident no charges would be filed against Rhonda. It was a slight fib, but one she felt justified in telling. She also told Norah about their current visitors and invited her and Nate to join them for dinner on Tuesday. "It won't be fancy. Probably just burgers on the grill."

"Yes!" Norah said. "We accept. Mom told me Ari's sister and her niece were staying with you for a while. We'd love to meet them. Let us bring dessert, okay?"

Carly laughed. "Now, there's an offer I can't refuse."

After they disconnected, Carly wondered if she'd been too hasty inviting them. So much was happening at the same time. Was she putting herself on overload?

She jumped when someone tapped her on the shoulder. It was Nina, her small face awash with worry. "Carly, you need to go home. Val and I can handle things here."

Carly shook her head. "I'm grateful for the offer, but I can't keep bailing on my own restaurant. I was gone all day Saturday. It's not fair to you guys, plus you still have a lot of unpacking to do."

Nina waved a dismissive hand. "No biggie. It doesn't have to be done all at once, right?"

Choked up, Carly gave her a hug. "Okay, then I'll take you up on that." She texted Ari to let him know she'd be leaving work soon.

By the time she arrived home, Ari had everything set up in the backyard and ready to go on the grill. Quinne was delighted that Carly was home earlier than expected. She couldn't wait to share some of the new French words she'd learned.

Within fifteen minutes, they were all gathered around the umbrella table eating hot dogs and French fries. Havarti was allowed a tiny sliver of Quinne's hot dog. She laughed when he leaped up to take it from her fingers.

Leslie seemed subdued, but she was sweet with Quinne. Carly was sure something was eating at her.

"Auntie Carly," Quinne said with a teasing smile, "do you know what Havarti is?"

"A cheese?" she guessed.

Quinne giggled. "Nope. *Un chien,*" she said proudly, pronouncing it *shee-EH*.

"Great French accent." Carly high-fived her.

Quinne pronounced a few other words for her, then Carly brought out four dishes of vanilla ice cream. She'd divided Tillie's pie slice four ways so they could each enjoy a sliver with their ice cream. She'd have to remember to thank Tillie, as the pie was even more scrumptious than she'd expected.

After they all finished, Leslie suggested they clean up and go inside. "Quinne, I have some work to do upstairs," she said, cupping the child's shoulder. "Can you watch a video on your tablet while I do that?"

"She's welcome to watch it on our TV downstairs with us," Ari offered, gathering up the dirty plates. "We'll download any video she wants."

Leslie agreed, and Quinne yelled, "Yay!"

With the dishes put away and everyone settled in the living room, Leslie quietly went upstairs. About a half hour through the Disney flick Quinne had chosen, Carly excused herself to bring a glass of iced tea upstairs to Leslie.

She climbed the stairs quietly and found the bedroom door slightly ajar. Carly knocked lightly. "Leslie? I brought you some iced tea, in case you're thirsty."

After a long pause, Leslie came to the door and opened it wider. Her face was streaked with tears, and her nose was red. "Oh, Carly, I think I'm in trouble."

With that, she dissolved into tears.

CHAPTER 8

CARLY WENT INTO THE ROOM AND CLOSED THE DOOR. LESLIE'S LAPTOP WAS open on the small corner desk. From where Carly stood, the document on the screen appeared to be a résumé.

She set down the iced tea on the bureau opposite the bed. "I had a feeling something was wrong. Is it anything I can help with?"

Leslie dropped onto the bed and Carly sat beside her.

"I don't have a job anymore," Leslie said in a wobbly voice. "My boss fired me five weeks ago. I've been getting by on the little savings I have left, plus my severance check." She blotted her eyes with a tissue.

Carly felt her heart clutch. No wonder Leslie had been so withdrawn. She slipped an arm around her shoulder.

Leslie sniffled. "For twelve years I devoted myself to that job, and to that man. My patients loved me. No one ever complained."

"Then what happened?" Carly asked.

"My boss said I'd been taking too much time off because of the adoption thing, as he called it. Which is partly true, but I had no choice. I had frequent appointments with social workers, plus phone calls during the day. Anyway, he called me into his office one afternoon, gave me a month's severance, and told me to look elsewhere for a job. He said he needed someone 'steady,' someone more dependable. I found out he'd already replaced me with a twentysomething fresh out of dental hygiene school. At a much lower salary, I'm sure."

Carly was horrified. "Leslie, I'm so sorry he did that to you. He's obviously not very understanding of what you're going through."

"No, he's not. I found out," Leslie went on, "that his receptionist slash bookkeeper, who's also his latest squeeze, had been monitoring my time out of the office. Whenever I was out, she kept track of my absences, right down to the nanosecond. The day he let me go, he showed me a list a mile long that she'd compiled. I felt so humiliated, like I had to defend myself."

She cried for another minute or so, then Carly asked, "Have you looked for a new job yet?"

Leslie sniffled. "I've been trolling the online employment sites, but so far no one's asked to interview me. I'm terrified I'll lose Quinne, Carly. What if my boss bad-mouthed me to all his dentist friends?"

Carly retrieved the glass of iced tea she'd brought up and handed it to Leslie. "I'm not even sure if it's legal to do that. Have you filed for unemployment?"

Leslie sipped from her glass. "Not yet. I was hoping I wouldn't have to, but if I don't get a job soon—" She shook her head.

Carly blew out a quiet breath. The pieces were coming together now.

Leslie's plea for a portion of the proceeds from Ari's house sale was born out of desperation, not entitlement.

"Leslie, why didn't you tell all this to Ari?" Carly asked her.

"Because I'm embarrassed, that's why," Leslie said bitterly. "Ari always told people how smart I was, how proud he was of me. He never approved of my marriage to my ex, but he supported my decision. Turned out he was right." She swiped at her eyes again. "If I tell him I'm jobless, he'll think I'm a total loser. Not to mention that Quinne's adoption could be jeopardized."

"Ari would never think that," Carly assured her. "He loves you dearly, and I know he wants to help you. Just think about telling him, okay?"

Leslie reached over and hugged her. "I will. Thank you, Carly. I'm so lucky you're going to be my sister-in-law. And I don't want you to worry about me, or about Quinne. You need to focus on your mom, okay?"

"That's a given," Carly said with a smile. "You'll get to meet her soon."

Carly went back downstairs, her thoughts ricocheting from Leslie to her mother and back to Leslie. The video was still playing on the television, but Quinne was fast asleep on the sofa. Her fingers were curled in Havarti's fur as the dog dozed peacefully beside her. The sight gave Carly's heart a twist. She marveled at how quickly the girl and dog had become nearly inseparable.

Ari gave her a worried look. "Everything okay?" he asked, making room for her in the overstuffed chair he was hunkered in.

She squeezed in beside him. "I hope so." She didn't want to divulge what Leslie had confided in her. She only hoped Leslie would take her advice and tell Ari everything.

Carly's phone pinged. She slid it out of her pocket and looked at the readout. "Hmmm, it's Grant. He wants to know if it's too late to call me."

Ari yawned. "It's only eight fifteen."

"Yeah, but we're all beat," she said, then frowned. "Except . . . he wouldn't ask if it wasn't important."

She hadn't spoken to Grant since they'd left the school together on Saturday. That seemed odd, given everything that had happened since. Was Grant avoiding her?

A lump formed in her stomach. She went into the kitchen and tapped his number.

"Hey," he said, "I'm sorry I didn't call sooner." He hesitated, then lowered his voice. "Carly, my folks are super ticked off about me being involved in another murder investigation. They were less than thrilled when that attorney came over to interview me today."

Ah, now she got it.

"I understand how they feel," she replied, "but what happened didn't have anything to do with you. You witnessed an argument. That's all."

"I know, but they—" His long sigh said it all. In his parents' minds, Carly attracted murder the way sugar attracted flies.

"Anyway," he went on, "I stopped by the restaurant this afternoon but you'd already left. Nina and Val told me about some other stuff that's going on with you. They're worried about you, bigly."

Carly gave a silent groan, and tears formed in her eyes. "I know. Everything's hitting the fan at once, but—"

"Before you say any more," Grant interrupted, "I'm going to work at the eatery tomorrow, *all day*. You don't even need to show up. I mean, it's not like I don't know the drill, right?" He tried to sound lighthearted, but his tone was laced with concern.

Carly's throat tightened. She wanted to tell him no, that it was too much to expect. But she knew he wouldn't listen, even if she insisted.

"How can I ever repay you?" she said in a near whisper.

"By taking care of your family," he responded, making her tears flow even harder.

"Get some rest tonight, okay?" Grant said before disconnecting.

Carly promised to try, just as low voices filtered in from the living room. She wiped her face with a napkin and went in to see what was happening.

Leslie was leaning over Quinne, urging her to wake up. "Come on, sweetie, time for bed. You can take your bath in the morning."

Quinne's eyelids fluttered, and she mumbled, "Can Havarti come with me?"

"Of course he can," Leslie said, the love in her voice unmistakable.

"Need help?" Carly asked her.

"No, I'll be back in a little while."

Quinne said her good nights and Leslie led the little girl up the staircase, Havarti trotting at their heels.

"She told me she wants to talk to me about something," Ari said, his brow furrowed. "It sounded serious. Do you know what it's about?"

"I do, but I'll let her tell you."

About ten minutes later, Leslie came into the living room. Carly dropped onto the sofa, while Leslie took the overstuffed chair next to Ari. Her face was drawn with anxiety, but at Carly's nod, she took a deep breath and launched into her story.

By the time she was through, Ari's face had paled beneath his tan. "Les, why didn't you tell me this before?" He reached over and gripped her hand.

"I didn't want to disappoint you," she muttered in a shaky voice.

He blinked. "You could never disappoint me, so don't say that. At least now we can help you, right, honey?" He threw a questioning look at Carly.

As Carly was turning over Leslie's problem in her mind, something occurred to her. Norah was an employment recruiter, with contacts in almost every occupation. She'd helped Gina find a store assistant who turned out to be a gem. Prior to that, none of Gina's employees had lasted very long.

Carly explained her idea about asking for Norah's help.

Leslie's face brightened, and she pressed her palms together as if praying. "I would be so grateful if she could help."

"I can't promise anything," Carly cautioned, "but my sister is a go-getter when it comes to job placement, and I know she has contacts all over New England. In fact—I haven't had a chance to tell you, Ari—she and Nate are coming over for dinner tomorrow evening. They want to meet Leslie and Quinne, and they're bringing dessert. I told them we'd have burgers on the grill."

Ari looked as if he could breathe again. "That's great," he said. "What about your mom and Gary?"

"Mom's holding off meeting our visitors." Carly smiled at Leslie. "She wants to be in a better frame of mind first. But believe me, she's going to love you both."

Leslie hugged her brother and then bade them both good night before heading back upstairs. Carly took advantage of her alone time with Ari to tell him about her meeting with Burt Oakley.

"I'm sensing you weren't impressed with him," Ari said.

Carly wasn't sure how to answer that. "He's got a big reputation, and an ego to match. I can't say he gave me the warm fuzzies, but then, that's not his job. He asked me if the scuttlebutt about my helping the police solve murders was true, and he didn't seem overjoyed with my answer."

"Hmmm. Makes me wonder what your mom thought of him."

"I'll talk to her tomorrow. Grant insists on replacing me tomorrow, so I won't be going to the restaurant. Maybe I can make some progress on Mom's case. And I'll contact Norah about Leslie's situation, too."

Ari sat up straighter, his expression serious. "And by helping Mom you mean . . ."

Carly felt her cheeks burn. "You know, things like . . . googling people to check into their backgrounds. Stuff like that."

He looked unhappy with her answer. Not that Carly expected him to jump for joy. More than once, she'd found herself in the clutches of a killer.

Ari took her hands in both of his. "Honey, that's exactly what worries me. If you left it at googling, that would be one thing, but you don't. And your mom doesn't have a *case*. She hasn't been charged with anything yet, remember?"

"But she could be, any time now. That's why I want to nip it in the bud."

Ari hung his head in defeat. "I know I can't stop you, but please, *please* don't do anything without telling me where you are first. Or at least taking someone with you."

Carly thought about the woman who was at the fundraiser with Brice—Yvette something. Don said he'd recognized her from the auto parts store. What harm could it do to stop by for a pair of windshield wipers? The ones on her

Corolla were definitely getting ragged. Well, sort of ragged.

"I will keep you informed if I decide to talk to anyone. That's a promise."

Ari sighed and closed his eyes, then wrapped her in his arms. "I guess that's better than nothing. I have a few jobs lined up this week, but I can postpone one of them if you need me. I still have Leslie's cash flow problem to work on."

Carly gave him a smile that was more reassuring than she felt. "We'll work on it together, okay?"

He swallowed, and his dark brown gaze captured hers. "What would I ever do without you?" he said hoarsely.

She reached up and touched his cheek. "Luckily, you'll never have to find out."

CHAPTER 9

CARLY GOT UP AT FIVE THIRTY TUESDAY MORNING. SHE'D CAUGHT UP ON some much-needed sleep and was ready to face the challenges of the day with a fresh outlook.

A steady rain was coming down, and the windows were dotted with droplets. The lawns were growing lush. The impatiens Carly had hung above the front porch were bursting with pink and white blossoms.

After everyone enjoyed a breakfast of cereal and fresh blueberries, Ari headed off to do a rewiring job at a local business, while Leslie worked on pumping up her résumé and checking out more online job sites.

Quinne was content to watch animated shows on PBS with her trusty sidekick, Havarti. Carly smiled at the two sprawled out on the living room carpet with their gazes glued to the TV. She was relieved to see the little girl adjusting to her new living situation, temporary though it would be. Carly sensed she was an indoor kind of girl who'd rather study French or watch a video on her tablet than explore a playground or visit a park. So long as Havarti was at her side, she was content.

Knowing that Grant was taking over for her at the eatery, Carly set up her laptop on the kitchen table and started googling. First on the list: Brice Keaton.

She wasn't surprised to find zero social media pages for him. Given his grouchy temperament, Carly wondered if the man had any friends at all.

Stop it, she berated herself. She herself didn't have a Facebook page or an Instagram account either. It didn't mean she was friendless or unlikeable. In her case, it meant that the restaurant's Facebook page satisfied her social media needs quite sufficiently.

She continued scrolling. The only thing that popped up was a link to a short article from a Manchester newspaper. Brice Keaton of Shaftsbury, Vermont, had been involved in an accident that past winter while working as a delivery person for Silverio Brothers Beverage Distributors. He was driving his company's delivery van when the SUV behind him failed to slow down on the icy road and plowed right into him. Despite sustaining a badly sprained arm and a small fracture in his wrist, he'd rushed to the vehicle that struck him to check on the other driver. The man hadn't been hurt but was later charged with DUI. The police later praised Brice for being "an exemplary driver as well as a good Samaritan."

It made his death seem all the more senseless.

Assuming he still worked for the same company, what made him want to sell beverages for a fundraiser? Did he secretly plan to keep the profits instead of donating to the cause? Even if that were true, he wouldn't have made enough money to make it worth his trouble.

Something wasn't adding up.

That was it for Brice. His obituary hadn't been published yet. Carly wondered who would write it. Did he have any family?

Disappointed at the dearth of information about him, Carly checked out Panda Bear Auto Parts. Just as Don had described, it was located on the southern end of the main drag in Balsam Dell. Their website didn't list employee names, but Don had sounded sure Yvette worked there.

Today would be a perfect day to nab her for a chat, if she was there. Should she ask Ari to go with her? He'd bought truck parts there before, so they might remember him.

She mulled it for a minute, then had a better idea. She tapped a saved number on her cell.

"Any chance you want to pay a visit to Panda Bear Auto Parts with me today?"

Don Frasco chuckled. "This was so predictable. You want to check out that Yvette woman, right?"

"You bet I do. I thought you might want to go with me since you're familiar with the place."

"What auto parts do you need? A pine-scented air freshener? A new cup holder?" Don loved yanking her chain.

"It so happens that my windshield wipers are practically falling apart," she said with mock annoyance.

"Ah, yes, your windshield wipers." The sound of papers being shuffled came through the line. "Well, you're in luck," Don said. "I have a free hour from two to three today. Will that work?"

Carly doubted that Don's schedule was that precise. His days revolved around setting up ads for his weekly paper, along with writing a few local interest articles. She knew he was helping Nina unpack this week, but she refrained from mentioning it.

"That works for me," Carly agreed. "Park in my spot behind the eatery at two and I'll pick you up."

"Will your poor windshield wipers survive that long?"

"Very amusing."

She ended the call just as Quinne came into the kitchen with Havarti trailing behind her. Instead of being in two tight braids, her red hair hung down her back in one thick braid secured with a green bow. She slid onto a chair adjacent to Carly's and set her tablet on the table.

"Hey, what's happening?" Carly closed her laptop.

Quinne smiled, and her eyes sparkled. "I found the coolest video about Paris. Wanna see it?"

"You bet I do," Carly said.

The video, which lasted about six minutes, was an aerial panorama of Paris, highlighted by fun facts.

"Wow, that *was* cool," Carly agreed when the video ended. "What was your favorite place?"

"The Eiffel Tower," Quinne answered without hesitation. "Someday I want to go to the tippity-top and take a million pictures of Paris!" She spread her arms high above her head, and Havarti gave a yip of approval.

"That's an excellent goal. Would you like some juice?" Carly offered.

"Apple juice, please. And can I have some of those vanilla wafers I saw in the cupboard?"

Carly smiled and fetched her treat for her. She couldn't help marveling at this little girl. Her early life had been filled with uncertainty and loneliness. Yet she'd found her own way to navigate through it by immersing herself in an exciting place she'd seen only in pictures.

Quinne finished her snack and returned to the living room with Havarti. "I'm going to look for more pictures of the Eiffel Tower," she announced.

As much as Carly loved spending time with the little girl, she had other matters that needed attention. She started by calling her mom, who sounded subdued.

"What did you think of Burt Oakley?" was Rhonda's first question.

Carly winced. "I'm not sure, Mom. He's experienced and he knows his stuff, that's for sure. And I was inspired by his confidence." She tried to sound encouraging, but her mom knew her far too well.

"But?" Rhonda said sharply.

"Well, he didn't seem thrilled about my past involvement with murders. And I didn't bring it up—he did. I also sensed that he views the police as the enemy."

"I got that feeling, too," Rhonda said with a long sigh. "Honey, what do you think I should do?"

Carly had no clue how to answer that. She was too close to the situation to be objective. She rubbed her hand over her face. "You haven't been charged with anything, so I'd say sit tight for now. Are you going to work today?"

"No." Rhonda sounded dejected. "Even though I'm only part-time, the library trustees want me to take some time off until the dust settles."

Until the dust settles? What did that mean? Carly thought crossly.

"Listen, Mom, I'm taking today off. Grant insisted on filling in for me. How about I treat you to lunch?"

Rhonda's smile came through the phone. "I'd love to, but Gary's picking up a pizza for us. We're going to spend the afternoon watching some of my favorite old movies. How are Leslie and Quinne doing?"

"They're doing okay. Quinne seems to be enjoying her visit with us. You should see her with Havarti. I swear, it's like they're glued together!" She laughed.

Rhonda promised to meet them soon and disconnected.

Feeling unsettled after the phone conversation, Carly went into her bedroom and called Norah. "Listen," she said, "I know you're coming over later, but can I run something by you?"

"Of course!" Norah replied.

Carly gave her a summary of Leslie's employment woes.

"That poor woman," Norah said, clearly disgusted. "I don't want to promise anything until I check out a few things, but I might be able to help her. I assume she wants to work where she lives in Rhode Island, right?"

"As far as I know," Carly said. "She's working on her résumé now. Quinne's looking for pictures of the Eiffel Tower on her tablet. She's teaching herself to speak French. I can't wait for you to meet her. She's such a bright little girl."

"Nate and I are excited about meeting both of them," Norah said. "Listen, I have a meeting at one with a new client, but after that I'll have some time. Can you ask Leslie to email her résumé to me? Even if it's not in final form, it'll give me a snapshot of her work history."

"You got it," Carly told her.

After the call ended, Carly headed upstairs to deliver her sister's message to Leslie. Armed with Norah's email address, Leslie thanked Carly profusely. She agreed to forward her résumé to her immediately.

Downstairs, Carly dusted and vacuumed her bedroom. She hadn't had a chance to do much cleaning. With her temporary guests there, she had even less time.

An early lunch of PBJs and milk—coffee for the adults—put a huge grin on Quinne's face. Carly explained to Leslie that she had an errand to run at two but would be back in plenty of time for supper.

The sky was clearing by the time Carly left. As he'd promised, Don was waiting for her behind the eatery. He hopped into Carly's Corolla and they set off for the auto parts store.

Panda Bear Auto Parts was a stand-alone building with a good-sized parking lot. The store itself was huge, with row after row of neatly appointed shelves of every product imaginable to make your vehicle run smoothly.

Don pointed to the rear of the store, and they walked along an aisle of auto accessories. At the back was a long counter, above which was a sign identifying it as the Sales & Service department. A youngish man with blond hair and a mustache greeted them. His name tag identified him as Cliff T. "Help you folks?" he asked with a pleasant smile.

Carly returned his smile. "I hope so. We're looking for Yvette. Is she in today?"

The man's eyes narrowed. "You looking for Yvette Carter?"

"Yes," Carly replied, hoping there wasn't another Yvette who worked there.

The man eyed them for a moment, then, "Are you with the cops? Because a detective was here earlier."

"Really?" Carly tried to sound surprised. "No, we're not with the police.

Yvette offered to help me with something a few days ago. She told me to ask for her."

"Wait here," the man instructed, then went through a door behind the counter.

It was a fib, but it worked. Even better, he hadn't asked for her name.

A minute or so later, Yvette emerged from the same door. The name tag attached to her flowered top read *Yvette C.*

When she saw Carly, a spark of recognition flashed in her brown eyes. She gave a nervous smile. "Hello, I'm Yvette. Can I help you with something?"

"Hi, Yvette," Carly said amiably. "I don't know if you remember me, but I met you on Saturday at the high school. I'm in desperate need of windshield wipers for my Toyota, but I'm totally clueless about which ones to buy."

Yvette fingered the silver chain that hung around her neck. Confusion, mixed with a touch of fear, crossed her features. "How did you know I worked here?"

Don quickly piped in with one of his rare smiles. "I was the dude taking pictures that day for the *Balsam Dell Weekly*. I recognized you from when I bought my new tire here a few weeks ago. When I saw you, it reminded me about the great customer service you guys give."

Carly had to resist an eye roll. Don was really laying it on thick.

Yvette's face relaxed a bit. "Okay, then. Can you give me the year, make, and model of your car?" she addressed Carly.

Carly supplied the details, and Yvette excused herself.

"Don," Carly said in a low voice, "I want to speak to Yvette alone, woman to woman. Can you start browsing around, pretend you're shopping for something?"

"Yeah, sure," he said. "I've got to make a phone call anyway." He strode off toward the front of the store, just as Yvette returned holding a package of windshield wipers.

"These should do it." She set them on the counter. "We offer free installation, if you're interested."

"That would be great, thanks." After Carly paid for the wipers, she leaned forward. "Yvette, when you get a break, can I treat you to a cup of coffee? There's something I want to talk to you about. It's important."

Yvette's face blanched. She toyed with a strand of her straight brown hair. "I-I already talked to the police," she hedged.

Carly adopted a worried expression. "Yvette, my mom is a strong suspect in Brice's death. I'm trying to help her because I know she's innocent. I just have a few questions about him, that's all." She gave her a pleading look.

Yvette swiveled her head and looked all around, then said, "I go on break in ten minutes. There's an employee snack room out back. We can have coffee there."

"Great," Carly said. "I'll be back in ten."

A customer was waiting, so Carly stepped back. She took advantage of the short wait by stepping outside and checking in with her team.

"Hey," Nina said in a concerned voice, "how's everything going?"

"So far, so good," Carly said vaguely. "I wanted to check on things, see if you needed me for anything."

"We are having a super day," Nina assured her. "Our customers are so happy to see Grant's smiling face that they're practically doing cartwheels."

"I can imagine." Carly laughed. "Okay, but I'm only a text away if you need me. Otherwise, I'll see you all early tomorrow."

Don finally returned, having bought nothing. Carly asked him to be patient a bit longer while she chatted privately with Yvette.

"No problem," he said. "I saw something I might want to buy."

After the customer left, Yvette signaled to Carly. "Let's go out back. Where's your friend?"

"He's browsing. I told him this was girl talk." She winked at Yvette.

They went through the door behind the counter and into a large storage room. Boxes were stacked everywhere, all neatly labeled and organized. At the rear, a doorway off to the right led into a small kitchen, complete with a fridge and microwave. The room smelled of burnt coffee and the remains of someone's greasy lunch.

Yvette tossed out the old coffee and made a fresh pot. While it brewed, she waved a hand at a rickety wooden table. "Have a seat."

Carly sat down and set her tote in her lap. Yvette waited for the coffee to finish, then poured some into two mugs. "What is it you wanted to ask?" she said, sliding a mug over to Carly.

"I know this is personal, but were you and Brice . . . a couple?" She took a creamer from a bowl on the table and opened it into her coffee.

Yvette's eyes narrowed. She looked flustered at the question. "It's hard to describe. There was a guy who used to work here—Theo Sullivan. We dated for a while, but the verbal abuse started almost immediately. My boss ended up firing him, and then I dumped him. Double whammy, right? Theo did not take it well. He blamed me for getting him fired. He started sending me creepy texts."

Carly was appalled. "Did you report him to the police?"

Yvette shook her head. "No, I was afraid he might escalate if I did. I figured if I ignored him, he'd eventually leave me alone. Unfortunately, he kept sending the texts, plus phone calls." She pulled in a shaky breath and took a sip of her coffee. "Then one day Brice came into the store. He needed a part for his delivery truck. We sort of . . . clicked, I guess."

"How long ago was that?" Carly asked.

Yvette shrugged. "I don't know. Maybe three or four months ago? Brice was so different from Theo. Once he even bought me flowers." She gave out a strangled laugh. "The thing is, he made me feel safe. As long as I was with him, I figured Theo would finally take a hint and leave me alone."

From what Carly had overhead on Saturday, it didn't sound as if Brice was much of an improvement, as boyfriends go. She remembered how he'd berated Yvette for being late.

Carly took another sip from her mug. Even fresh, the coffee was terrible. "So Theo found out about Brice?"

"Yeah, he saw Brice pick me up at my apartment one day. That's when I realized Theo had been watching me." She gave a hard shiver. "He got out of the car and screamed at Brice, told him to leave his 'girl' alone."

A frisson of fear for Yvette's safety rushed through Carly. "Yvette, this man sounds dangerous. He shouldn't be getting away with this. The police should know about his threats."

Yvette rubbed her eyes with her fingers, and her cheeks reddened. "I know. It's just . . . I figured with Brice in my life I didn't need to. He'd given me a key to his house, and I stayed there a few times. Whenever he knew he'd be home late, he'd ask me to feed Moxie."

"Moxie?"

"His cat. Brice lives—lived—in Shaftsbury. I always said yes because I care about the kitty." Tears leaked from Yvette's eyes, and she blotted them with a napkin. "Brice loved that cat so much."

"Who's taking care of Moxie now?" Carly asked.

"Brice's brother Phil is. He drove here on Sunday from New Hampshire after he saw the news about his brother on TV. Supposedly he's been working with the police. For the time being, he's staying at Brice's house."

A brother. Now that was an interesting twist, Carly thought.

"Have you met him?"

"Once," she confirmed. "Weird thing is, I didn't even know Brice had a brother until, you know, he died. Ever weirder, his brother's his twin. I mean, why didn't he ever tell me he was a twin?"

"What did you think of him?" Carly asked.

"He seemed like an okay guy but he wasn't terribly friendly. He told me he'd take care of Moxie, so I didn't have to go over there anymore. I got the feeling he didn't want me there while he cleaned out Brice's belongings. The thing is, I left some of my own stuff there and I need to get it back." She shot a nervous glance at the doorway.

Carly sensed she was getting antsy over the questions, so she cut to the chase. "Yvette, after you and Brice left the fundraiser on Saturday, where did you go?"

She toyed with the handle of her mug. "We met somewhere for lunch and then I went home," she said testily. "He said he'd call me, but—" She gulped down a mouthful of coffee.

"But he didn't?"

"No, he didn't," she said in a barely audible voice. "He never called me again." Her eyes filled.

Carly felt terrible for everything Yvette had gone through. The woman seemed to have zero luck with boyfriends. "I'm so sorry." She tried to gauge whether Yvette was genuinely mourning Brice's death, or if she was only going through the motions. But there was something else she needed to know.

"Yvette, Brice seemed super angry that day at the fundraiser. Was he really there to raise money for the school? It didn't seem as if he wanted to be there."

"I asked him that, too," she replied, "but he acted real annoyed that I even asked, so I dropped it. I didn't need any more grief."

So why did Brice agree to take part in the fundraiser? Carly mused. Did he have an ulterior motive?

"If I'm not prying, Yvette, what did the police ask you?"

Yvette shifted uncomfortably on her chair. "You know—stuff like, were we close, had we argued lately, did I know anyone who had a grudge against him."

The last question was telling. It meant the police weren't one hundred percent sold on Rhonda being the culprit.

"Did you? Know of anyone?"

"Other than Theo, no. I finally told the police about him, so I'm hoping he won't bother me anymore." Yvette gulped down the rest of her coffee. "Look, I'm sorry about your mom, but I really gotta get back in the store. Drive your car around to the side and pull up to the first carport, okay? I'll buzz Elijah and let him know. He'll have those wipers on in no time." She picked up both their mugs and rinsed them in the sink.

"Thanks, that would be great." Carly reached into her tote and pulled out her cell. "Would you mind if we took each other's cell numbers? That way, if you think of anything, you can text me?"

After a hesitation, Yvette said, "Um, I guess that would be okay."

Their cell phone numbers exchanged, they retraced their steps back into the store. Don was standing near the sales counter holding a brown bag. "I paid for this down front. You ready to go?"

Yvette quickly swooped in to help a waiting customer. She looked relieved to see Carly leaving.

"I am, but I have to drive around to the side to have my wipers installed." She held up the bag.

They got into the Corolla, which felt like the inside of a furnace. Carly blasted the AC, then drove around to the side of the building. A husky, muscular man wearing safety goggles motioned her toward the open carport, then held up a hand for her to stop at the entrance.

Carly powered her window down. "You must be Elijah."

He flashed a toothy smile. "Guilty as charged. Got the wipers?"

She handed him the package, and in less than two minutes the new wipers were on. Carly started to thank him until she noticed that his gaze was fixed on a black sedan with a silver hood ornament that had driven into the lot. His stubbled jaw hardened, and he held up a curled fist.

Carly glanced in her rearview mirror. The sedan cruised slowly behind her. It idled for a few moments, then abruptly took off like a jet.

"Yeah, you'd better get out of here, Sullivan," Elijah muttered in a menacing tone. Looking flustered, he turned back to Carly. "Sorry about that. That lowlife's been warned to stay away."

"That's okay. I heard you call him Sullivan."

Elijah nodded. "Theo Sullivan. He's been harassing Yvette. If I see him here again, I'm gonna punch his lights out."

"Do you think he's dangerous?" Carly prodded.

Elijah shrugged. "Hard to tell. Guy like that? Probably just a coward, like all bullies." He gave a contrite smile. "Sorry to rant like that, miss. You have a nice day."

Carly rolled up her window, feeling goose bumps sprout on her arms. But it wasn't from the car's AC kicking in.

It was the appearance of Theo Sullivan that'd given her the sudden chill.

Don gave her an anxious look. "Come on. Let's get out of here."

CHAPTER 10

CARLY BACKED HER CAR OUT SLOWLY, THEN HEADED INTO TOWN. DON HAD been strangely silent throughout the exchange. It wasn't like him. Typically, he'd be all over anything he thought might be a juicy story.

She looked at the bag he was holding. "What did you buy?"

His freckles darkened in a blush. He pulled out a beaded strand attached to a sparkly butterfly. "It's a sun catcher," Don told her. "It's for a car, but I thought it would look cool in Nina's kitchen window."

Carly smiled at him. "That's sweet of you. I think she'll love that."

He shrugged and dropped it back into the bag. "So, tell me about your meeting with Yvette."

Carly related the highlights of their conversation and then explained who Theo Sullivan was.

Don grimaced. "Yikes. So he was the guy in the black car? He sounds like a loose cannon."

"I know. That's why I'm worried for Yvette." Carly bit down on her lip. "So, what's the rest of your day looking like?"

"Nothing exciting. Setting up the paper to bring to the printer tomorrow. I made a whole centerfold of pics from the fundraiser."

"What about Brice's death?" she asked. "You must've written a piece about that."

He shrugged. "I reported what I knew, but as usual, the cops aren't sharing much."

Carly's heart slammed in her chest. "You didn't mention my mom's name, right?" she yelped.

"No, I did not," Don said smugly. "A lesser reporter might have, but I have respect for the truth. When the real killer is caught, I'll blast it all over the front page."

She felt her heartbeat slow to an almost normal pace. "Thank you, Don. I don't say this often, but you're a good friend."

He raised an eyebrow at her. "Actually, you never say it."

Ouch. That got Carly where it hurt. "You're right. My bad." She gave his arm a playful tap with her fist.

Don gave her a crooked grin, then turned serious. "When I get home, I'm going to google Theo Sullivan. He sounds like a shady character."

"Thanks, and while you're googling, can you check out Brice's brother, Phil Keaton? He lives in New Hampshire. That's all I know."

Don nodded slowly. "Sure, but was he even in town when Brice was murdered?"

"Not according to Yvette," Carly replied, "but I think we should check him out anyway. And while you're at it, maybe check out Yvette, too."

"Gotcha," he said. "I'll let you know what pops up."

She thanked Don for his help, dropped him off at his car, and made a quick visit inside the eatery. Three booths were occupied, and a lone customer sat at the counter. The aroma of golden grilled cheese tantalized her senses, and suddenly she had a craving for one.

"Hey, what are you doing here?" Valerie greeted her after wiping down a table. "This is your day off."

"I know, but I couldn't resist popping in."

Nina barreled out of the kitchen carrying a rectangular container of salad. "I thought I heard your voice! How's your day been going?"

"Pretty well," Carly said, ambling toward the front of the restaurant. "I'm going to grab a lemonade and then get out of your hair. After I say hi to Grant."

Grant flipped over a sandwich and looked up at her. "Hey, what're you doing here? Checking up on me?" he teased.

"Never," Carly said. She didn't want to say it aloud, but she simply missed the place. And the team she'd grown to love.

When she first opened her eatery, she had only two part-time employees. Now she had two full-time employees and a part-time server. She'd expanded the menu from its original few choices to a wider array of grilled cheese delights—thanks largely to Grant's culinary creativity. Adding a salad had been a popular choice for the health-conscious, and Nina's homemade sugar cookies were a welcome addition.

Carly nabbed a lemonade from the cooler, then stopped to greet a few patrons before leaving through the rear door. She still had to pick up supplies for the barbecue, so she made a fast trip into Telly's Market.

When she got home, only Havarti was there. He bounced off Carly's knees all the way into the kitchen, where she fed him a few doggy treats and refreshed his water.

Leslie had left a note for her on the kitchen table. *Quinne and I went to see a puppet show at the community center. Be back by four thirty! Les—*

Carly smiled. They'd found a local activity that Quinne would enjoy. She hoped it was a sign that Leslie was feeling more optimistic about her future.

She poured herself a spring water and began putting away the groceries. The burgers were all made. All they'd need to do was slap them on the grill. Carly was chopping onions for the burgers when she heard the front door open. Havarti raced toward the foyer with rocket-like speed.

Carly wiped her hands on a towel and followed the dog. Quinne was already on the floor in the living room, giggling with joy as he licked her face.

Leslie smiled. "They're a pair, aren't they?"

"They sure are," Carly agreed, though she worried about how Quinne would feel when she and Leslie had to return to Rhode Island. From the moment they arrived, Havarti had been Quinne's nearly constant companion.

Pushing the thought aside, Carly said, "So, how was the puppet show?"

"Oh, Quinne loved it." Leslie dropped onto the sofa and ran a hand through her hair. "They performed the *Tale of Peter Rabbit*, and the narrator did a super job. Afterward they gave out Popsicles to the kids."

Carly grinned. "I'm glad you both had fun."

Leslie toyed with the fringe on the nearest throw pillow. "I really enjoyed driving around town today, pointing out some of my old haunts to Quinne. I'd forgotten what a great little town this is. I didn't appreciate it when I was young, but I'm seeing it through different eyes now. I love that nothing much has changed, you know?"

Carly did know, although she herself had left her hometown to marry Daniel and move to northern Vermont. It wasn't until he died in a tragic accident that she returned to Balsam Dell. She understood exactly what Leslie was feeling.

"Want something to drink?" Carly asked, pushing away the memory.

"Nah. I'm good. Quinne, you want a juice?" Leslie asked.

Quinne was sitting on the floor, her little arms wrapped around Havarti's neck. "No, thank you. I'll wait for supper."

Leslie rose from the sofa and signaled to Carly. "Let's go in the kitchen. I want to tell you about my convo with Norah."

They sat at the kitchen table, and Carly set out some water crackers and cheddar squares. Leslie's demeanor had undergone an amazing transformation. Her face was animated and her eyes sparkled—such a difference from only that morning.

Leslie plucked a cheddar square off the plate. "Carly, your sister is a dynamo. After she got my email, she did some research and then called me. She's working on tweaking my résumé, but then it's full steam ahead to nail down some interviews."

A surge of pride in her sister swept through Carly. "Les, that's fantastic. I'm so glad Norah's helping you." She bit a cracker in half and crunched it between her teeth.

"She's hoping to match me with one of the larger dentistry groups," Leslie explained. "There's more variety, and better benefits." She shook her head and picked up a cracker. "All these years I stuck with one dentist because I thought he valued me. Look what it got me." She pursed her lips but then smiled. "I'm *so* looking forward to meeting Norah in person."

Despite her faith in Norah, Carly hoped Leslie wasn't getting her hopes up too soon.

• • •

Ari came home around four thirty, and Leslie gave him her news. He wrapped his sister in a hug. "I think that calls for a celebration," he said, and poured them each a short glass of wine.

Norah and Nate arrived about an hour later. As always, Norah was stylishly garbed—this time in a flowered sundress that brushed her knees, and sandals with matching fabric. Quinne gawked up at Nate, who was well over six feet tall. It wasn't long before she'd completely warmed up to both him and Norah.

"And this is yours." Norah presented Quinne with a pink, tissue-stuffed gift bag.

Quinne's eyes widened. "This is for me?"

Norah grinned. "You bet it is. Check it out!"

Quinne separated the crinkly tissue and peeked inside. Her eyes widened as she removed a child's Paris-themed tote bag emblazoned with a pink Eiffel Tower. "Auntie Leslie, look!" she cried, holding it aloft. "Isn't it beautiful?"

"Oh, my." Leslie gaped at Norah. "Where did you ever find that?"

Norah looked thrilled at Quinne's reaction. "We have a shop downtown called Pugs and Purses. They have a great selection for children."

Leslie folded her hands over her chest, her eyes moist. "What a lovely thing to do. Thank you, Norah. And Nate."

Nate laughed. "Hey, this was all Norah. I'm only in charge of dessert." He held up a large paper bag, which he immediately stashed in the fridge.

After everyone had gushed over Quinne's gift, they trailed into the yard for the barbecue. Carly was pleased at how easily Leslie had gained a comfort level with Nate and Norah. As for Quinne, she seemed to be growing more comfortable in her new surroundings every day.

Once everyone had eaten, Nate announced, "Time for dessert! I'll be back in a jiffy." He returned minutes later with all the fixings for strawberry shortcake.

"Yay, I love strawberries!" Quinne chirped as Nate gave her the first helping. She offered Havarti a speck of whipped cream, which the dog licked gently from her finger. Watching them together, Carly got a lump in her throat.

After everyone had finished dessert, Carly and Ari cleaned up the dishes. The rainfall of earlier in the day had scrubbed the landscape clean. Squirrels darted up and down the big maple, and a mild breeze sifted through the leaves.

"Would anyone mind if Leslie and I went inside for a private chat?" Norah asked, with a meaningful look at Leslie. "I have a few more things to discuss with her. It won't take long."

"Not at all," Nate said, leaning over to plant a quick kiss on her cheek.

The two headed into the house, while Nate entertained Quinne with stories of Paris, a city he'd visited several times while appearing at one of the opera houses. His animated tales had Quinne's mouth dropping open with wonder.

Twenty minutes later, Norah and Leslie returned to the table, both grinning as if they shared a secret. Then hugs were exchanged, and Norah and Nate left, promising to see them again soon.

Leslie took Quinne upstairs for her bath and a bedtime story, Havarti trotting behind them. The child looked tired, but happy.

"Our faithful companion has abandoned us again," Carly joked as she and Ari settled onto the sofa.

Ari squeezed her knee and smiled. "But for a good cause. Quinne adores him, don't you think?"

Carly nodded, then rested her head on Ari's shoulder. "Did you find it odd that Norah never even mentioned Mom? It kind of bothered me."

Ari pulled her close. "I was thinking that too, but maybe in Quinne's presence she didn't want to bring it up."

"I suppose," Carly said, turning as Leslie came back downstairs.

"Hey," Leslie said, then cleared her throat nervously. "I need to talk to you both. Is this a good time?"

Carly's mental antennae went on high alert. "Sure," she and Ari said in unison.

Leslie perched on the arm of one of the overstuffed chairs. "First off, I want to say how grateful I am to both of you for having us here. It's truly been a lifesaver."

"We'll do whatever we can, Les," Ari said warily. "You know that."

Leslie twisted her hands in her lap. "I know. The thing is, after Norah and I talked today, she did some research on regions that have the biggest need for dental hygienists. Turns out Vermont has a shortage of them, right now at least. I've already graduated from an accredited hygiene program, I have a bachelor's degree, and my experience speaks for itself. If I were to move to this area, I'd have to pass a licensing exam, but once I get that I could apply for a job."

"Wait a minute," Carly said. "You're saying you want to move back here? What about Quinne?"

Leslie sagged. "I'd have to wait until the adoption is final. That's the biggest hurdle."

Ari looked gobsmacked. "I don't know what to say, Les. It seems so sudden. If that's really what you want, then go for it. But I think you need to give it careful consideration. The process could take a long time."

"I know, and I don't want to make a hasty decision. I guess . . . I just wanted to know if you'd be supportive if we moved close by. Not financially," she added quickly. "Just . . . as family."

Ari rose from the sofa and slung an arm around his sister. "My God, Les, you seriously have to ask that? You're my only sister. Having you and Quinne living near us would be fantastic. As long as you're sure it's what you truly want."

"Honestly?" Leslie asked, a catch in her voice.

"Leslie, I feel exactly the same as Ari," Carly reassured her. "You and Quinne are family. I would love it if you moved to Vermont."

She was already picturing so many benefits of having them settle nearby. They'd celebrate holidays together. Quinne would gain a loving extended family. Unfortunately, the timing of it all couldn't be worse. Between Rhonda being a murder suspect and a wedding nipping at their heels, how much more could she juggle?

Leslie looked as if she wanted to say more, but instead she bade them good night and hurried upstairs.

Ari dropped back onto the sofa and took Carly's hand. "Honey, I know you're worried about your mom, and about our wedding. Tell me anything I can do to help, okay? And I mean anything."

The concern in his voice tore at Carly's heart. She'd never had a chance to tell him about her and Don's visit to the auto parts store, so she gave him a brief recap.

"At least Don went with you," Ari said with a sigh, "but it still worries me that you're asking questions. Especially with that creepy character hanging around Yvette."

"I know." She wanted to reassure him that nothing bad would happen, but the appearance of Theo Sullivan had thrown a monkey wrench into the mix.

Something else was nagging at Carly. She'd tried to push it out of her head, but it hung over her like a hammer about to drop.

Deep down, in the pit of her gut, she didn't trust Burt Oakley.

CHAPTER 11

ON WEDNESDAY MORNING, CARLY LEFT FOR WORK EARLIER THAN USUAL. Leslie had made pancakes, which delighted Quinne. Ari was off to finish the job he'd started on Tuesday.

Even at seven thirty in the morning, the air was moist and warm. The mercury would hit the low nineties before the day was done.

The night before, while Ari was taking his shower, Carly had booted up her laptop and googled Burt Oakley.

Link after link had pulled up news clips about the lawyer's cutting-edge tactics in court. He had an uncanny ability to break down witnesses until they wept for mercy. Some of the clients he'd defended were hard-core—the worst of the worst. Even in cases where their guilt had been certain, he'd "gotten them off," either on technicalities or by tweaking hard facts to create reasonable doubt. Carly doubted the lawyer had made many friends in the law enforcement community.

Once inside her eatery, Carly turned on the AC and brewed a pot of coffee. The aroma wafting from the pot instantly relaxed her, like a potpourri designed to soothe the senses. The pot had just filled when Nina let herself in through the front door. When she saw Carly, she immediately went over and encased her in a hug. "Hey, girl, you doing okay?"

Carly stood back and flashed a weak smile. "I am," she said, noting the dark lines beneath Nina's green eyes. "How about you? Did you stay up late unpacking?"

"You got me," Nina said and chuckled, grabbing two mugs. She poured coffee for each of them, and they sat at the counter. "It's just . . . I love the place so much I can't wait till everything looks perfect, you know? I want to invite you all over for a housewarming."

Carly plunked a creamer into her mug. She'd felt the same way after the reno work was completed on their own home. The two-family house where she'd once rented the upstairs apartment was now the lovely, one-family it had been decades earlier. A generous offer from Joyce Katso, her former landlady, had enabled her and Ari to purchase it. They were thrilled when the work was completed in time for them to enjoy their first Christmas in the beautiful vintage home.

Nina stirred her coffee. "Any news about your mom?"

Carly shook her head, her throat tight. "We seem to be in a holding pattern. She's hunkering down at home, praying no charges will be filed against her."

"What did her lawyer say?" Nina asked. "If it's not too personal."

"A lot of lawyer-y stuff, none of which gave me any comfort."

When Carly didn't elaborate, Nina slid off her stool. "We're all here for you, sweetie, and that includes Grant. Anything we can do—"

"I know, and I appreciate it."

Carly grabbed her mug and hurried into the kitchen before she teared up. She had a business to run. Despite the fears roiling inside her, she had to keep her emotions in check.

Valerie arrived shortly after that, accompanied by a surprise visitor. Carly had just emerged through the swinging door from the kitchen when she saw Chief Holloway. A momentary wave of panic shot through her. Was he here to give her bad news?

"Hey, Carly," he said in an amiable voice, "can we chat privately for a few?"

"Sure," she said, not fooled by his tone. This was going to be a difficult conversation. She waved him toward the rear booth and they both sat down.

Valerie delivered a mug of coffee to him, then left the two alone.

"Don't worry. I'm not here with any dire news," he began by saying. "But before you start getting involved and asking people questions, I wanted to tell you where we are."

Carly blew out a slow breath. If her visit to Yvette counted, she'd already started asking questions. "I appreciate that, but why now? Brice's death was on Saturday."

Holloway took a sip from his mug. "I know, but I held back until more information came to light. We got a report yesterday of a woman fitting your description stopping by Panda Bear Auto Parts. She was accompanied by a young man with distinctive auburn hair and freckles."

Carly felt her cheeks heat. "I-I needed windshield wipers. Mine were getting worn."

A smile danced on the chief's lips. "Did Don help you pick them out?"

She threw up her hands. "Okay, Chief, you got me. I wanted to talk to Yvette, the woman who was with Brice at the fundraiser. I asked Don to go with me."

"I see." The chief nodded slowly. "Did Yvette tell you that a state police detective had already interviewed her?"

"I think she just said police."

Holloway leaned forward in the booth. "Did you learn anything?"

"Yes, I learned that a scary guy named Theo Sullivan has been harassing Yvette, and that Brice was afraid of him, too." She gave the chief a summary of their conversation, ending with the sudden appearance in the parking lot of the scary guy himself.

It struck Carly that she should have reported the incident to the chief immediately after she dropped off Don. But her head was so jammed with family issues she'd dropped the ball.

"Yvette told me that Brice has a brother named Phil," Carly went on. "He's been staying at Brice's house since Sunday. But I'm sure you know all that."

"We do. What we didn't know was that Sullivan showed up at the auto parts store yesterday. Maybe it's time for another chat with him."

"So, he's already been interviewed?" Carly asked.

"At length, but here's the thing. Keaton's TOD—time of death—was between three thirty and four that day, give or take. Sullivan was at the Nickel and Bear in Bennington—one of those trendy new pubs. Two witnesses and the bartender swore that he was sitting at the bar watching a Red Sox game until after seven. He nursed a few beers, ate a ton of free pretzels, then left."

"So, he's off the hook?"

Holloway's smile was flat. "Not totally. Witnesses sometimes have agendas, if you get my meaning. Sullivan and the bartender are supposedly good buds. There was also a lot of drinking going on during the game, which could've affected witness testimony."

"Chief, let's cut to the real issue—my mother." Carly lowered her voice. "You've known my family for a very long time. You don't seriously believe she strangled Brice Keaton with her scarf, do you?"

"Ah, Carly, we've been over this before. It doesn't matter what I think. The state police are going to follow the evidence."

"But—"

He held up a hand. "I know what you're going to say. The evidence is circumstantial. Anyone could have stolen the wig and scarf and used the scarf to kill Brice."

"Exactly! Mom left them in an unlocked locker." She held up a finger. "Wait. What about fingerprints on the locker?"

"Wiped clean. Probably with the scarf."

Carly wanted to scream. "Doesn't that suggest that someone other than my mom removed the wig and scarf? I mean, why would she wipe the prints clean?"

Holloway looked as if he'd rather eat broken glass than answer the question. "Carly, your mom's car was seen tearing out of the school parking lot only moments after the squad cars arrived at the school."

A lump of bile climbed toward Carly's throat. "What time was that?" she choked out.

"Four thirteen," the chief said. "I'm sorry, but you needed to know."

Carly felt as if her head was swimming in a sea of sharks. Everywhere her mind traveled, she swam smack into another one.

"There's something else," Holloway murmured, "but I'm not at liberty to disclose it. I can reveal this, though. Keaton sustained a blow to his forehead before he was killed. We think the culprit slammed his head into a locker door first, then used the scarf to finish the job."

• • •

Carly stumbled into the kitchen, her mind in a daze. Holloway's words had cut through her like a shard of shrapnel.

If what he said was accurate, then her mom had clearly lied to her. But why? Didn't she know Carly was on her side? That no matter what, she'd do everything in her power to help her?

Unfortunately, the police had a solid witness. One of the officers dispatched to the scene spotted Rhonda's car soaring out of the school parking lot. He'd gotten a clear look at her vanity plate—her three initials—as she sped away. Even more strange, a man was seen running from the parking lot into a side door to the school. He was later identified as Andy Fields, the teacher who orchestrated the fundraiser.

Carly needed to talk to her mom, ASAP. She poured herself a glass of leftover iced coffee and plopped onto a chair at the table. She felt her heart thumping so hard she was afraid it might burst through her chest. Fingers shaking, she punched in her mom's number on her cell.

"Mom?" Carly tried, and failed, to keep her voice even.

"Hi, honey." Rhonda sounded slightly better than she had the day before. "Uh-oh. I can tell from your voice something's wrong."

"Mom, why didn't you tell me you stopped at the school on your way home from Debbie's on Saturday?"

For a long moment, there was stark silence. Then, "I can explain that. When the gals and I left the school that afternoon, Lorraine insisted on driving Vivian and me to Debbie's. She wanted to show off that new Lincoln of hers. It seats about four hundred people," she said dryly. "Debbie and I had driven separately that day, so my car was still in the school parking lot. Lorraine promised to drive me back to my car in plenty of time for me to get home and ready for dinner."

"What about Vivian?"

"She stayed at Debbie's. They'd decided to watch a movie together."

Carly turned it all over in her mind, trying to make sense of it. Lorraine, Rhonda, and Vivian went from the school to Debbie's in Lorraine's car. After they had drinks, Vivian stayed at Debbie's, while Lorraine drove Rhonda back to her car.

"Mom, what did you do after Lorraine dropped you off?"

"What do you think I did?" Rhonda said sharply. "I went home. Carly Hale, are you insinuating something?"

"No, absolutely not." Carly softened her voice. "Mom, I'm sure the police told you that your car was seen tearing out of the parking lot at four thirteen that afternoon. An officer noticed your vanity plate and reported it."

"I . . . honey, you know I have a lead foot sometimes. When I realized how late it was, I rushed home to shower and get ready for dinner. We have a standing reservation at six thirty and Gary hates to be late. I probably did drive a little too fast."

A headache was forming between Carly's eyes, and she rubbed it with her fingers. "Mom, did you speak to anyone at the school after Lorraine dropped you off? Did someone talk to you in the—"

A faint voice in the background that sounded like Gary's made Rhonda interrupt. "Honey, I can't talk about this right now. I was hoping you'd invite us to meet Leslie and Quinne later."

That was an abrupt change of topic, Carly thought. "Ari and I would love that, but you and I still need to talk alone."

"Great! We'll stop by after you're all done with dinner. Is seven thirty okay?"

"Seven thirty is fine. See you then."

Carly would have to leave work early again, but she knew Nina and Valerie wouldn't mind. At least she wouldn't have to worry about making dinner for her mom and Gary.

She tapped Ari's number on her cell. "Hey, remember me?" she teased.

Ari laughed. "You're the beautiful woman I'm going to marry," he said in a low voice. "Everything okay?"

Carly explained that her mom and Gary wanted to meet Leslie and Quinne that evening. She'd tell him the rest privately, when they had time to be alone.

He readily agreed, then said, "I'm sorry we haven't had much time to ourselves these past few days."

"It's no one's fault, Ari. We want to take care of our families, right?"

"Right. Hey, I had an idea about supper. Why don't we order takeout from Canoodle the Noodle? They have healthy choices, and Quinne can pick out whatever she wants."

"Sounds perfect. I'll see you when I get home."

Dinner plans made, they ended the call.

In the dining room, Valerie was cleaning the grill, and Nina was scrubbing the bathroom.

Valerie poured a mug of coffee for Carly and set it on the counter. "Fred told me you'd need some privacy, so Nina and I left you alone. Are you okay?"

Carly slid onto a stool and dumped a creamer into her mug. She was far from okay, but she needed to keep it together. "I'm hanging in there, but I'll need to leave early again today."

"You know Nina and I are fine with that," she said with an understanding nod. "Is there anything I can do to help?"

"Everything you do helps, Val."

Valerie looked ready to cry, but she sucked in a breath and deftly changed the subject. "You know how you said Quinne loves everything about Paris? Well, I had an idea for a French grilled cheese I'd like to try."

Carly's curiosity was piqued. "What is it?"

70

"It's a *croque monsieur*. It requires a béchamel sauce, but that can be made ahead. The rest is easy cheesy."

"Go for it," Carly encouraged. She reflected for the umpteenth time on how lucky she was to have Valerie as a friend and team member.

A knock on the front door made Carly turn. Don Frasco's freckled face stared back at her.

"Hey," she said, unlocking the door.

He strode inside and looked around before heading to the refrigerated case for a bottle of root beer. "I have some info you might be interested in. Got a few minutes?"

"For you, more than a few."

Carly grabbed her mug and they slid into the rear booth, their usual spot to chat.

Nina emerged from the bathroom, her smile a yard wide as she homed in on Don. "I thought I heard your voice." She went over and ruffled his gelled hair.

"Hey, Nina. How's the apartment?" he said.

"About the same as it was when you left last night. I'll leave you guys alone."

Don's freckles deepened in color. "I was only there to put her bookcase together," he mumbled, booting up his new tablet. "She bought it online, but it said 'some assembly required.' Which usually means you need an engineering degree to figure it out. Anyway, I found out a few things, but I'm not sure they're helpful."

"Starting with . . ." Carly prompted.

"Starting with our friend Theo Sullivan. Now there's a piece of work. He has a slew of moving violations, mostly for excessive speed, but he's also been arrested for assault a few times."

"Not really surprising," Carly noted.

"Nor is his arrest for stalking a woman last year," Don added meaningfully. He swallowed a mouthful of root beer.

That got Carly's attention. "Was it Yvette he was stalking?"

"No, a woman in Woodford. For some reason, the charges were dropped. Nothing about Yvette."

Carly remembered Yvette saying she didn't report him to the police.

"Not much else on Sullivan," Don reported. "Of course, there's only so much I can find out from the online police logs."

"What about the brother?"

"Phil Keaton," Don said, pulling up a different link. "Owns a family restaurant in Hancock, New Hampshire, with a souvenir shop attached. He bought out the former owner ten years ago and it's been going strong ever since." He showed Carly a photo of Phil's Place, a gray and white structure flanked by neatly trimmed shrubs. Another picture showed a grinning Phil Keaton with his arm around a teenaged boy.

Carly sucked in a breath. If she didn't know better, she'd think she was looking at Brice Keaton. Phil's head was shaved, but aside from that, the brothers bore a startling resemblance to one another. The boy he was posing with had earned a year's worth of free hamburgers for rescuing a family of ducklings from a sewer drain.

Don's eyes glittered. "Phil looks like Brice, doesn't he? The restaurant is on Facebook and Instagram, but no personal pages for Phil. I guess he likes to keep a low profile."

"A lot of people do. I only have the eatery's Facebook page. Nina does a fantastic job keeping it current."

"Why am I not surprised?" Don smiled. "Nina rocks."

The scent of bacon sizzling on the grill drifted from the front of the restaurant. Carly took a sip of her now-cold coffee. "Does he own a house?"

"Oops, I almost forgot. Yes, he does," Don said. "I got the info from the town assessor's office. Nice little ranch house, worth about three hundred thou. The house is in his name alone."

"He sounds like a cookie-cutter version of the quintessential good guy. What about Yvette Carter?"

Don puffed up his cheeks and blew out a breath. "She's another one who's not on social media. It's like she materialized out of the ozone two years ago, around the time she started working at the auto parts store. I found some online reviews praising her for her excellent service and knowledge of the products, but that's about all."

Carly mulled over Don's findings. Unless she was missing something, nothing he'd turned up had raised any red flags, though she appreciated his efforts. "Can you send me those links?" she asked him.

"Already did. Check your email."

"Efficient as always," Carly said with a smile. "Anything else?"

"Nope. I have to get the paper over to the printer today, so I've gotta bounce."

As if on cue, Nina came over holding a paper bag. "Bacon and tomato sandwich. You can eat it for breakfast or save it for lunch. And I stuck a cookie in there, too. My treat."

His face lit up. "Thanks, Nina." He packed up his tablet and finished his root beer. "Catch you guys later, okay?"

In a flash, he was gone.

Carly grinned at Nina. "You know you don't have to treat him. Don's food is always on the house."

"I know, but this time I want to. He's been a lifesaver helping me get my apartment in shape."

It was more than that, Carly suspected, but she kept her thoughts to herself.

With Don gone, Carly's mind immediately jumped back to her mother's situation. She needed to brainstorm with someone, and she knew exactly who that someone was.

Cell phone in hand, Carly went into the kitchen and punched a saved number on her cell.

"Everything okay?" Gina greeted her.

"Could be better. Hey, can you get away for an hour this afternoon? I need to run something by you."

"It so happens that your timing is impeccable," Gina said, a smile in her voice. "I have something to show you."

They agreed to meet at Gina's apartment at two.

Suzanne came in a few minutes early, and they opened promptly at eleven. It wasn't long before customers began filling the booths—partly, Carly knew, because the steamy day drove them into the air-conditioned restaurant. Tourist season was kicking into gear, and the sidewalks bustled with browsers and shoppers.

At the front of the eatery, Nina had written the day's featured sandwich on the whiteboard she'd set up. It had been her idea a few months earlier to offer a special of the day. Customers welcomed the lower price, which included a free sugar cookie. Today's offering was the Farmhouse Cheddar Sleeps with the Fishes—the eatery's tangy version of a tuna melt.

Carly was seating a gaggle of teenaged girls when a familiar face beamed at her from the entrance. She gave the girls their menus and then went over to greet the newcomer. "Tillie, how nice to see you again."

"Yeah, long time no see." Tillie laughed. Her blond hair, with its pale blue streak, framed her face in a trendy bob. "Hey, you never texted me about whether or not you and Ari liked the pie." She pushed out her lower lip in a faux pout. "I was afraid it might've been awful, and you didn't want to hurt my feelings."

"Oh my gosh, are you kidding? That pie was delicious! Ari's sister and her niece were visiting, so we shared it with them. Everyone praised it to the heavens."

"Whew. What a relief." Tillie's face relaxed.

"I apologize for not texting you. Things have been hectic at our house lately. Are you here for lunch?" Carly asked her.

"I sure am. Can I have a booth?"

She followed Carly to a vacant booth near the restroom. "I'll have today's special with an iced tea," she said, sliding onto the bench.

"You got it. It'll be up shortly."

Carly gave her order to Valerie, who was flipping sandwiches at the speed of light. "I'll need more tuna pretty soon," she said.

Turning on her heel, Carly went into the kitchen. She was removing a large container of tuna salad from the fridge when she remembered that Tillie knew Rhonda from working at the library. Could she have seen something at the gym that day? Someone skulking around the lockers maybe?

When Tillie's order was ready, Carly delivered it to her, along with an iced tea and a cellophane-wrapped cookie. Tillie was busy scrolling through her cell phone, but she slipped it into her purse when Carly set her plate down in front of her.

"This looks amazing," Tillie breathed. "I might be the pie lady, but you are the grilled cheese queen!" She reached for a sandwich half and bit off a large corner. "Mmm," she moaned, closing her eyes.

"I'm glad you like it," Carly said. "I'll leave you to eat your lunch in peace."

Tillie held up a finger. "Wait, can you sit for a few minutes? I wanted to ask how your mom is doing."

It was the opening Carly'd been hoping for. "Sure." She sat down opposite Tillie and folded her hands on the table. "Mom's doing okay, but I'm extremely concerned about her. The investigation seems to be in a holding pattern, which puts Mom in limbo."

"I heard the library suspended her temporarily," Tillie said. "That is *so* unfair." She shook her head while she munched on a potato chip. "So, the police haven't made any progress finding the real killer?"

"Not that I've been told, and I appreciate your faith in her," Carly said. "I'm sure there are gossips in town who've already assumed she *is* the real killer."

"They wouldn't if they knew her," Tillie tsked. "Your mom is a terrific lady, Carly. So kind and supportive. She's the one who encouraged me to expand my pie business."

That didn't surprise Carly. Her mom was big on supporting women-owned businesses. "So tell me, what made you choose baking pies as a business?"

Tillie swallowed another bite of her sandwich. "Long story, but I'll give you the mini version. First mistake—getting married right out of high school to a world-class loser. Thankfully, we split not long afterward. After that I found myself floundering, you know? No clue what I wanted to do for a job. I worked retail—hated it—then got a job at a car washing place. Ugh." She rolled her eyes. "After that I bounced from one boring job to another. I could barely afford my studio apartment, and my car was a piece of junk." She took another sip of her iced tea.

"So anyway," Tillie went on, "one day when I was feeling especially rotten about my life, I consoled myself by baking a pie. A coconut cream pie, to be exact."

"Ooh, that sounds scrumptious," Carly remarked. "With toasted coconut on top?"

"Exactly. Carly, I ate the whole thing in one day. Which upset my stomach to no end, but . . . anyway, after that I tried baking different pies. Pretty soon, a lightbulb went off in my brain." She tapped a finger to her head.

Carly grinned. "You discovered you were good at it."

"No. I discovered I was fantastic at it." Tillie's eyes glittered. "I'd bring pies to work, and everyone would beg for more. I started taking orders from coworkers, and I could barely keep up. I even saved up enough to buy a better car." She went back to eating her sandwich.

"That's a great story, Tillie," Carly praised. "You found your passion and you went for it. I truly admire that."

Tillie shrugged. "Thanks, but right now it's only a side business. I'm lucky I work at a place where I can use the commercial kitchen for free."

"Where do you work?" Carly asked.

"I'm the supervisor at a private cafeteria at Gazebo Insurance Company. You know, they own that massive blue building right off the highway? The owner lets me use the commercial kitchen on Sundays to bake my pies for the week. So long as I supply my own ingredients and leave the kitchen spotless, I'm golden."

"Nice arrangement," Carly noted. "Is this your day off?"

Tillie shook her head. "My yearly physical and a dental appointment were scheduled for today, so my boss told me to take the whole day."

"That worked out well," Carly said. "Tell me about your pies. Where do you sell them?"

"Small businesses, mostly. It's kind of hit-or-miss. Hey, if you ever decide to add pie to your menu, let me know." She gave Carly a hopeful smile.

Carly had thought about expanding the eatery's dessert offerings beyond the scope of Nina's buttery sugar cookies. With more pressing issues on her mind, it wasn't something she wanted to pursue just then. But it was an idea to ponder for the future.

"I will," Carly told her. "Are you originally from Balsam Dell?"

"No, I grew up in the wilds of the Green Mountains." Tillie took a sip of her iced tea. "So, Carly, you're getting married soon. Are you excited?"

A week ago, Carly would have answered that question with a resounding "Yes!" Now, with tension and uncertainty swirling around her like a swarm of locusts, any excitement she felt had been dampened by worry.

"I am, but right now I'm more stressed than anything. My fiancé's sister and her niece are staying with us for a while, and with Mom's situation being up in the air, I'm juggling a lot."

"I'm sorry," Tillie said, her eyes creased with sympathy. "If you think of anything I can do to help, will you let me know?"

"Now that you mention it," Carly said in a low voice, "can I get your thoughts on who might have wanted Brice Keaton dead?"

Tillie looked surprised at the question. "Me? I don't have a clue. I only met him that day. But you saw the way he treated people. Clearly someone had it in for him." She bit off another chunk of her sandwich.

"Did you go into the locker room at all?" Carly asked.

Tillie nodded and swallowed, then took another swig of iced tea. "Actually, I did. I'd brought a few extra supplies in case I needed them, so I stuffed them in one of the lockers. Turned out I didn't need them after all."

"So you picked them up before you left?"

"Yup. I ran out of pie early, so I packed up my things first and made a trip out to my car. When I went back inside for the rest of my stuff, I remembered the locker, so I went in there for my—" Her mouth opened, and her blue eyes popped wide. "Oh, Carly, I just remembered something. Your mom must've shoved her wig in the locker next to mine. I recall seeing a strip of red fabric sticking out."

Red fabric. Carly's heart bounced in her chest. "That must've been Mom's scarf. That means anyone could have noticed it and stolen it to kill Brice."

But why a random scarf? If the murder had been premeditated, the killer would have come prepared. Carly could think of a dozen items that would have made a better weapon.

"Did you mention that to the police?" Carly asked.

Tillie winced. "No, I didn't remember it until just now. Do you think I should tell them?"

"I do," Carly told her. "Can you pinpoint the time when you saw it?"

"Not really," Tillie hedged. "But it had to be sometime around two."

That wasn't much to go on, but at least it was something. And then it hit Carly. Had the killer recognized Rhonda's scarf sticking out of the locker and used it to frame her for the murder? Or was her mom simply the unwitting victim of the culprit's desperate and sudden need for a weapon?

Tillie gave her a distressed look. "Carly, I hate that this is happening to Rhonda. She *so* doesn't deserve this. How can the police not see that?"

"I guess they look at it from a different angle," Carly said, her spirits drooping again.

"It still doesn't make sense." Tillie shook her head with disgust.

She finished by eating half her cookie and stuffing the other half into her purse.

"Your lunch is on me today," Carly told her.

"Are you sure?"

"Absolutely. I appreciate your insight on what happened Saturday."

With a promise to tell the police what she'd remembered about the scarf, Tillie hugged her and went off to her afternoon appointment.

CHAPTER 12

BEFORE SHE HEADED UPSTAIRS TO GINA'S APARTMENT, CARLY ASKED NINA to prepare a daily special, sans the cookie, to bring along. She knew Gina would be glad to share the tuna melt with her. They'd both been trying to curb calories in anticipation of the wedding.

Gina was already home when Carly climbed the stairs to her apartment. Carly set the packaged sandwich on the kitchen table, smiling as Gina's adorable black cat padded over and issued a loud meow.

"Hey, KitCat, are you smelling the tuna?" Carly lifted the cat and nuzzled her fur, then gently set her on a vinyl-covered kitchen chair. Resting on the Formica table was a large gold box, tied with a white bow.

Carly gasped. "Oh, good gravy, are those—"

"Yes, but don't touch them until you put these on." Gina handed Carly a pair of white cotton gloves.

With eager fingers Carly slid them on, then untied the bow and lifted the cover off the box. Inside were the most gorgeous wedding invitations she'd ever seen. She carefully removed one.

On a background of thick cream-colored paper, Gina had used the quilling art she'd perfected to create a border of yellow buttercups woven through delicate green vines. The design was similar to that of Carly's tea-length wedding dress—sage green with a chiffon overlay embroidered with tiny yellow flowers.

Carly began reading the elegant script. "Together with their families, Carly Hale and Ari Mitchell would love for you to join them as they exchange . . ." She stopped and pressed her gloved fingers to her lips, her eyes growing moist.

Gina stared at her. "Is something wrong? Is there a printing error?"

"No! Oh my gosh, are you kidding? Gina, these are beyond fabulous. It's obvious you put your heart and soul into them. I can't tell you how much I love them." Fighting tears, she went over and hugged her friend.

"Thank goodness," Gina said, looking relieved. "Each one is slightly different to make them unique. I know some people like to frame them."

"I can't wait to show Ari. Can I bring this one home?"

"Of course! And don't forget to show your mom. I want to know what she thinks." Gina removed plates and glasses from her cupboard. "Iced tea okay?"

"Sure." Carly removed the cotton gloves and slipped the invitation into her tote.

Gina poured them each a glass of iced tea, and they divided the sandwich.

"Carly, what's wrong?" Gina asked, sitting at the table. "Other than the obvious, something else is bothering you. Come on, spill the tea. Not the iced tea, though."

Carly picked up her sandwich half and set it down again. "The chief stopped by the restaurant this morning to have a chat with me." She told her friend what Holloway had revealed about Rhonda's car being spotted in the school parking lot.

Gina's normally rosy cheeks paled. "And that was right around the time Keaton was . . . killed?"

"As near as they can estimate. When I called Mom and asked her about it, she got all defensive, then cut me off because she wasn't alone." She repeated the gist of what Rhonda had told her, then bit off a tiny corner of her sandwich.

"Do you think your mom's hiding something?" Gina asked.

"She has to be, right?" Carly groaned. "We'd already gone over everything that happened that day, in detail. Why would she omit that?"

Gina lowered her gaze. "You don't think . . . there's someone else, do you? I mean, your mom and Gary are such a perfect match. I can't even imagine it."

Carly gawked at her friend. "No! I never thought that, not even for a second. Come on, Gina, you know Mom as well as I do."

"I know," Gina said, hanging her head. "I'm sorry I even said that. But you need to talk to her again, Carly."

"I know I do." Carly's stomach pinched with dread. It was a conversation she wasn't looking forward to. "Listen, I never had a chance to tell you—Ari's sister and her niece have been staying with us the past few days."

"What? Are you freakin' kidding me?"

Carly explained the circumstances, and why she and Ari wanted to help Leslie. "I can't wait for you to meet Quinne. She's the sweetest child, and so bright."

"Oh, man," Gina said, "you're always putting other people first. But Carly, you have your mom's problem to deal with—not a small one, I might add—and your wedding coming up next month. Something's gotta give."

"I know, I *know*. But we can't ignore Ari's family. They're my family, too," she added softly.

Her cell pinged with a text. Carly excused herself and checked the message. She typed a quick response and tucked her cell back into her tote.

"That was Sissy from the bakery. She wants me there tomorrow at two to choose our wedding cake. I'll be doing some taste testing."

Gina's dark brown eyes sparkled. "Ooh, what a hardship. I can't wait to see what you pick. Remember, all the world loves chocolate. Will Ari go with you?"

Carly smiled. "You sound more excited than I am. I'll ask Ari, but I have a better idea. I'm pretty sure he'll be pleased with it."

They quickly finished their lunch, though Carly had to choke hers down. Gina rinsed their dishes and stuck them in the dishwasher. Although her furnishings were throwbacks to the 1960s, she'd installed a dishwasher that did everything except mop the floor.

"I'm going to spend the afternoon addressing the invitations," Gina said, loading the box carefully into a shopping bag. She'd also perfected the art of calligraphy, which she would use to write out the invitations. "Your mailing list is complete, right?"

"It is," Carly confirmed. "But maybe hold off on mailing Leslie's. I'm not sure how long she'll be here."

"Gotcha." Gina paused. "What are you going to do about your mom?" she asked gently.

Carly slung her tote over her shoulder. "She and Gary are coming over later, after dinner. I'm going to pin her down for a private confab and squeeze the whole truth from her."

"The whole truth and nothing but the truth," Gina emphasized. "Accept no less."

Carly chuckled. "Maybe she should have you for a lawyer."

The two hugged, and Carly thanked her again for the beautiful invitations. Gina hadn't offered any mind-blowing solutions to the problem with her mom, but sorting through everything with her friend had helped bolster her courage.

All she had to do next was to interrogate her mom.

Oh, joy.

• • •

The dining room was quiet, typical for midafternoon. Three booths near the front were occupied. One of Carly's favorite customers, retired fishmonger Buck Heffernan, was seated at the counter enjoying the special of the day—the only sandwich he ever ordered.

"You're late today, Buck," Carly greeted him with a smile.

He waved a hand and scowled. "The wife made me go for a hearing test. Waste of time, if you ask me. I told 'em they could keep their hearing aids because I'm not buying 'em. Do you know what those things cost?"

Carly smiled at the rhetorical question and patted Buck lightly on the shoulder. She'd noticed lately that she had to raise her voice when speaking to him; otherwise, she had to repeat whatever she'd said.

Until a few years ago, her mom had stubbornly resisted wearing hearing aids. One day a light dawned, and she realized how much better her life was when she could hear what was going on around her.

Oh, Mom, what happened that day in the parking lot? What is it you're not telling me?

The question buzzed through Carly's mind as she busied herself clearing dishes off vacated tables. She was carrying a tray of dirty dishes into the kitchen when her cell rang in her pocket. She scurried through the swinging door and set down the tray before answering the call.

"Carly?"

"Yes, is this Yvette?"

"It is," she said, sounding glum. "I wanted to tell you that Brice's brother arranged a memorial service for Friday morning. It'll be at the funeral home in Shaftsbury. I didn't know if you'd be interested in going, but I thought I'd let you know, just in case."

"Thank you. I appreciate that. Do you know what time it starts?"

"Yeah, nine o'clock. Kind of early. The funeral parlor's right on the main street, but I can give you directions if you need them." Her tone was bleak, devoid of any inflection.

"I'm sure I can find it," Carly said. "Yvette, you sound kind of down. How are you dealing with Brice's passing?"

"Passing?" Yvette sniped. "It wasn't a passing, it was a murder." She sniffled loudly. "And I could deal with it better if Phil would let me in the house to get the things I left there. I mean, it's not like they're valuable or anything, but they're mine, you know? And I want to be sure Moxie's okay."

Carly felt for her, yet she couldn't help thinking that Yvette's grief seemed more about the loss of her personal possessions than the loss of Brice. "Don't you still have a key?" Carly asked her.

"I do, but Phil is always there, cleaning out the place. Shaftsbury's, like, a fifteen-minute drive for me. Both times I went there and tried to get in, he acted like I was some sort of . . . gold digger, hoping to grab whatever I wanted for myself. Yeah, like Brice had so many valuables," she snorted.

"So, he didn't let you in?"

Yvette issued a noisy sigh. "He said I can come back for my things after he's done loading all of Brice's stuff into the van he rented. Does that make sense to you?"

"Not really," Carly said, but she suspected that wasn't the whole story.

An idea tripped through her mind—one that wouldn't make Ari happy. Any hesitation she had was instantly overridden by thoughts of her mom's predicament.

"Yvette," Carly said, "would you feel better if I went over there with you? Maybe between the two of us, we could convince Phil you're only there to retrieve your personal items. I can even bring some boxes to pack your things in, if that helps." She and Ari had at least a dozen empty boxes in their upstairs storage space. They could easily spare one or two.

After a long pause, Yvette said, "You would do that for me?"

"I would," Carly confirmed. "I can see you're in a bind."

Yvette let out a relieved sigh. "Thank you. That would be great. We might strike out, but . . . it's worth a shot."

Before ending the call, they agreed to meet behind the eatery at seven thirty the following morning. Carly wasn't sure what she was getting herself into, but she'd already decided to follow Yvette there instead of driving with her. If they got separated in traffic, she could use Brice's address and her GPS to find his residence.

She didn't expect Ari to be thrilled with her plan. He'd probably try to talk her out of it. But if it could help her glean some intel about Brice's death, it was an opportunity she couldn't pass up.

Her mom's freedom was at stake.

CHAPTER 13

CARLY HAD ORIGINALLY HOPED TO WORK UNTIL CLOSING TIME, BUT WITH her mom and Gary coming over at seven thirty, she'd have to leave a bit sooner.

"You're the boss," Nina reminded her when Carly told her about leaving early. "You get to call the shots. Besides, you've been on overload lately. Val and I aren't going to turn into pumpkins if you leave an hour early."

Carly smiled at her and went back to tidying up the tables. "I know, and I appreciate the sentiment. But Ari's picking up takeout for all of us from Canoodle, so at least I don't have to worry about what we're going to eat tonight."

As much as Carly wanted to see her mom, she was dreading the conversation they needed to have.

It was close to four o'clock when another familiar face came in. Hands in the pockets of his trousers, Andy Fields paused and looked around. His eyes brightened when he spotted Carly, although his face was pale and dotted with stubble.

"Andy, it's nice to see you again," Carly greeted him.

"Same here," he said, skimming his gaze over the counter space. "This place is so nice. I don't know why I never ate here before."

"Well, I'm glad you're here now." She grabbed a menu. "Would you like a booth?"

"I would," he said, following her toward the back. "I was so impressed with how helpful you were at Saturday's fundraiser that I promised myself I'd come in for a nice grilled cheese this week."

Carly escorted him to a booth toward the back and gave him a menu. He immediately chose the daily special, and she gave his order slip to Valerie.

When she returned with his iced tea, he was texting on his cell phone. He quickly slipped it into his pocket. "No rest for the weary," he said with a weak laugh.

"Are things still chaotic at the school?" she asked him quietly.

Andy's shoulders drooped. "Not anymore, thankfully. The police finally removed the yellow tape from inside and from the parking lot. I turned over copies of the available video images to them. I've asked a couple of times if they found anything significant, but they keep telling me they're still reviewing the footage." He shrugged and took a sip of his iced tea.

Still reviewing the footage after four days? Carly mused. That seemed like a long time, but then she was only vaguely familiar with police protocol for studying videos.

"I'm sorry," Carly said. "This has to be tough on you."

He rubbed a hand over his face. "I'm still kicking myself, Carly. If I hadn't asked the beverage company to set up a soda stand at the fundraiser, this never would've happened. As unpleasant as he was, I still can't help blaming myself for poor Brice . . ."

Carly slid into the booth opposite him. "It was you who suggested they set up a soda stand?"

"Regretfully, it was. We'd had vendors signing up for all the diner-style foods we'd hoped for, but no one to sell soda pop. I really wanted it to be as authentic as possible for the people attending," he said miserably.

Carly wasn't sure soda pop was the missing puzzle piece to the success of the fundraiser, but Andy had obviously thought otherwise. She suspected he was a conscientious teacher who cared about his students and the school.

"How did Brice end up being the person doing the selling?" she asked him.

Andy heaved a sigh. "My fault, I'm afraid. I'd seen an online article from the Manchester paper about him being injured when his delivery truck was rear-ended. It was back in the winter, one of those icy days. Even with a sprained arm and a cracked wrist, he'd gotten out of his vehicle to help the driver who hit him. Pretty heroic, if you ask me." He plucked a handful of napkins from the dispenser and set them on the table. "Anyway, when I asked the beverage company's head guy if Brice could represent the company at the fundraiser, he readily agreed. He said Brice owed him a favor anyway."

Ah, now Brice's surly attitude was beginning to make sense. He hadn't wanted to be there in the first place. Carly wondered what the favor was that Brice owed his boss.

"By the way," Andy said, pride rising in his voice, "thanks to you and the other vendors, we made a little over five thousand dollars at the fundraiser. At least one good thing came from that awful day."

"That's great, Andy. I'm glad I could do my small part."

"Well, since I'm the assistant basketball coach, having a new gym floor means a lot to me."

"You must be very dedicated to do that and teach," Carly said. "What do you teach?"

"The scintillating subject of earth science," he said with a dry chuckle. "Not a favorite as classes go, but it helps the seniors fulfill their science requirements for certain college majors."

Nina came by with his daily special. She set down a mug of coffee and a creamer for Carly.

"Ah, this looks delicious," he said, thanking Nina.

Carly lifted her mug and the creamer and started to slide off the bench. "I'll let you enjoy your lunch in peace, Andy."

He held up a hand. "Please don't go on my account," he pleaded, picking up a sandwich half. "Truth be told, it's been cathartic to talk to someone who was there that day. You're a very good listener."

Carly nodded and remained where she was, adding the creamer to her coffee. She'd just been handed the perfect opportunity to question Andy more about the videos, especially the ones from the parking lot.

Andy took a large bite of his sandwich and closed his eyes as he chewed. "My goodness," he said after he swallowed. "This is the best tuna melt I've ever had." He washed it down with a swig of iced tea.

As he continued eating, Carly mulled how to broach the subject.

"Andy," she said, after he'd finished a sandwich half, "did the police say why it's taking them so long to review the videos?"

He shook his head. "They didn't come right out and say it, but it sounded like there was a glitch of some sort. But they assured me it was nothing, and that their expert at the state police would figure it out."

A glitch. That could mean almost anything.

Frustration bubbled up in Carly, making her want to tear out her hair. And what was the detail the chief claimed he "wasn't at liberty" to share? Did it have anything to do with the glitch?

And then she remembered something.

"Andy," she said evenly, "did you go out into the parking lot around the time the police arrived?"

He grimaced. "Actually, I did." After a long hesitation he said, "I didn't want to mention this, Carly, but I already told the police. After the custodian found Brice's body that day and I called nine-one-one, I started looking out the windows toward the parking lot so I'd know when the police got there. I was surprised to see a lone car still out there. Even more surprised when Rhonda got out and started heading toward the school at a pretty fast clip. I knew the police would be arriving at any moment, so I ran out to warn her not to come inside. She thanked me, got back in her car, and drove off."

"But someone in a patrol car spotted her, didn't they?"

And swabbed his lips with a napkin. "Yes," he said glumly. "But I only found that out later, when the police questioned me. It was unlucky timing on Rhonda's part, I'm afraid."

Carly digested that while Andy continued eating his tuna melt. She waited until he swallowed and said, "There's something I don't understand. Why did you feel you had to warn my mom that the police were coming?"

His face turned crimson. "I . . . I don't know. I mean, I just thought—"

"You thought Mom might have killed Brice, didn't you?" Carly said, a tremor in her voice. "You recognized the scarf, and you assumed the worst." She covered her mouth with her hand.

"No," Andy said forcefully. "I promise you, Carly, that's not what happened. I just didn't want her getting tangled up with the police in case they saw her. Which, as it turned out, they did."

Carly tried to calm herself, but her nerves felt like they'd been swiped over a cheese grater. She forced herself to take deep, slow breaths. She'd had no right to jump down his throat the way she did. She only wanted to know what happened.

After another deep breath, she gave him an apologetic smile. "I'm so sorry, Andy. I didn't mean to upset you. I was totally out of line, wasn't I?"

"Of course not," he said kindly. "After all, she's your mom. I understand completely."

"Andy," Carly said carefully, "did she tell you why she was going into the school?"

His face reddened and he dropped his gaze to his plate. "She said she needed to use the bathroom. She didn't think she could wait till she got home."

With that, Carly felt even worse. She'd practically attacked the poor man, then pressured him into revealing something he found embarrassing.

I'm losing it. I've got to pull myself together.

Andy motored through the last few bites of his sandwich. He probably regretted asking Carly to sit with him, but that ship had already sailed. As he was gulping down the last few drops of his iced tea, Carly thought of something else.

"Andy, when you told my mom the police were on their way, did she ask why?"

For what seemed an eternity, he seemed to ponder the question. Finally, he said quietly, "No, she didn't."

CHAPTER 14

ON THE SHORT DRIVE HOME, CARLY'S MIND SWIRLED WITH EVERYTHING she'd learned from Andy Fields. Initially he'd been eager to chat. That'd changed quickly when Carly questioned him about meeting her mom in the parking lot on the day of the murder. One positive thing came from his visit, though. He'd promised to let her know if he learned anything new from the police.

After succumbing to pressure from Nina and Valerie, Carly left work at four thirty instead of waiting until six. It was a race to see who greeted her first—Quinne or the little Morkie trailing at her heels. Carly pulled Quinne into a hug and kissed the top of her head, then lifted Havarti and gave him a noisy smooch before setting him back down.

"Auntie Carly, we're getting supper from a noodle place," Quinne chirped. "Uncle Ari said I could order anything I want! Guess what I picked?"

"Um, let's see." Carly pretended to think. "Gummy worms with a side of jelly beans?"

Quinne giggled. "No, silly! That's not supper. I'm getting cauliflower spaghetti with green pesto sauce."

"Whoa. Sounds radical."

Canoodle the Noodle made their pasta with veggies such as cauliflower and spinach. They offered a wide variety of sauces and side dishes, along with heavenly rolls made with Greek yogurt.

Quinne's laughter as she skipped into the kitchen lifted Carly's mood. The tantalizing aroma of pasta and marinara sauce reminded her that she was hungry. Aside from the tuna melt she'd shared with Gina, she'd eaten almost nothing since breakfast. She was ready for a real meal.

Leslie had set the kitchen table for four, and a bottle of Chardonnay sat on the counter. A clean glass rested on the place mat where Quinne always sat.

Ari came in through the back door and promptly kissed Carly on the cheek. "I heard your car drive in. Everything go okay today?"

Loaded question, Carly thought grimly.

"Things went great at the restaurant, but I need to have a serious chat with Mom when she and Gary come over. I found out something today that might be a problem."

His face fell, and he pulled her close. "I'm sorry, honey. Whatever it is, you know I'll do anything I can to help."

Carly stepped back and touched his cheek. "I know you will. By the way, what were you doing outside?"

"Outside? Oh, um, just wiping down the umbrella table in case we decided to eat out there. But Leslie already set the table, so I guess we'll eat in the kitchen."

"With pasta, it makes more sense to eat inside," Carly said.

Quinne tugged on Carly's sleeve. "Auntie Carly, can I use your bathroom to wash my hands?"

"Sure, you can," Carly told her, glad to have a minute alone with Ari.

Quinne dashed off, the dog right behind her.

Carly pulled Ari aside. "Before we all sit down, I have a question." She told him about her cake-tasting appointment, and her idea for bringing along a companion.

Ari's dark brown eyes softened like warm chocolate. "I love that idea. You tell her at dinner. As for the other stuff, we'll talk later."

Leslie came downstairs and joined them. Garbed in a blue tee and beige shorts, she looked relaxed, and her eyes sparkled. "I thought I heard you come in." She gave Carly's arm a light squeeze. "I'm still polishing my résumé, thanks to your sister's brilliant suggestions. I swear, if I tweak it any more it's going to sprout legs and run away."

"That's great, Les," Carly said. "Sounds like you and Norah are getting along swimmingly."

"She's as wonderful as you are." Leslie inhaled deeply. "Hey, since you're home, why don't we eat? Everything's warm, and I'll set out the rolls and salad." She bent down and smiled at Quinne, who'd just returned from the bathroom. "Sweetie, go upstairs and wash your hands before supper, okay?"

"I already did," she said proudly, holding up her clean hands. "Auntie Carly let me use her bathroom."

Carly took a few minutes to wash her own hands and then returned to the kitchen. Ari poured three glasses of wine and filled Quinne's glass with milk.

"By the way," Carly said after they were all seated at the table, "the bakery called me today. They want me to do some taste testing tomorrow for our wedding cake. I have a problem, though. I need someone to go with me. Someone who *really* loves cake."

Ari buttered a roll. "I love cake, but I'm working tomorrow."

Carly smiled and fixed her gaze on Quinne, who looked ready to spring off her chair. "Can I go, Auntie Carly?" she asked. "Cake is my favorite dessert!"

"Why, that's an excellent idea," Carly said. "We have to be there at two."

Leslie was beaming from ear to ear. "I can drop her off at the restaurant first. Will that work?"

With their game plan in place, they finished their meal. Quinne cleaned her plate, leaving only traces of the pesto sauce that coated her shell-shaped pasta. Ari had bought a carton of strawberry gelato, so they each enjoyed a big helping.

After they'd all helped clean up the table and load the dishwasher, Quinne headed upstairs to fetch the new book Leslie had bought her.

Carly quietly told Leslie, "My mom and stepdad will be here in a little while.

They're anxious to meet you and Quinne. The thing is, at some point I'll need to pull Mom aside for a private chat. Something came up that we need to talk about."

"Gotcha," Leslie said. "By the way, thanks for inviting Quinne to the cake testing. I can tell she's over the moon. That was a kind gesture on your part."

Carly waved a hand and laughed. "Hey, it's a tough job, but someone has to help me, right?"

Leslie hugged her, her eyes glistening. "I wish it hadn't taken this long for us to meet. Quinne and I should've visited a long time ago."

"That's okay," Carly said, blinking. "We'll make up for lost time.

• • •

"We're here!" Rhonda announced as she stepped into the foyer. A strand of her brunette hair had slipped out of her decorative comb and curled around her right eye.

Gary came in behind her, his smile looking more forced than genuine. Behind his wire-rimmed glasses, his gentle blue eyes were bloodshot. Carly suspected he was short on sleep and long on stress.

Ari greeted them warmly, shaking Gary's hand and hugging Rhonda. Carly embraced her mom next, a lump filling her throat. "I'm so glad you guys finally came over."

Quinne was there instantly, smiling and holding up her new book for everyone to admire. "Hi, my name's Quinne. My Auntie Leslie bought this for me at the used bookstore today. The books are cheaper there."

They all chuckled, and Carly's heart warmed at the sight of Quinne introducing herself. The child was becoming a social butterfly.

Over Quinne's chatter, Leslie managed to greet everyone, and they all strolled into the living room.

"Okay now, let me see that book!" Rhonda plopped onto the sofa and signaled for Quinne to join her. Havarti claimed the spot on the other side of Quinne, while Gary chose one of the overstuffed chairs.

"I'll read the book from up here," Carly said, leaning over her mom's shoulder.

"It's a children's book, so it's short," Quinne informed them, turning to the first page. "It's all about the Eiffel Tower."

As the little girl slowly turned the pages, Rhonda oohed and aahed over the colorful illustrations. The narrative was beautifully written, describing the pains that were taken in designing and constructing the tower. After Quinne turned the last page, Rhonda and Carly clapped.

"Lemonade for all," Ari announced, carrying a tray into the living room. They each took a glass, and for a while engaged in small talk. Gary kept glancing at his phone. Given his impeccable manners, it was extremely unlike him.

After Carly had drunk half her lemonade, she set her glass on an end table and asked her mom to go into the kitchen with her. Her eyebrows drawn together, Rhonda excused herself and followed her daughter.

"We have a little Chardonnay left," Carly said. "Enough for one glass. Would you like it?"

Rhonda dropped onto a chair at the table. "I'll take it."

Carly poured the wine into a glass and set it down in front of her mom. Rhonda immediately took a long gulp, then wiped her lips with her fingers.

Carly smiled and took the adjacent chair, hoping to put her mom at ease. "First of all, Mom, no one on earth who knows you would ever think you murdered someone. That's not why I want to talk to you."

"Then why do I have to go over this again?" Rhonda said wearily.

"Because the police and another witness," Carly explained quietly, "claim that you talked to someone in the parking lot that day, sometime after four o'clock."

Rhonda's face blanched. Her fingers trembled around the stem of her glass.

"So can we just go over it again?" Carly said when she didn't respond. "Please? So I can get it straight in my own head?"

Rhonda swallowed another mouthful of wine, then rested her hands flat on the table. "Okay, listen, honey. After Lorraine dropped me off that afternoon, I sat in my car for a minute trying to decide if I could make it home without using a bathroom. I'd had a boatload of iced tea at Debbie's, and I was getting desperate. When I decided I couldn't wait that long, I got out of my car and started toward the school. I'd barely walked a few yards when I saw someone running toward me. As soon as I realized it was Andy Fields, my guard immediately went up. I told him why I was going inside, but he said I couldn't, that the police would be arriving any moment and I should get out of there."

Carly took in a breath. "Did you ask him why the police were coming?"

Rhonda stared at her daughter as if she had a few bolts loose. "No! Are you kidding me? I was too scared to ask. I mean, what if there was about to be a shootout or something? At that point, all I wanted was to get out of there, and fast."

Carly sat back in her chair and digested her mom's response. In a way, it made sense. Her mom didn't have the innate curiosity about crime and criminals that Carly had. It was a source of constant annoyance to Rhonda that her daughter had a disturbing knack for stumbling upon murders—and then getting involved in solving them.

"Okay, I totally get that," Carly replied. "Why did you say your guard went up when you saw Andy Fields?"

Rhonda took another gulp of wine. "Because he invited me to have lunch with him some Saturday. Can you imagine? I'm old enough to be his gra—

mother! I haven't felt comfortable around him ever since."

"He . . . asked you out?" Carly gasped. If she'd had a thousand guesses, that one wouldn't have made it to the list.

Rhonda sighed. "It was a few months after I'd started visiting the school to talk to the kids about books. From the get-go he always gushed over my visits. He claimed they made a huge difference in the kids' attitudes toward reading." She toyed with the stem of her glass. "Then one day as I was leaving the school, he pulled me aside. He asked if he could treat me to lunch some Saturday. He couldn't do it during the week because of his job."

Carly shook her head in disbelief. "What did you say?"

"Tell you the truth, I was at a loss for words. Which is rare for me, as you know." Her brief smile faded to a frown. "He'd caught me unawares, as the saying goes. I thanked him but told him I was happily married and declined his invitation."

"How did he take it?" Carly asked.

"His face turned bright red," Rhonda replied, "and he apologized profusely. He said he'd seen my wedding ring, but he'd only asked as a friend, nothing more."

Not only a wedding ring. Rhonda sported a stunning antique diamond that had been handed down in Gary's family for decades. It had once adorned his great-grandmother's ring finger.

"Did he ever invite you to lunch again?" Carly asked her.

Rhonda drained her wineglass. "Thank goodness, no. But the next few times I visited the classes with my usual spiel about books, I caught him staring at me. You know, that puppy dog sort of stare? I was probably being paranoid, but it made me uncomfortable. I decided not to go back there."

Carly didn't know what to make of this new information. On its face it seemed harmless, but she knew better than to make such an assumption. If Andy had developed an obsession with her mom, could he have killed Brice in some misguided "knight in shining armor" act?

She tried to remember if Andy had witnessed Rhonda's rant against Brice that day. Or maybe he'd seen the video that spread through the internet like wildfire not long after it was taken.

Rhonda eyed her daughter with suspicion. "You said the police and another witness saw me going into the school. Was the witness Andy Fields?"

"It was," Carly admitted. "In fact, he came into the eatery this afternoon." She gave her mom a summary of their conversation.

"So . . . he thought he was protecting me by stopping me from going into the school?"

"I might have been wrong, but that's the sense I got," Carly said.

Rhonda reached over and grabbed her daughter's hand. "Honey, why is this happening to me?" she said tearfully. "What did I do to deserve this?"

Carly went over and encased her mom in a hug. "You didn't do anything, Mom. We're going to figure this out. I promise." She kissed Rhonda's hair, and her mom latched on to her arm. "Does Gary know about Andy?"

"He does now. I didn't tell him before because I knew he'd worry. But in light of everything that's happened, I decided I had to."

"How did he react?"

Rhonda sucked in a breath. "He got this sick look on his face that broke my heart. Like I didn't trust him enough to tell him in the first place."

Carly felt sick, too. Her mom and Gary adored each other. Neither of them deserved this torment.

Carly straightened and went back to her chair. "What about your lawyer?"

"Oh, that's another thing," she said sourly. "Gary had him checked out more thoroughly. Turns out he almost never represents a woman. He favors male defendants—the more hardened the better. He's made his reputation that way."

So, a woman who's clearly innocent isn't his cup of tea? The thought made Carly furious.

"Apparently, he took my case because a good buddy of Gary's asked him to." She waved a hand. "The good news is, he's history. The bad news is, I still need a lawyer."

"You fired him?"

"Gary did it for me. I didn't want to talk to him ever again."

A faint knock on the doorframe made them both look up. Gary paused and then came in and wrapped his arms around his wife. She pressed her face against his chest. A tear leaked down his cheek into Rhonda's hair.

Carly struggled to maintain her composure, but it was more than she could bear. She started to bolt from the kitchen when Gary held up a hand. "Carly, wait. I have something to tell you both."

She sat down again, an ache in her chest. Gary stood between the two women.

"Moments ago, I spoke to Chief Holloway. I'd been waiting for his call. As you know, he's been a longtime friend to the Hale family, which has put him in an untenable position. His daughter Anne's partner, Erika, is an experienced attorney who's represented criminal defendants with much success."

"But—" Carly began.

"However," Gary interrupted, "because of her close relationship to the chief, she felt it wise not to represent Rhonda. She recommended her former law partner, a woman named Shania Worthington, who, as Erika puts it, is a 'kick-butt defender of the wronged.'" He offered a tiny smile. "She said it a bit differently, but I'm paraphrasing."

Rhonda looked at Carly, a twinge of hope in her eyes. "That's exactly what I need," she said hoarsely.

91

Gary cupped his wife's shoulder. "If you're willing to meet with her, I've arranged for her to be at our house tomorrow morning at eight. No obligation, just an introductory meeting. I can easily cancel her if you want me to."

Rhonda rose and threw her arms around her husband. "No, I want to meet her. I have a good feeling about this." She kissed his cheek and stood back, a genuine smile lighting her face.

"We're not out of the woods yet," Gary cautioned. "But at least this time we'll have a proper guide."

A tsunami of relief washed over Carly. No, they weren't out of the woods yet. But on the optimism meter, she'd gone from zero to sixty in a flash.

Murmuring a silent prayer, she thanked whatever gods had worked their magic to bring Gary into her mom's life.

CHAPTER 15

CARLY HAD BEEN RIGHT ABOUT ARI. HE WAS FAR FROM JOYFUL WHEN SHE related her plans with Yvette for Thursday morning.

"This is serious, Carly. You don't even know his address," Ari pointed out.

"I know," she said, "but Yvette will give it to me before we leave. I'll text it to you immediately."

He'd muted the television so they could talk, but now he turned it off. "I know I can't stop you, but, honey, you need to be super aware of everything around you. Keep your phone at your fingertips, and your pepper spray where you can reach it in a split second. If anything feels the least bit off, you run out to your car and get the heck out of there."

"I will. I promise. Besides, it'll be broad daylight. We're only going to collect Yvette's belongings and leave." She kissed his cheek and snuggled into him, hoping to reassure him.

He grumbled and returned the kiss, then pulled her even closer.

The house was quiet. Leslie and Quinne had gone to bed early, Quinne still chirping excitedly about her cake-testing date the following day. Carly was glad she'd invited her, and even more happy that Ari had embraced the idea. He would make a wonderful dad someday. If it ever happened.

Carly gazed around, reflecting on how much she loved their newly renovated home. She and Ari had added their own special touches, keeping in mind the vintage features its former owner had treasured. She could never thank her former landlady enough for making the purchase possible. It was a blessing to know that Joyce was thriving in her new assisted living community.

"Hey," Ari said with a chuckle, "do you think we'll ever get our pup back?"

Not as long as Quinne is here, Carly thought.

"Of course we will," she assured him. "Leslie and Quinne are only temporary residents. I'm sure one day they'll have a pup of their own."

In truth, Carly was worried about how Quinne would fare without Havarti once she and Leslie returned to Rhode Island. Havarti would miss the child, too, but he'd still have Carly and Ari. The little girl had endured enough loneliness in her short life. Would she feel lost without her canine companion?

In all the hoopla over her mom's situation, Carly had allowed Leslie's problems to take a backseat in her mind. She and Ari had never spoken about the money Leslie asked for. Was that question off the table now?

Carly realized that the gears of her mind were running on empty. They needed fuel in the form of a solid night's sleep. A night without the intrusion of the oddball dreams she'd been having.

She nestled even closer to Ari. "Can you believe it? In a little over a month, I'll be Carly Hale Mitchell."

He took her hand in his and kissed her fingers. "Are you sure you want to add the 'Mitchell'?" he teased.

It was a good question. When Carly married her first husband, she'd retained her maiden name of Hale. As much as she'd loved Daniel, she felt differently about Ari. He was the soulmate she believed would never come into her life.

And then one day he did.

"I am," she said firmly. "Heretofore, my initials shall be C.H.M."

"I like the sound of that," Ari said in a husky voice. "But remember, it won't hurt my feelings if you don't take my name. Didn't Juliet say to Romeo 'what's in a name'?"

That which we call a rose by any other name would smell as sweet.

She hadn't read the play since high school, but the words instantly came back to her.

"I know that," Carly replied softly, "but that's what I choose."

• • •

The weather turned muggy Thursday morning, with rising temps projected to hit the low nineties. Carly murmured a silent thank-you to the person who invented air-conditioning, whoever that blessed soul was.

Before she left home, she texted Valerie and Nina to let them know she had an early appointment and hoped to be at work by ten. Since Ari knew of her plan, she didn't see the need to explain further. It would only worry them needlessly.

Right on time, Yvette was waiting for her behind the eatery at seven thirty. Her window rolled down, she sat inside an older sedan that had seen better days. She thanked Carly again for agreeing to go with her. Carly explained her plan to drive herself to Brice's home. "I might have to do a few errands on the way back," she fibbed, "so I'll follow you there."

Yvette nodded and gave Brice's address to Carly, who entered it into her cell phone and immediately texted it to Ari.

"By the way, I brought two boxes," she told Yvette. Ari had brought them down from their upstairs storage space early that morning and tucked them into the backseat of Carly's Corolla.

"Thank you," Yvette said with a grateful smile. "Two should be plenty. There's really not that much stuff."

Carly got into her car and followed Yvette onto the main drag, where they picked up Route 7 North. The route was so direct that Carly had no trouble following her. Yvette was also a poky driver.

It was only about fifteen minutes before they crossed the town line into Shaftsbury. The picturesque town boasted quaint shops, pristine lawns, and a general store with a front lawn sign that advertised farm fresh eggs.

About a mile beyond that, Yvette flicked on her signal and made a careful right turn onto the tree-lined street where Brice had lived. They passed a few homes before his mailbox came into view—identified only by the number 18 on the side. A large rental van with its doors flung open hunkered near the side entrance. The inside of the van looked choc-a-bloc with boxes and furniture. A man was stuffing a large fan into the back when Yvette pulled into the driveway. He turned around, and Carly did an abrupt double take.

Except for the shaved head, the man was an exact replica of Brice Keaton.

For a moment it knocked the breath out of her, until she remembered something. Brice had been a twin.

Carly parked on the street and got out of her car, then walked up the short driveway. Her tote on her shoulder, she checked to be sure her phone and her pepper spray were within easy reach. Not that she was worried, but she'd made a promise to Ari and she intended to keep it.

Yvette remained in her own car until Carly was standing beside her, then got out and quietly closed her door. The man loading the van, who had to be Phil Keaton, was already striding toward them with a sour expression.

His face was overly tanned, his mouth turned down into a hard scowl. Wearing faded jeans and a sweat-stained tee, he fixed Yvette with a hostile look. "You're back, I see. Well, I'm not done packing, so you'll have to wait till after the memorial service to get your stuff. I'll be outta here by tomorrow night. It won't kill you to wait another day."

Yvette's lower lip trembled. "I'm sorry, Phil, but I really need my things today. They're mine, and I have a right to them. Besides," she said in a sudden spurt of courage, "you can't stop me. I have a key."

Carly silently applauded Yvette for standing up for herself. Before Phil could protest, she stuck out her hand and gave him a saccharine smile. "Hi there, I'm Carly Hale. I came along to help Yvette. With the two of us working, I'm sure it won't take too long to pack up everything. If you'll just do us the courtesy of allowing us inside . . ."

Phil eyed her critically, then gave her hand a loose-fingered shake. Before he could voice another objection to their entering, she blurted, "I'm so very sorry for your loss, Mr. Keaton. I can't imagine how hard this is for you."

As if a light switch had suddenly flicked on inside his head, he pointed a forefinger at her. "I've seen your face. You're in that video of the woman who was threatening my brother."

Carly swallowed. "Yes, you're right. I was there that day. Mr. Keaton, if there's anything at all I can do to help—"

"You wanna help?" he said through clenched teeth. "Then find the SOB who killed my brother." He waved a hand toward the house and glowered at Yvette. "Go ahead and get your things. I'll give you ten minutes."

Carly looked at Yvette. "Is ten minutes enough?" she whispered.

Yvette nodded, then lifted her chin and said, "Where's Moxie?"

"Don't worry. She's fine. I closed her in the spare bedroom so I could pack the van without worrying about her scooting outdoors."

With that, Carly hustled back to her car and retrieved the boxes. She and Yvette hurried inside the house, using the front entrance instead of the side door.

It stymied Carly that Phil was so cantankerous. The articles Don had found on the internet had made him out to be a generous, caring citizen—a real people person. She could only surmise that his twin brother's murder had turned him into a spiteful, vengeful man.

They stepped into a small living room that looked as if a hurricane had swept through. Torn papers and crumpled fast-food bags had been strewn willy-nilly all over the floor. Pizza boxes were stacked in a corner, alongside discarded drink cups. If the house had air-conditioning, it wasn't obvious. The damp air was stifling, making breathing a challenge.

Yvette glanced all around, dismay etched on her thin face. "Brice never kept it like this," she said sullenly. "That pig Phil did this."

"Let's just get your things so we can get out of here," Carly urged.

"Wait! I want to check on Moxie first."

Carly followed her down a short hallway. The first room they passed was the bathroom. The door was open, and Carly couldn't help wrinkling her nose as they passed it. Meadow-fresh it was not. At the end of the hallway were two doors, one on either side. Yvette opened the one on the right, and Carly followed her inside, quickly closing the door behind her.

Yvette flipped up a wall switch. Light from an overhead fixture bathed the room in a dim glow. A beautiful gray kitty lounged on the bedspread, giving herself a bath. She sprang up when she saw Yvette, who scooped the kitty into her arms. "Moxie! Are you okay, sweet girl? Did you miss me?" She held the cat to her chest and kissed her furry face, tears forming in her eyes. In return, Moxie purred loudly and clung to Yvette.

Carly moved her gaze over the small room. Aside from the bed, the only furnishings were a tall chest of drawers and a bedside table. A large fan resting on the table was going at full blast. Boxes were stacked in one corner, each one taped shut. If there'd been any smaller items, Phil had probably already loaded them into the van.

Against one wall was a kitty litter box that looked freshly scooped. Water and food bowls rested nearby, both filled to the brim. To Carly's relief, it appeared the cat was being adequately cared for. She smiled and went over to pet the gray kitty, who studied her with big green eyes.

Yvette sniffled and set the cat gently on the bed. "We need to hurry before Phil throws us out."

After closing the door firmly behind them, they left the room and each took a box.

"I'll start in the bathroom," Yvette said. "You go into Brice's bedroom and take everything out of the bottom right drawer of the bureau. Whatever's in there is all mine."

Box in hand, Carly opened the door to the other bedroom and perused the room's contents. Aside from a twin bed, a tall lamp, and a battered bureau, the room was empty. A large black suitcase, zipped shut, sat on the bed. Carly set her tote next to the suitcase, then stooped down in front of the bureau. When she tried to pull out the bottom right drawer, it stuck. After three hard yanks, she managed to force it open, but not without landing on her rump.

Inside the drawer she found two lightweight tops, a pair of girly flip-flops, and a handful of greeting cards still in their envelopes. She gathered up the envelopes and shuffled through them. They'd all been postmarked within the last few months. Each had been addressed to Brice and opened, with Yvette's name and address scribbled at the upper left. She shot a quick glance at the doorway, then pulled out a card from one of the envelopes.

The image of a smiley-faced cat adorned the front. Inside was a printed greeting that read *Missing you!* Below that was a message written in purple ink: "Saturday was fun. Hope we can do it again soon. Yve." A whimsical heart had been sketched beside her name.

Carly grabbed her tote off the bed and pulled out her phone. She took a quick photo of the inside of the card, then set her phone down on the carpet. She didn't dare read the other cards. There wasn't time, and Yvette might catch her in the act. She counted the envelopes. There were nine in all. Would Yvette miss one?

She plucked one from the middle of the batch and shoved it into her tote. She was tucking the remaining cards into the packing box when she spotted something at the bottom of the drawer. Lifting it, she saw that it was the back of a photograph. She flipped it around to see a faded color picture of two children, a boy and a girl, sitting on the grass with their legs extended. The boy looked about eleven or twelve; the girl about nine. The boy was gaunt, but the girl had a pudgy face and fleshy limbs. Their unsmiling faces radiated a sadness that Carly could almost reach out and touch. Peering at it more closely, she noticed that the two were clasping hands on the grass.

Was the little girl in the photo Yvette? The child was so young it was impossible to tell.

Carly turned over the photo. Unfortunately, there was no writing on the back, nor was there a date. She held it up to the light. On closer inspection, it looked as if something might have been written on the back but later erased. Carly aimed her cell at the photo and took a few pics, then dropped the photo into the box.

Yvette had instructed her to empty the bottom right drawer but didn't mention the other drawers. Noises coming from the bathroom told her that Yvette was still packing. As quietly as she could Carly opened the other drawers, which luckily slid open easily. She sagged with disappointment when she found nothing. Phil had obviously removed his brother's personal belongings. Given his surly demeanor, she was surprised he hadn't taken the cards Yvette had written to Brice.

"Did you get everything?"

Carly's heart jumped at the voice. She turned to see Yvette standing in the doorway, her arms wrapped around a box with the flaps still open. The business end of a hair dryer stuck out from the top.

"I sure did," Carly said, "but there wasn't much else in the bureau. At least Phil saved your stuff for you. Is anything else in the house yours? What about the kitchen?"

Yvette shook her head. "No, that should be everything. Come on, we better go. It's so freakin' hot in here."

Carly had been hoping for a chance to question Phil before they left, but she sensed he wasn't in any mood to chat. She didn't blame him for being angry. His brother had been taken from him in a horrible way. Imagining herself in his place, she knew she'd feel the same way.

Before closing the box, Carly reached inside and pulled out the photo. "I found an old photograph of two kids at the bottom of the drawer." She smiled at Yvette and held it out. "Is this you?"

Still clutching her box, Yvette went over and took it from Carly. Her lips pursed, she stared at it and said, "I have no idea who these people are. But that's definitely not me. You can keep it if you want." She dropped it on the floor. "We should go before Phil gets antsy."

Whoa, Carly thought. The mild-mannered Yvette had developed a 'tude.

Carly picked up the photo and slipped it into her tote, along with her phone. They made it as far as the living room when Phil Keaton stopped them in their tracks.

CHAPTER 16

"GET EVERYTHING?"

To Carly's relief, Phil sounded friendlier this time. He'd even managed a weak smile as he met them in the living room.

Carly returned his smile with a bright one of her own. Maybe she could put him at ease enough to talk. "Yes, we did, I think. Yvette, is this everything?"

Yvette fidgeted with the box she was holding. "Yeah, we got everything. Um, Phil, what are you gonna do about Moxie? I don't want her going to a shelter."

"Here, let me help you with that," he said, taking the box from her. "No worries about the kitty, Yvette. I love cats as much as Brice obviously did. I'm taking her home to New Hampshire with me. Believe me, she'll be treated like a princess."

Yvette looked both relieved and sad. "Okay, if you're sure . . ."

Phil nodded and shifted his gaze to Carly. "Miss . . . Hale, is it? I apologize for snapping at you the way I did. It's not like me to treat people so rudely. It's just . . . I've been emptying out Brice's things nonstop since Sunday. My head feels like a bowling ball someone threw into the gutter a few too many times." He barked out a short laugh. "I spent so much time sorting and packing that I've been living on takeout. Hence, all the junk food boxes strewn around. I've arranged to have the house professionally cleaned after I leave. Once that's done, I'll turn in my brother's key to the landlord and be done with this place forever."

Keeping her tote on her shoulder, she rested her box on a nearby chair—partly to give her arms a break, but also to keep him talking. "No need to apologize, Mr. Keaton. It's perfectly understandable. You've been through so much this past week. Have the police made any progress with the investigation?"

"Please, it's Phil," he said. "They brought in a few suspects for questioning, but so far nothing's come of it. The lack of progress is making me nuts."

Because they're determined to pin it on Mom, Carly thought dismally.

"What about Theo Sullivan?" Carly pressed, although she knew he'd supposedly produced an airtight alibi.

"Yeah, I kept asking that, too. Turns out Sullivan's a creep, but he can account for his whereabouts when Brice was killed. A bunch of witnesses confirmed it."

"But he threatened Brice!" Yvette cried.

"True, but threats don't make him a killer." Phil set Yvette's box down on the floor and pulled out his cell from his jeans pocket. "Carly, while you two were packing, I checked out this video again of the woman threatening my brother." He held it up and showed it to her. "I know she's your mom."

Carly swallowed. "Yes, she is. But I assure you, Phil, she did not harm your brother. Believe me, she's all bark, no bite."

"I do believe you," he said gently. "Listen, operating a family restaurant for over ten years has taught me a lot about human nature. I've thrown bullies out on their ear and warned them never to return. I've also rewarded people for doing the right thing."

Like the teenager who rescued the baby ducks from a drain, Carly remembered from the news article.

"Bottom line," he went on, "your mom was only defending you, which she had every right to do. I can tell she doesn't have a mean bone in her body."

A wave of relief flushed through Carly. Not that Phil had any influence over the police, but at least he was intuitive enough to recognize the truth.

"Phil, I got thinking about something. Is there anyone from your brother's past who might have held a grudge against him?"

Phil's eye twitched. He shoved his phone back into his pocket. "I'm sorry to say Brice and I have been estranged for a long time. I tried getting in touch a bunch of times, but he never responded. I finally gave up. It's like"—he swallowed and his eyes misted—"it's like we were never brothers."

"I'm so sorry," Carly said. "If you don't mind my asking, were you two close when you were kids?"

Phil shook his head. "Not at all. Even as twins, we were like night and day. By the time we got to middle school, Brice started hanging with kids who were always in trouble. It was like he resented being a twin, you know? He did whatever he could to show he was different from me. Meanwhile, I was getting better grades, playing sports. It made him despise me even more."

Carly was surprised by Phil's revelations. She'd always thought that twins, especially identical ones, had an inseparable bond.

Phil swiped his hand over his forehead. "When he was fifteen, he ended up in juvie. Our parents were devastated."

Yvette's face blanched. She stared openmouthed at Phil but remained quiet.

"What did he do?" Carly asked.

"Brice and another troublemaker snuck into a neighbor's garage one afternoon. They started playing with an open gas can, tossing lighted matches into it. They didn't notice that the woman who lived there had come in through a side door." He swallowed, and his eyes turned glassy. "The fumes from the gas can ignited. It might have gone out on its own, but other flammable materials were nearby."

Carly almost gagged. "The woman . . . ?"

"She should have run out of there, but she didn't. Instead, she tried stomping on the flames to extinguish them. The hem of her skirt caught fire, and she—" He shook his head.

"What about the boys?"

"They did the cowardly thing. They booked it out of there as fast as their legs would carry them. The woman's husband had been inside the house. He worked nights and slept during the day. When he heard the commotion, he ran into the garage. He tried to rescue his wife, but he tripped—right into the flames. They both . . . perished. The man died that day. The woman died about three days later."

Carly felt suddenly lightheaded. Her morning coffee climbed toward her throat. She swallowed several times, hoping to tamp it down. Between that and the airless room, her legs started to wobble. She stumbled sideways.

Phil quickly gripped her upper arm to keep her upright. "Easy, there. Are you okay?"

Carly nodded. "Yes, thank you. I think the humidity is getting to me."

Once she was steady on her feet, Phil released her arm. "Gosh, I'm sorry. I don't know what made me tell you all that. It was such a long time ago. Water over the dam, as they say. Speaking of which, let me get you ladies some water before you leave."

Phil dashed out of the room and returned with two bottles of water, handing one to each of the women. "I'll help you take the boxes to the car." Without another word, he lifted Yvette's box and went out through the front door.

A dazed-looking Yvette followed in his wake. Carly slipped her water bottle into her tote, then lifted the other box from the chair and shuffled off behind them. Phil's awful story, combined with the humid weather, was making her insides throb.

Yvette opened the rear door of her car, and Phil set both boxes on the backseat. He closed the door and looked at them both, his shaved head speckled with beads of sweat.

"Yvette, I'm sorry I gave you such a hard time," he said, sounding contrite. "I'm struggling to process what happened to Brice, but I can tell you cared for him. I shouldn't have taken my anger out on you."

She offered a quick nod, then said, "Just take good care of Moxie. That's all I ask." She slid inside her car and slammed the door.

"Bye, ladies," Phil said, then started toward his van.

"Phil, wait," Carly called to him. "What were the names of the couple that died in the fire?"

Phil turned and stared at her. "Why would you ask that?"

"I just wondered . . . maybe it's important."

"I can't see how it matters now. Brice and I were fifteen when it happened. Our folks made me finish high school in a different town. They didn't want me tainted by ugly gossip."

"That must've been hard on you," she said quietly.

"More than hard. Sports-wise, it was a disaster for me. I'd been a key player on the JV soccer and basketball teams in my hometown. After I switched schools, I didn't have the heart to play sports anymore. Any chance I had at getting a sports scholarship to a good college went right down the hopper. I settled for a two-year business degree. The worst part was, rumors went around my new school that I was the real culprit, not Brice. If you could've seen the scathing looks I got—" He swiped the heel of his hand over his eye. "Shoot, I don't even know why I'm telling you all this. As to your question, I've blocked the memory of that day as much as I could. The couple who died had a French name, but that's all I remember."

"Phil, one last question," Carly said. "What happened to the other boy? Did he end up in juvie, too?"

Phil's eyes narrowed to slits. "Yeah, he did. I don't know where he went after he was released, but I heard that he died in a freak accident not too long afterward."

"What kind of freak accident?"

He shook his head. "I can't remember. Carly, I really have a lot to do today."

Carly saw that she wouldn't get any further with Phil. He was either hiding something or there truly was a gap in his memory. Either way, she felt heartsick for everything he'd endured.

"Okay, thanks, Phil. I'm sorry for everything you've gone through."

He paused and stared at her, then turned again and strode toward the van.

Carly went back to Yvette, who was sitting in her car with the engine running, her window rolled all the way down. Her lips were trembling.

Carly reached in and put a hand on Yvette's shoulder. "Are you okay to drive?"

Yvette gave a quick nod. "Don't worry. I'm fine." She looked up at Carly with a bleak expression. "Thank you for coming here with me. It . . . means a lot."

"You're welcome. You know, I saw a coffee shop just up the road from here. Do you have time to meet me there? I'll treat you to breakfast." Carly gave her an encouraging smile.

After a brief hesitation, Yvette said, "I guess that would be okay. I'm working a late shift today, so my morning is free."

They agreed that Yvette would follow Carly this time.

Once inside her car, Carly immediately called Ari, who was relieved that she was leaving Brice's house and heading back. Next, she contacted Nina to let her know she was on her way to the eatery but had to run an errand first.

On the way to the coffee shop, Carly's mind filled with terrible images, triggered by Phil's revelations. Even worse was the expression on his face just before he walked away from her. She could think of only one word to describe it.

Haunted.

CHAPTER 17

THE COFFEE SHOP WAS A BREATH OF SPRING AIR AFTER THEIR EXPERIENCE at Brice's house. Green and white gingham valances hung over the multipaned windows, and the walls were the color of celery. Collectibles such as antique license plates and signs from long-gone eateries graced the walls. The dual aromas of bacon and coffee began to restore Carly's appetite.

She and Yvette got into the only remaining booth. A perky teenaged server with purple hair and inch-long eyelashes flashed a smile and took their orders for coffee and blueberry muffins, then brought them each a steaming mug.

"I wish you hadn't asked Phil about their childhood," Yvette said, clasping the handle of her mug. "Brice never told me any of that stuff. Now I won't stop thinking about it."

"I know, and I'm sorry," Carly murmured, adding a creamer to her coffee. "It surprised me, too, that Phil revealed those things. Maybe it was something he needed to get off his chest. I'm sure he's been carrying those painful memories around for a long time."

Yvette gave a slight shrug. "I suppose," she mumbled. "Do you think he'll really take good care of Moxie?"

"I think he will," Carly replied. "Beneath all the bluster, he struck me as a kind man." She stirred the creamer into her mug. "Yvette, I know this is difficult to talk about, but I've been meaning to ask you something. The police believe that Brice was killed sometime between three thirty and four on Saturday. The thing is, my friend Grant, who was helping me that day, told me Brice left with all his stuff a little after two, and that you left with him."

Yvette's lips tightened. "So? What's your point?"

"My point is that after you and Brice left, he obviously went back to the school. Do you know why he did that?"

The question seemed to fluster Yvette. "Look, all I know is, after we left the school we met at a sub shop for some lunch. I was driving my own car that day. We were almost done eating when he got a phone call. After he hung up, he looked seriously PO'd. He told me he had to go back to the blankety-blank school. Someone noticed he'd left a case of his soda there and he needed to go back and pick it up. He took off like a bat out of you-know-where and said he'd call me later."

Their blueberry muffins arrived. Yvette sliced hers in two and slathered one half with butter.

"Did he say who it was that called him?" Carly prompted.

Yvette blew out an exasperated breath. "No, he didn't, and I already told all this to the police. Why are you asking me this stuff?"

"I'm sorry," Carly said, "but my mom, who would never hurt a soul, is still a suspect in Brice's death. I'm only trying to figure out what really happened."

For a long moment, Yvette was silent. "Okay, I get it. But I'm pretty sure the police have Brice's cell phone. You should be bugging them with these questions, not me." She bit off a chunk of her muffin.

Carly took a bite of her own muffin. It was warm and loaded with blueberries. She glanced over at Yvette, who was scarfing down hers at warp speed.

"I'm glad we stopped here," Carly said, hoping to put Yvette at ease. "This is a really good muffin, isn't it?"

Yvette gave a slight nod, and they both went back to eating.

"Something else I meant to ask you," Carly said. "Did Theo Sullivan ever show up again? I know he was bothering you for a while."

A look of panic filled Yvette's eyes. "Why, did you see him?" Her voice rose to a high pitch.

"I . . . no, I just wondered if you had."

Yvette relaxed, but her eyes remained wary. "I thought I saw him following me in his car a couple times. It's hard to miss that stupid hood ornament."

"Did you report it to anyone?"

Yvette shook her head. "Who would I tell?"

Carly wasn't sure. Except for Sullivan's prior actions when they were dating, Yvette didn't have much evidence to go on. After a few minutes of silence, she switched to a different matter. "Yvette, I sense that you truly cared for Brice. Those cards in the bureau drawer were all from you."

Yvette's cheeks flushed. If she was annoyed that Carly had looked at them, she gave no indication. "Okay, I admit it. I did like Brice. A *lot*." Her eyes took on a dreamy haze, as if she was reminiscing. "He could be moody sometimes, but he was also a super-sweet guy. I've been hurt by guys in the past, so I didn't want to get my hopes up. But I did think Brice was special." She offered up a faint smile. "I was hoping he'd see how good I was for him when I made that dumb sign with all the soda bottles." She shook her head. "He barely acknowledged it."

Carly took a slow sip of her coffee. Brice's behavior at the fundraiser hadn't indicated any warm feelings toward Yvette. "Do you think he tried to turn his life around after . . . you know, what Phil told us?" she finished quietly.

"How would I know?" Yvette said crossly. "I didn't really know him all that long, so I can't speak for the past. He mentioned he had an issue with his boss at work, but he didn't act like it was anything major. A misunderstanding, he called it."

That was interesting, Carly thought. She recalled Andy Fields saying that the "head guy" at the beverage company claimed Brice had "owed him a favor." It was the only reason Brice agreed to host a table at the fundraiser.

They finished their coffee and muffins in awkward silence, and Carly paid the tab.

Yvette gathered up her purse. She foraged around inside, then tipped it on its side and jiggled it. "Where the heck—oh, here it is." Along with a tube of lip gloss, her driver's license and a packet of tissues had fallen out. As she uncapped the tube and swiped the gloss over her pale lips, Carly sneaked a look at her license. Her name was shown as Mabel Yvette Carter.

Yvette closed the tube and shoved everything back into her purse. "You saw my name, didn't you?" she said with an embarrassed smile.

"I'm sorry, sometimes I'm a bit nosy," Carly said lightly. "It's a nice old-fashioned name, though. Names like that are coming back into style."

"I hate it." Yvette pouted. "My folks named me after both my grandmothers, but they should have put the 'Yvette' before the 'Mabel.' Like, what were they thinking? Anyway, that's why I go by Yvette now. I don't want people to know I have that frumpy name."

Carly didn't know what to say, but a part of her felt sorry for Yvette. She seemed to have a lot of pent-up anger.

Yvette's face softened. "Hey, thanks for breakfast, Carly. I'm sorry if I got a little testy before. You've been really nice to me, and I won't forget it."

"Don't give it a thought. Considering everything you've been through, it's perfectly understandable." She hoisted her tote onto her shoulder.

"Are you going to the memorial service tomorrow?" Yvette asked.

"I plan to, yes," Carly replied, sliding out of the booth, "if I can get someone to cover for me at my restaurant."

"Good. I hope I'll see you there." After hesitating briefly, Yvette said, "That day, when Brice and me ate lunch together in the sub shop? That was the last time I ever saw him." Her eyes turned glassy. "I was alone again. Alone again in the world . . ." Her voice was so childlike, so forlorn, it made Carly want to cry.

Before Carly could respond, Yvette turned and made a mad dash outside to her car. Her rush to leave without saying goodbye took Carly aback.

Carly was getting into her own vehicle when she noticed a car idling at the far corner of the parking lot. Her blood ran cold.

It was a black sedan with a hood ornament.

Sullivan followed her here, was Carly's first terrifying thought. Her heart thumping, she removed her cell from her tote and took a quick photo of the sedan. It might not even be him, but if it was, she'd have evidence that he was following Yvette.

She started her car and flipped on the AC. As she drove slowly out of the parking lot, she glanced again at the sedan. It hadn't moved. Maybe it wasn't Theo Sullivan. Maybe she was letting her mind get carried away by her concern for Yvette.

As she made her way back to Balsam Dell, thoughts of Theo Sullivan slipped from her mind. Something else had been nudging at her brain ever since they'd left Brice's. Whatever it was had gotten overshadowed by other dark thoughts.

But then, in a flash, it came to her. In her last conversation with Phil, he'd implied that because of his brother's actions, his final few high school years had been a living nightmare. He'd abandoned sports, and his classmates had regarded him with suspicion.

In Carly's mind, it was a darn good motive for murder.

• • •

Carly was so relieved to step inside her eatery that she had to stifle the urge to drop down and kiss the diamond-patterned floor. The trip to Brice's house had done a number on her nerves.

"Yay, you're back," Nina greeted, a smile lighting her face. Today she sported grilled cheese sandwich earrings the size of golf balls.

"Hey, those are cute." Carly dropped her tote onto the counter.

"Thanks." Nina swung her head from side to side. The earrings came within millimeters of slapping her in the mouth. "Don't worry," she said, seeing Carly's expression. "They're papier-mâché. They weigh next to nothing. I got them from one of those online shops."

Nina fixed her a mug of coffee and sat with her at the counter. Carly loved seeing her assistant manager so bubbly. She suspected Nina's new living quarters had something to do with it, not to mention the growing friendship she was cultivating with Don.

Carly glanced up at the wall clock behind the counter. Quarter to three. She groaned. The old clock had given up the ghost weeks earlier, and she'd never had a chance to shop for a new one. One more thing to add to her mounting list of chores.

A tantalizing aroma drifted from the kitchen. Something different from the usual scents of bacon sizzling on the grill or tangy tomato soup. "Is Val making something?"

Nina giggled. "She asked Grant to give her a lesson in making béchamel sauce. They've been in the kitchen for half an hour."

Carly hopped off her stool. "Oh boy, this I've got to see."

She marched into the kitchen with Nina close at her heels. At the work counter, Grant and Valerie were peering into a saucepan. They couldn't have looked more blissful if the pan had been brimming with solid gold coins.

Grant looked up, his dark eyes beaming. "Hey, you guys, you gotta sample what Val made."

"Is this the béchamel?" Carly asked.

"Yup, but Grant's the one who made it," Val said dryly, her topknot bobbing a little. "It was so much simpler than I thought it would be. Now I definitely want to experiment with a croque monsieur."

Spoons in hand, they each tasted the sauce. Moans of delight went around.

"Decadence, thy name is béchamel," Carly murmured.

"Best of all, it can be made ahead and refrigerated for up to a week," Grant explained. "I'd suggest freezing it though. At the inn we prepare the sauce daily, but we use reusable bags to freeze any leftovers in small batches. The bags should lie flat in the freezer. Be sure to label them with the date."

"Will it be just as good after it thaws?" Nina bit down on her lower lip.

"It'll be a tad watery, but if you whisk it over low heat, it'll go right back to its original consistency." He wiped his hands on a towel. "Once this cools, I'll show you how to do it. By the way, I plan to hang out here through the lunch crunch, so whatever you need, let me know."

Hang out. Carly knew it was code for "work my butt off."

"Thank you, Grant," Carly said gratefully. She hadn't asked him to work today, but he seemed to know instinctively when his help was needed.

Carly snapped her fingers. "Hey, I just remembered. I have a cake-tasting appointment at two. Quinne is going with me. She's so excited. You should've seen her face when I asked her."

"I'll finally get to meet her then." Grant gave the pot another careful stir.

• • •

The morning flew by. Grant made a large pot of tomato soup, along with two heaping batches of salad.

Carly refrained from eating even a small lunch. She wanted to save her taste buds for all the varieties of cake and frosting she'd be sampling at Sissy's Bakery.

At one thirty, Leslie and Quinne came into the eatery. Quinne looked adorable in a bright pink dress with white polka-dots, and a pair of pink sneakers to match. Leslie had gathered Quinne's hair into a high ponytail from which her long auburn curls cascaded down her back. The little girl's Eiffel Tower tote dangled from the crook of her elbow.

"Uncle Ari gave me the money to make a deposit on the cake," she told Carly seriously.

Leslie winked at Carly, who immediately got the gist. "She's so looking forward to this. I can't thank you enough for inviting her."

"Well, I needed an assistant," Carly said, "and Quinne was perfect for the job."

Leslie bent toward her niece. "Remember what we talked about. Don't overdo the tasting, or you might end up with a sick tummy. Cake has a lot of sugar."

Quinne wrinkled her nose. "I know. I remember."

Suzanne and Nina instantly descended on Quinne, telling her how sweet she looked, and how lucky she was to be chosen as a cake taster. Quinne was shy with her thanks, but it was obvious she was basking in the attention.

Grant came out of the kitchen with a container of prepared salad. When he saw Quinne, he set it down behind the counter and introduced himself. "Hi, I'm Grant. *Comment vous appelez-vous?*" He pronounced it with a perfect French accent.

Quinne's lips widened into a huge grin. *"Je m'appelle Quinne!"* she replied.

He held up his hand in a high-five gesture. Quinne tapped it with her palm and giggled.

"I heard you're going to help Carly choose a wedding cake," he said. "That's a very important job."

"I know, and she's really my Auntie Carly," Quinne corrected.

"Grant, it's nice to meet you," Leslie said. "Thank you for speaking French to her."

He grinned. "I'm lucky I remembered that much. I've picked up bits and pieces from some of my instructors at culinary school."

Carly ushered her visitors into the kitchen so they could have more privacy. She removed her apron and tossed it into the laundry bin. "We'll leave in about ten minutes," she told them. "Shall I drive Quinne home after we finish up at the bakery?"

"That would be great," Leslie said, smiling at her niece. "By the way, I'm making dinner tonight. You and Ari won't have to lift a finger. It's nothing fancy, but it's a favorite of Quinne's. And we won't even have to turn on the oven."

"Hey, I like the sound of that." Carly grinned. "Shall I bring a dessert from the bakery?"

"Oh, please do."

Leslie hugged Carly and gave Quinne a kiss.

Minutes later, Carly and Quinne were on their way to the bakery.

CHAPTER 18

SISSY'S BAKERY WAS A FAVORITE HAUNT OF CARLY'S. THE OWNER, SISSY Patel, had opened the bakery years earlier in partnership with her brother. He'd since moved on to pursue a different career, so Sissy was now the top banana, as she liked to joke.

A long row of glass display cases boasted handmade cinnamon rolls, oversized cookies, and pastries and muffins of every kind. Quinne's eyes widened as they moved along the display.

Behind the counter, a woman with thick black hair pulled into a tight bun burst into smiles when she spotted Carly. Sissy had just finished boxing up six raspberry muffins for a customer. She tied the box with bakery string and asked her assistant to ring up the order.

Sissy scurried around the counter to hug Carly, then beamed down at Quinne. "Hi there, you must be Quinne. I'm Sissy. I understand you're going to help Carly choose a wedding cake today."

Carly had texted Sissy earlier to let her know Ari wouldn't be joining her, but that she was bringing along a young helper.

"Yup," Quinne said proudly. "She needed an assistant, and she picked me."

"Then let's get started!"

Sissy led them into a room where five gorgeously decorated cakes, each about eight inches in diameter, rested along one side of a cloth-covered table. A few months earlier, Carly and Ari had perused the bakery's photo album of wedding cakes. Next to each photo was a detailed description of each available style and flavor. They'd narrowed it down to their five favorites and presented their choices to the baker.

Sissy set out plates and forks and invited them to sit.

Clutching her tote in her lap, Quinne gawked openmouthed at the cakes. "Are we going to eat all of these?"

Sissy gave out a hearty laugh. "No, sweetie, even I couldn't manage that." She patted her slightly rounded abdomen. "But we are going to sample each one." Quinne accepted the offer of a glass of milk, but Carly declined any beverage. "You don't have to finish each slice, unless you want to," Sissy said. "But if you do, you might end up on sugar overload. I would suggest tasting only a few mouthfuls of each cake."

After describing each of the flavors, Sissy cut them each a thin slice of the chocolate raspberry truffle cake.

Quinne's face registered instant approval, but Carly wanted something lighter. She'd already texted Sissy a copy of their wedding invitation, asking if she could adapt the theme when frosting the cake.

The fruitcake was a thumbs-down. Carly laughed at the face Quinne made.

By mutual agreement, they finally chose a three-layer marble cake with a vanilla buttercream frosting. A line of yellow buttercups, woven through delicate green tendrils, circled its way along the layers from top to bottom. It was almost an exact depiction of the quilling design on their wedding invitations.

"And now, I have a surprise," Sissy said.

She brought over a square white box and set it on the table. When she removed the cover, Carly gasped. "Sissy, where on earth did you find that?"

Quinne clapped her hands and grinned. "Auntie Carly, it's you and Uncle Ari and Havarti!"

The porcelain wedding topper depicted a bride, a groom, and their little white dog. Even the hair coloring matched Carly's and Ari's.

"You don't have to take it," Sissy said with a sly smile, "but I took a chance and ordered it. I'm sure I can sell it if you don't like it."

"Are you kidding? It's absolutely perfect."

"Great!" Sissy winked at Quinne. "Now, let's get down to the serious stuff. Which cake would you like to take home?"

Quinne looked awestruck. "We can take one of these cakes with us?"

"Whichever one you'd like," Sissy told her.

Carly was tempted to suggest the marble cake but wanted it to be special for their wedding. "What do you think, Quinne? It's your decision."

The little girl scrunched her face. "Um, let's take the chocolate one with the raspberries. I know Auntie Leslie will love it." Her face lit up at the thought.

"Excellent choice. I'll box it up for you." Sissy lifted the cake off the table. "I'll be right back."

Carly kissed the top of Quinne's head. She was such a sweet girl, thinking of Leslie first. She sent up a silent prayer that the adoption would become official soon.

"Wait!" Quinne called to Sissy, who was heading into the bakery with the cake. "Don't you need the deposit?"

Sissy turned to Carly with a quizzical look, and Carly gave her a meaningful nod. She'd paid the deposit weeks earlier, but Sissy got the message.

"Oh . . . right, the deposit. I almost forgot about it." Sissy wiggled her eyes. "I don't know where my head is today."

"That's okay," Quinne said. "Sometimes I space out too." She pulled a five-dollar bill from her tote and gave it to Sissy. Then she swung her head toward Carly and said in a loud whisper, "Should I get a receipt?"

"Never fear," Sissy assured the child with a smile. "I'll bring you a receipt. Carly, if it works for you, I'll write up the order and email it to you tomorrow for your approval."

Carly agreed, and she and Quinne left the bakery with a cake box in hand.

As they drove back to the house, Quinne chattered from the backseat about her fun experience at the bakery. Carly felt her throat tighten. For the umpteenth time, she imagined a future with her and Ari riding around town with their own little girl or boy.

Numerous times since their engagement, they'd talked about having a kid. Discussed all the pros and cons. Ultimately, they decided that after they were married, they'd let nature take its course. If it happened, their lives would be filled with joy. If it didn't—

That was the "if" Carly didn't want to think about.

• • •

By the time Carly returned to the eatery, Grant had left for his job at the inn.

Only two of the booths were occupied. At the counter, two uniformed police officers who'd just finished their shift were each enjoying a Smoky Steals the Bacon. They'd eaten there before, but Carly noticed lately that their visits were getting more frequent.

The sandwich, one of the eatery's most popular choices, was made with asiago bread, smoked gouda, and several slices of bacon. A generous sprinkling of Parmesan cheese on the grill ensured that the sandwiches were crisp and golden.

"My wife doesn't cook bacon at home unless it's vegan," one of them griped. "That's why I love this place."

His partner laughed. "I don't have a wife, but I can't make a decent grilled cheese to save my soul. I either burn them or the cheese doesn't melt." He took a large bite of his sandwich.

Carly couldn't resist smiling to herself. She loved overhearing conversations like this one. Although in this case it was more like eavesdropping.

"Gentlemen, would you like more iced coffee?" she offered.

They both nodded, and Carly replenished their drinks. The men raised their glasses in thanks.

"By the way," the first one said to his partner, "did you see the brother of that guy who was murdered? He came into the station today to pick up his brother's belongings."

"Yeah, I did. Man, he looks exactly like the guy who was murdered, doesn't he? Wouldn't it be wild if one of them pulled a switcheroo?"

They both laughed and went back to their sandwiches.

A switcheroo.

Carly's heart pounded. Could the officers be on to something? They'd spoken in jest, but the fact was, Brice and Phil were identical.

What if Brice had grown tired of his life? Tired of carrying the emotional burden of what he'd done as a teenager. His brother was a respected businessman with a thriving restaurant. Did Brice long for the life his brother was enjoying?

The only physical difference Carly could discern between the two men was that Phil shaved his head. Easy enough to accomplish with a razor. Or a barber.

A shiver ran down Carly's spine.

No, it wasn't possible. Was it?

For starters, Yvette would have recognized Brice. There was no way he could have fooled her. And second—

No, she refused to go there. It was a ridiculous thought.

Shaking it off, Carly went into the kitchen. Two tubs of dirty dishes were waiting to be rinsed and loaded into the dishwasher. After she did that, she tidied up the worktable and checked the fridge, making a list of items that would need replenishing before the week was out.

Nina came flouncing through the swinging door, munching on a grilled cheddar sandwich. "I am *so* starving," she announced, plopping down at the kitchen table. "I haven't eaten all day! Val just whipped this up for me."

"It's no wonder you're hungry," Carly told her. "You hardly ever take a lunch break."

"Yeah, I know. Hey, I've been meaning to tell you something," Nina said, waggling her eyebrows.

"Ooh, is it juicy?" Carly sat down adjacent to her and rested an elbow on the table.

"Yeah, it is, in a weird way. Last night Don asked me over to his apartment so I could see the wall shelf he put together. It's one of those DIY jobs from a kit he ordered online. He said if I liked it, he'd buy another kit and put it together for me. He even offered to paint it whatever color I wanted." She glowed as if the ghost of Michelangelo had offered to paint her ceiling.

"Very generous of him. Did you like it?"

"I did, but wait till you hear this. While I was waiting for him to get our root beers from his fridge, I noticed a photo album in his bookcase. I pulled it out and asked him if it was okay if I looked at it. He said 'sure.' Carly, I couldn't believe my eyes. There's a picture of Don in there when he was like, five or six, and he's eating a grilled cheese sandwich!"

"What!" Carly slapped her hands on the table. "You're sure it was a grilled cheese?"

"Yup, positive. I teased him about it, but he just shrugged it off. When I pressed him further, he said that his tastes had matured."

"This is big." Carly drummed her fingers on the table. "We need to find out the real story. All this time . . . he could've been eating our delicious grilled cheese sandwiches!"

"I know. It's like he went cold turkey on grilled cheese at a very young age. What's that about?"

Nina gobbled down the rest of her sandwich, and they both returned to the dining room.

Another mystery to solve, Carly thought.

At least this one didn't involve murder.

CHAPTER 19

When Carly arrived home, the kitchen table was set for four. It was starting to become a familiar sight. She realized it was one she looked forward to. Having meals with the two additions to her family gave her a case of the warm fuzzies.

Speaking of family, where was everyone?

The question had no sooner popped into her head than Quinne, Leslie, and Ari trooped into the house from the backyard. Quinne had changed into shorts and a striped tee. Havarti led the way into the kitchen, his short tail sticking up behind him. He leaped at Carly's knees as if he hadn't seen her in a year.

"Oh, so you remember your mom now?" Carly stooped down and hugged him to her chest.

When she rose, Ari gave her a light kiss and smiled. "I heard you and Quinne had a delectable cake-tasting session."

"Oh, did we ever." Carly said.

"And I helped pick out the wedding cake!" Quinne beamed as if she'd been chosen to select a diamond-studded tiara for one of the royals.

Leslie scrubbed her hands in the sink. "Carly, would you like to eat now, or unwind a little first?"

Carly didn't want to admit that the cake tasting had taken the edge off her hunger. Knowing that Ari was probably ravenous, she said, "Sure, let's eat! Give me a minute to wash up."

"Quinne, you wash up, too," Leslie said.

Quinne dashed upstairs, and Carly went into her own bathroom. When she returned, a large platter sat in the center of the kitchen table. Four colorful wraps, sliced in half, had been placed in pinwheel fashion on the dish.

"These are my special chicken wraps," Leslie said, a touch of pride in her voice. "I bought rotisserie chicken so I wouldn't have to heat up the kitchen. They're made with chicken, spinach leaves, sun-dried tomatoes, mozzarella cheese, and a special sauce. I made them once before and Quinne loved them."

Everyone sat down and helped themselves to the wraps. After the first bite, Carly's taste buds sprang to life. "Wow, you have got to share this recipe, Les."

"Thanks," Leslie said, looking pleased. "I was hoping you'd like them."

After the adults had eaten their wraps, Carly noticed that Quinne had finished only half of hers. The little girl was gazing down at her plate, a worried expression in her eyes.

"Sweetie," Leslie said, "you don't have to eat the other half. That's an adult-sized meal, and you're a kid-sized person."

Quinne hunched her shoulders. "But won't it go to waste?"

"Not at all. In fact"—Leslie winked at her brother—"Uncle Ari looks like

114

he's ready to pounce on it and gobble it down in a second."

"You bet I am," Ari told Quinne. "If you're sure you don't want it."

Quinne's shoulders relaxed, and she gave Ari her plate. He attacked the wrap with gusto, making everyone laugh.

Leslie stroked Quinne's hair. "Why don't you go outside and play with Havarti for a while? Later we can have some of that chocolate cake you brought home."

"I can still have dessert?"

"Of course you can." The love in Leslie's gaze made Carly's heart go all squishy.

Carly jumped up and gave Quinne two dog cookies. "Take these for Havarti's dessert."

"Thanks, Auntie Carly. Come on, Havarti. Let's go play with your ball!" Quinne and the dog raced outside.

After the back door closed, Leslie sat down and clasped her hands on the table. "While Quinne's outside, I have something to tell you both. I got some news today. I think it's good news."

Ari swallowed the last bite of Quinne's wrap. "Well, don't keep us in suspense, Les. What is it?"

Leslie took a deep breath. "This afternoon, I got a call from my contact person at the DCYF—the Department of Children, Youth, and Families. The so-called powers that be are holding a meeting tomorrow, and Quinne's adoption is on their agenda. Keep in mind, we've already jumped through all the major hoops—the home study visits, the background check—everything they need to approve it." Her voice grew soft. "That's why I went into panic mode when my boss let me go. For obvious reasons, I have to be gainfully employed to adopt a child."

Ari reached over and gave Leslie's arm a supportive squeeze. She clasped his hand in return.

"Anyway," she went on, "here's the good part. The social worker agreed to video chat with Norah this afternoon. Carly, your sister is a powerhouse! Do you know she's already lined up three dental practitioners anxious to interview me? And they're all within easy commuting distance of our apartment complex."

Carly and Ari exchanged smiles. "Les, that's fantastic news," Carly said.

"So where does the adoption stand now?" Ari asked.

"Well, that's the thing. Quinne and I will need to drive back to Rhode Island this weekend. Our social worker plans to do one final home visit either Monday or Tuesday. But after that, I'm hoping the adoption will be approved. At least conditionally, until I have a new job. And that's the other good thing—I have a job interview on Tuesday!"

Ari leaped off his chair and gave his sister a bearlike hug. "I'm so proud of you, Les. I love you."

Leslie laughed. "Well, we can't celebrate yet. But my social worker sounded very upbeat. If all goes as I hope it does, Quinne and I can start planning our future."

Despite being elated for both of them, Carly felt her insides sink a little. She'd been nursing a tiny hope that before long, Leslie and Quinne would be living in Vermont. In the short time since they arrived in town, she'd grown seriously attached to them, especially to that sweet little girl.

"What about your idea of moving to Vermont?" Carly asked her.

"I spoke to the social worker about that, too," Leslie said. "I told her about my very supportive family, and how positive such a move would be for both of us. I'd have to get the court's consent to relocate out of state, but it's definitely possible. And, of course, I'd need a job that can support Quinne and me."

"You'll make it work," Carly said. "I know you will."

"Thank you." Leslie blinked hard. "Let me clear off the table and we can enjoy that wonderful cake you brought home."

Together they rinsed the dinner dishes and loaded them into the dishwasher. Ari dashed outside to check on Quinne.

"Les," Carly said, adding soap to the dishwasher, "Quinne seemed anxious about not finishing her chicken wrap tonight. Do you think living here this past week has been a strain on her? Things have been a little hectic."

"No, Carly, not at all," Leslie assured her. She swiped a damp cloth over the table. "Let me explain something. Quinne wasn't even four when her grandmother got custody of her. The grandmother was an old school type, you know? You had to eat everything on your plate before you left the table. Otherwise, you didn't get dessert."

Carly winced. She wasn't a fan of that style of parenting. Her own mom went out of her way to make healthy meals that were also appetizing. It wasn't easy. It took patience and love. Rhonda Hale Clark had both in abundance.

"I've had talks with Quinne about it, but I think that mindset has been ingrained in her." Leslie blew out a tired breath. "Maybe she was worried that you and Ari would be upset if she didn't 'clean her plate,' so to speak."

"Oh, Les, that would never happen. Not in this house," she emphasized. "She's only a little kid, for heaven's sake. I could barely finish my own wrap."

"I know." Leslie rinsed the dishcloth in the sink and wrung it out. "Don't worry. As she gets to know you better, she'll see that, too."

When the cleanup was finished, Carly removed the cake from the bakery box and set it on a glass plate. From the slot where Sissy had cut two sample slices, they could see that a rich raspberry filling was nestled between layers of dark chocolate cake.

Leslie's eyes nearly leaped out of their sockets. "Be still, my chocolate-craving heart. Quinne chose this one?"

"Of the five choices, she said you would like this one best."

Leslie blinked. "Oh, Carly, how did I get so lucky?"

"You're both lucky, to have each other."

Leslie went over and slung her arm around her future sister-in-law. "One of these days, you and Ari will be, too. I feel it in my bones."

• • •

Quinne took a sip of milk from her nearly empty glass, then set it down. A milk mustache coating her upper lip, she looked at Leslie with a serious expression and said, "Auntie Leslie, when we get home, can I change my name to Eiffel?"

Carly had an urge to giggle, but she kept her face blank. She was happy to let Leslie field this one.

Leslie coughed and choked at the same time, nearly spewing out her mouthful of cake. She swiped a napkin over her lips and said, "But you already have a lovely name. Why would you want to change it to Eiffel?"

Quinne shrugged. "Because I like it better. There's a girl at school whose name is Wyoming. Her mom named her after the state."

"Wyoming is an unusual name," Carly put in. "But I love the name Quinne."

"Did you know," Leslie said, "that your own mom named you after her great-aunt? Her name was Quinnetta, and she owned a button shop."

Quinne's eyes grew huge. "She did? Did she sell lots of buttons?"

"I'm sure she did. Back then, people made clothes at home more than they do now. For that, they needed buttons."

"Can we go see her?" Quinne bounced on her chair.

"I'm afraid she passed away a long time ago, sweetie. Way before you were even born."

Quinne mulled this, then forked up another mouthful of cake. "Okay, I'll think about it then. I guess Quinne is sort of a good name. But I still like Eiffel better."

CHAPTER 20

CARLY HAD ARRANGED FOR GRANT TO WORK A FEW HOURS AT THE EATERY Friday morning. Although the restaurant didn't open until eleven, she wanted extra coverage to help Val and Nina with food prep and other culinary chores. Grant was tickled that she'd asked him. To him, culinary tasks were the stuff his dreams were made of.

The night before the memorial service, she'd googled the directions to the funeral home. As Yvette had said, it was on the main road in Shaftsbury, although Carly didn't recall having passed it on their trek to Brice's house the day before.

Ari had a job in Bennington that would take up most of his day. Norah was meeting Leslie at the house in the morning for coffee and to review employment options. To Carly it was a positive sign that, employment-wise, things were looking up for Leslie.

The drive to the funeral home was more trafficky than Carly expected, though it didn't surprise her. During the summer, people flocked to Vermont's lakes and campsites at the start of each weekend.

Shaftsbury Funeral Home was a low red-brick building flanked on both sides by rows of sugar maples. The shrubbery near the entrance was immaculately trimmed. A hearse was parked just beyond the entrance.

Arriving shortly after eight thirty, Carly was surprised to see so many cars in the parking lot. Brice must've had more friends than she imagined. She wondered how many were his coworkers from the beverage distributor where he'd worked.

"Good morning." A thin man wearing a dark gray suit greeted Carly in the lobby. "Are you here for the Keaton service?" he asked in a somber tone.

"I am," Carly confirmed.

The man gestured toward a doorway to the left. "Please sign the guest book. The service will begin promptly at nine."

Carly thanked him and walked over to where the guest book rested on a mahogany pedestal. She took her time signing her name. It gave her a chance to peruse the other guest names.

Her gaze glided up the list. At least a dozen people had already signed in. The most notable was Yvette, whose name was near the top. None of the other names rang a bell with Carly.

She entered the room where Brice's closed coffin rested on a raised platform. Two floral bouquets sat at the foot of the coffin. Phil Keaton stood just beyond that, his hands clasped at his waist and his head bowed.

"Phil," Carly murmured, touching his arm lightly. "I'm so very sorry for your loss."

He lifted his head and gave her a surprised look. His eyes were puffy, his shaved head sunburned. "Carly, I didn't expect to see you here." He accepted her brief hug.

"Well, I didn't really know Brice, but I wanted to pay my respects—and offer my condolences again."

Phil nodded and cleared his throat. "Thank you," he said, his voice raw. "A lot of the people who worked with him are here. Also, a bunch of women from the animal shelter where he volunteered. One of them praised Brice for how caring he was with the cats, especially. They all said they're going to miss him." His eyes watered.

"I'm sure they will. Phil, was there an obituary published for your brother?"

He shook his head. "Only on the funeral home's web page. It was short and concise. Given my brother's early background, I didn't want to put anything in the local paper."

"I understand," she said.

Carly felt the man standing behind her edge forward. She moved past Phil and glanced around at the rows of chairs. Yvette was sitting in the last row, staring into her lap. Carly walked up the aisle and touched her shoulder gently. Yvette jerked her head up, then her body relaxed. "Oh, I didn't see you come in. Sit with me, okay?" She patted the fabric-covered chair beside her.

Carly moved past Yvette's thin legs and sat down. "Are you holding up okay?" she asked her quietly.

Yvette gave her usual shrug. Her eyelids were puffy and her hair looked unwashed. "I guess so. I'm not really sure it's all sunk in yet." She fingered the hem of her flowered top, which she wore over beige pants. "I feel weird wearing this, but I don't have any black clothing. Will people think I'm awful?"

"No, not at all," Carly assured her. She herself had worn lightweight black pants and a subdued green top. "You're here to mourn Brice's passing, and you look fine. Besides, no one has a right to judge what you wear."

Yvette looked relieved at Carly's comments. "I'm really glad you're here, Carly. I hated the thought of being here alone."

"Likewise. Yvette, after you told me about Theo yesterday, I got worried. Have you seen his car around?"

"I . . . no, but this morning when I was leaving, I found an egg splattered on my rear window." She twisted her hands in her lap. "It was probably just kids, though. Right?"

Maybe, although Carly was suspicious of the timing.

"You live in an apartment?"

"Yes. There's a few teenagers in my building," she hurried to add. "They're always blasting music from their cars. I'm sure that's all it was."

Carly didn't want to frighten her, so she gave her a bland smile. "If anything like that happens again, you should report it."

"That's probably a good idea," Yvette said without much enthusiasm.

Carly flitted her gaze around the room. Only about half the chairs were occupied. A podium stood beside the casket. A silver microphone rested on top.

From an unseen source, soft organ music began to drift through the room. More people had trickled in. A group of women came in together. The mourners formed a line, waiting to offer their condolences to Phil. One of them, a short, middle-aged man with thinning hair, was crying into a handkerchief. When he reached Phil, he grasped his arms and sobbed even louder.

Phil froze for a moment, then patted the man lightly on the back. The man finally moved along, stumbling over a chair leg as he seated himself near the front.

"Do you know who that man was?" Carly asked Yvette.

Yvette shook her head. "I don't have a clue. Never seen him before."

It was close to nine o'clock when a familiar figure lowered himself onto the seat beside Carly. She suppressed a gasp. "I didn't even see you come in."

"Good morning, Carly." Dressed in plain clothes, Chief Holloway was probably unknown to most of the mourners. Since this wasn't his town, he could blend in with ease.

"See anything interesting?" he asked Carly, a tiny edge to his voice.

"Chief, I'm only here to pay my respects," Carly replied evenly. "All I've seen so far are people who're very sad about Brice. One man was sobbing. I felt terrible for him."

The organ music suddenly grew louder, and a somberly attired pastor strode up behind the podium. Then the music stopped, and the pastor spoke in a comforting voice. He thanked everyone for attending the service. After murmuring a short prayer, he offered a few platitudes about Brice's untimely passing. After that, he asked if anyone would like to say a few words or share any memories.

Low murmurs rose from the mourners, but no one offered to speak.

Yvette pressed a tissue to her eyes. "This better be over soon before I totally lose it," she said in a shaky whisper.

Carly let out a silent breath of relief when the service ended. The burial was going to be private, so there wouldn't be a procession to the cemetery—wherever it was. People began filing out. Some nodded a thank-you to the pastor. A few stayed behind to offer a few last words to Phil.

The chief rose from his chair and turned to Carly. "I'll see you in the parking lot," he said, and moved toward the exit.

Yvette gave Carly's arm an impatient tap. "Aren't you ready to leave?"

"Sorry. I was daydreaming," Carly fibbed. She gathered her purse and followed Yvette down the aisle toward the exit. When they neared the casket, Carly stopped short. The man who'd sobbed into his handkerchief was kneeling at the coffin, his hands clasped in prayer. His lips moved, but he was murmuring so softly she couldn't make out what he was saying.

Two men filing out in front of her glanced over at the bereft man. One of them rolled his eyes at the other. "Phony jerk," he muttered.

"Yeah, you said it," the other one retorted.

Hmmm, that was interesting, Carly thought. Were they referring to Brice or to the man mourning him?

Now Carly was curious. As she moved closer to the man at the coffin, she noticed tears streaming down his cheeks. She caught the word *forgive* but the rest was swallowed up in a harsh cry. After he crossed himself and rose, Carly went over to him.

"Sir, I can see that you're struggling," she said gently. "Is there anything I can do? Would you like some water?"

The man looked at her with red-rimmed eyes. He wiped them with the hankie he seemed to be clutching like a life raft.

He cleared his throat. "Thank you," he said, his gray eyes dewy. I just need to collect myself before I leave."

"Can I get you some water or a cup of coffee? I think I saw a beverage stand out in the waiting area."

"Maybe some coffee would clear my head. If you could show me where . . ."

Carly took his upper arm and led him out of the room. They were the last mourners to leave, she noticed. Phil and the pastor had both disappeared.

They made their way to the lobby. A small table was set up in the adjacent waiting area. "Ah, a coffee machine," Carly said. "Have a seat and I'll get you a cup."

"Thank you. Black coffee will be fine."

Carly popped a pod into the coffee machine and made him a cup. He sipped it slowly, grimacing a little.

"It's strong," he said, "but I needed that. You're so kind to help me. You must think I'm an old fool."

If Carly had to guess his age, she'd say somewhere in his fifties. "You're neither old nor a fool. You must have cared deeply for Brice."

His eyes welled up. "It's my fault that he died. I'm the one who made him go to that fundraiser. If I hadn't, he'd still be alive." His face a mask of misery, he set the cup on the table beside him. "Oh, dear, I'm such a clod. I haven't even introduced myself. I'm Victor Silverio. I own the beverage company that employed Brice."

Brice's boss. The one who'd supposedly had an "issue" with Brice.

"Mr. Silverio, you can't blame yourself. You weren't even there that day, were you?"

"Well, um, no, but you don't understand. And please—it's Victor. You see, I discovered he was giving away cases of soda to people who'd never ordered them. He'd been doing it for several weeks. When I found out, I was furious. I thought he would deny it, but he didn't." Victor threw up his hands. "I didn't know what to do, so I told him I would either deduct the losses from his paycheck or fire him."

"What did he say?"

"He agreed to the deductions," he said dismally. "He needed the job."

"Most employers wouldn't have given him the choice," Carly pointed out.

"I know, but he was a good worker. Anyway, a short time after that I got a strange phone call. It was from a man at the school in Balsam Dell. He was recruiting vendors for a fundraiser. He saw an article online about Brice performing a good deed after someone crashed into our delivery van. This man from the school asked me if Brice would sell soda at the fundraiser and donate the proceeds to the school." He swallowed another mouthful of coffee.

"Brice obviously agreed."

Victor's mouth turned down. "I told him if he would do so, I would forgive the debt he owed the company. I would even donate the soda to the school. All he had to do was drive the soda there and sell it."

"That sounds like a generous offer," Carly told him.

"Maybe, but the problem was, he had a conflict. The animal shelter he volunteered for was having an outdoor fair that day to raise money. He'd been looking forward to helping them out."

Brice's surly behavior at the fundraiser was now beginning to make sense. The two events had been scheduled for the same day. Although the timing was no one's fault, Brice apparently resented the role he'd agreed to play.

Victor's face was more animated now. Unloading his guilty conscience to a willing listener seemed to have a cleansing effect on him. "I also found out something else. The missing soda? He was giving it to the volunteers at the animal shelter. He said they worked hard to save animals. He said he didn't think I'd mind."

Carly felt her heart pinch. Despite everything she'd learned about Brice's past, his devotion to helping animals showed him to be a caring person. He might have made poor choices, but his heart was in the right place.

"But it still wasn't right," Carly countered. "He should have asked you first before giving away the soda."

"Of course! I would have been glad to give to the shelter. It would have been a tax deduction for the company." He looked at Carly with a wounded expression. "Young lady, I can see you have a good head on your shoulders. May I ask you something?"

"Sure, you can."

He swallowed hard. "Do you think he forgives me?"

Carly hadn't expected the question. "He? Do you mean Brice?"

Victor nodded.

"I feel sure that he does," she said softly. "He knew that he worked for a good man, a good company. What happened to him had nothing to do with you, Victor. Please believe that."

Victor gave her a grateful smile. "I'm glad I met you. You've helped ease my mind." He threw his empty cup into a nearby trash receptacle, and together they walked toward the exit. "I wish I had a case of soda in my car I could give you."

"Not to worry," Carly said with a smile. "I own a small restaurant in Balsam Dell, so I'm well-stocked with soda."

Victor paused at the exit. "You know, when I first saw the brother, Phil, I came close to collapsing." He gave Carly an odd look. "I thought for sure I was looking at the ghost of Brice, coming back to haunt me."

No such thing, she was tempted to say. But was she really sure?

After they bade each other goodbye, Victor strode off into the parking lot. Carly retraced her steps and went off to find the restroom. Minutes later, as she was heading outside toward her car, she spotted the two men who'd made derogatory remarks that appeared to be about Victor. Puffing on cigarettes, they lingered near the front of the building.

Carly nodded politely at them. "Hello, gentlemen. I saw you both at Brice Keaton's service. May I ask you a question?"

The shorter of the two shrugged. "Yeah, sure. What do you want to know?"

"I don't mean to be nosy, but when everyone was leaving the service, I overheard you say someone was a jerk. Can I ask who you were talking about?"

The man scowled. "The *jerk*—and that's a polite word for him—is Victor Silverio. I hope you didn't fall for his crying act. He's the biggest hypocrite you ever met."

"Really?" Carly was surprised. Victor's grief had seemed genuine. Was he that good an actor? Or did these two have an axe to grind?

The other man picked up the thread. "He treated Brice like dirt, found fault with everything he did. Like this one time, Brice was ten minutes late for work. That creep docked his pay!"

Carly winced. "Do you both work at Silverio?"

"Nah, but we used to." The first one dropped his cigarette and crushed it with the toe of his scuffed loafer. "We both got different jobs last year. Couldn't stand working for that clown anymore." He narrowed his eyes at Carly. "Were you a friend of Brice's?"

"No, I only met him recently. I came here to offer my condolences to his brother." She lifted her tote farther onto her shoulder. "Thanks for answering my question. Have a great day."

They mumbled "goodbyes," and she made her way to her car.

Her mind was a jumble of conflicting information. Was Victor Silverio a good guy or a bad guy?

Or something in between?

CHAPTER 21

YVETTE HADN'T WAITED FOR CARLY, BUT SOMEONE ELSE HAD. THE CHIEF'S SUV crept up next to her driver's side, and she powered down her window. "I see you waited for me."

"I did. Got time for a chat?"

Carly shut off her engine and climbed out of her car. She slid onto the chief's passenger seat. The engine was running, the AC blowing frigid air from the vents.

"You were a long time in there," Holloway commented.

"Not that long," she countered. "I stopped to talk to the man Brice Keaton worked for."

"Ah, I should have guessed. Victor Silverio, right?"

"The very same." Carly pulled the visor down. The sun was glaring in her eyes. "He's devastated over Brice's death. He blames himself for making him do the fundraiser that day. The odd thing is, I found out he's not all that popular as a boss. I overheard two of his former employees trashing him."

"You learned all that since the service ended?"

"Well, like you say, Chief, I'm good at getting people to open up to me." She gave him an innocent smile.

"That you are," he said with a shake of his head. "Did you find out anything interesting at Brice's house yesterday?"

Carly felt her face flush. "Who told you I was there? Phil Keaton?"

Holloway gave her a knowing smile but said nothing.

"Okay, so I offered to help Yvette Carter retrieve her belongings. When I was cleaning out a drawer in Brice's bedroom, I found some greeting cards that Yvette had mailed to him. I didn't have a chance to read them all. But the one I did read told me she cared for him more than she'd been letting on."

"That's not a surprise," Holloway quipped. "The first day I spoke to her I picked up on that."

"Chief, I found something else in that drawer. It's a photo of two kids, an old photo of a boy and a girl. Nothing written on the back, but it looked as if someone might have scrawled something in pencil and then erased it. I thought the little girl might be Yvette, but she denied it."

"Knowing you, you took a copy of it."

"Even better. I have the actual picture. Yvette didn't want it, so I took it." She gave him a sly smile. "Would you like to see it? It's in my bag."

"Actually, I would—although I'm guessing it's not going to lead anywhere. Two little kids, no legible writing on the back. Never hurts to check it out, though. Leave no stone unturned, as they say."

From the far side of the funeral home, two men came around the corner wheeling the casket with Brice's remains. In keeping with their grim task, both men wore somber expressions. After sliding the casket into the back of the waiting hearse, they closed the doors.

A wave of raw emotion gripped Carly. Only days ago, Brice was hawking soda at the high school. Now he was on his way to being lowered into the ground. The finality of it, the utter senselessness, brought a lump to her throat.

Who disliked him enough to want to end his life? What did the killer gain?

"Dream weaving?" the chief said.

"No," she said. "I was just wondering where he's being buried." An icy shiver sprinted along her arms. She rubbed it away with her hands.

Holloway turned down the AC. The car was beginning to feel like the North Pole, but that wasn't the reason she shivered.

"His brother's having his remains transported to New Hampshire," the chief explained. "He's arranged for a private burial near his own home."

How sad, Carly thought. Alienated from his brother in life, Phil could now visit him any time he chose—in the cemetery. The irony of it was crushing. Carly shifted in her seat. "Chief, how much do you know about Brice's background?"

Holloway rested his arm on his steering wheel and gave her a curious look. "How much do *you* know?"

Carly knew the tactic. Answer a question with a question to delay a real response.

"I know that he ended up in juvie when he was fifteen. And I know the reason."

"Then you and Phil Keaton must've gotten pretty chummy yesterday."

"Not at all," she said. "I asked him a simple question about his and his brother's childhoods, and he blurted the whole ugly story."

Holloway shook his head and chuckled. "I gotta hand it to you, Carly. You do have a way of getting people to pour their hearts out to you. What else did he tell you?"

She thought back to her prior conversation with Phil. "He told me that his brother's bad deed had a damaging effect on his life, too—especially his last few high school years." She gave him a brief recap of what Phil had revealed about himself.

A chilling thought occurred to her. "Chief, is there any chance it was Phil Keaton who killed his brother? Could he have carried his own grudge all these years?"

Holloway blew out a heavy breath. "Given the brothers' estrangement, I wondered the same thing. But we've checked his whereabouts every which way, and it doesn't wash. He was definitely at his restaurant in New Hampshire when his brother was murdered."

Carly closed her eyes and thought for a moment. "What do you know about the teenage boy who started the fire that day with Brice? Phil said he died in a freak accident not long after he got out of juvie."

Holloway moved his hands to the top of the steering wheel. "Why, what're you thinking? That Keaton's death was some sort of revenge killing?"

"I'm not thinking anything," she said with a groan. "Mostly I'm feeling discouraged because my mom is a prisoner in her own home. Everyone in town is probably gossiping about her. And—forgive me for saying this—it doesn't seem like the investigation has progressed very far."

"Okay, first of all, that kid you referred to? The state police already looked into it. He ran his car off the road and crashed into a pole. His alcohol level was off the charts. It wasn't a freak accident at all—just a tragic, preventable one."

Carly sighed. "Okay, I appreciate the clarification. It was only a wild thought."

"As for Rhonda," Holloway went on, "she was released on her own recognizance, so she's technically not a prisoner. We've asked her to stay in town, but that doesn't seem like a hardship."

He was right. It was Rhonda who was sequestering herself. Despite all the support she'd been receiving from family and friends, she was still too embarrassed to face the world.

"Is she the only suspect?"

"No, she's not. We're looking at other possibilities, but right now I'm not at liberty—"

"To tell me who they are. I get it." She rubbed her hands over her cheeks in frustration. "Chief, are the police sure that Theo Sullivan couldn't have done it? Yvette Carter thinks he might be following her." She told him about Yvette finding the egg on her back window.

Holloway gave out an exasperated breath. "I wish she'd report things like that to the police. If nothing else, it would give us a reason to keep a closer eye on him. But as for the murder, Sullivan's alibi's been confirmed. Too many witnesses saw him at the pub that afternoon. He even took a selfie of himself posing with a woman there. It was taken right around the time Keaton was murdered."

How convenient, Carly thought with suspicion. Was it possible he took the selfie to throw the police off his trail? Which led her to another question.

"I forgot to ask you this earlier, Chief. Did Brice have a laptop, or a tablet?"

Holloway shook his head. "I'm afraid not. His home was searched every which way. They found nothing. Given that he wasn't on any social media, it wasn't surprising. All he had was a cell phone, and a basic one at that."

"Any photos on it?"

The chief laughed. "Mostly of his cat. A few taken at the animal shelter where he volunteered. None of Yvette Carter."

"Too bad," Carly noted, wondering why he didn't have a single photo of his girlfriend. "Have the investigators finished reviewing the video footage from the high school parking lot?"

The chief's right eye twitched. "For the most part, yes," he said carefully. "But there's still a few unanswered questions. I'm not trying to be evasive, Carly, but right now, that's the status of things. I know on TV shows, crimes are committed and solved within an hour's time. It doesn't work like that in real life."

"I understand," she said. "Is there any chance I can watch the video? I know it's a long shot, but maybe I'll pick up on something the investigators haven't. It's worth a try, right?"

He shook his head. "Ah, Carly, if it were my choice, I'd say yes. But the lead investigator would never go for it. He's a stickler for protocol. Besides, your mom's attorney watched it on Monday and didn't have any comments. None that he shared, anyway."

"You mean . . . Burt Oakley?"

The chief nodded.

"Chief, Mom dumped him. She met with her new attorney yesterday morning—a woman named Shania Worthington."

Holloway's eyebrows shot up. "Really? Worthington's an excellent criminal attorney. As for Oakley, I only know him by reputation, but I can tell you one thing—he's not exactly loved by most cops."

"Really?"

"He had a case a few years ago," the chief explained, "in which he knowingly selected a juror he knew personally. Oakley was sanctioned by the judge, and the juror was dismissed."

"That's all? No other repercussions?"

"Not that I'm aware of."

Carly felt her blood simmer. "I am *so* glad Mom fired him."

Something else suddenly occurred to her. Why hadn't she remembered it before?

"Chief, the day of the fundraiser, Brice supposedly got a phone call after he'd already left the school. Someone told him he left a case of soda there, so he had to go back for it. Did the police trace that call?"

Holloway looked annoyed. "Where did you hear that?"

"Oh, um, from Yvette. We stopped for coffee after we left Brice's house yesterday."

He let out a guttural sigh. "Carly, did it ever occur to you that Yvette Carter might be a suspect?"

"Is she?"

"At this stage, we have a few persons of interest. And yes, she's on the list, so please do not contact her again. Or accept calls from her."

Carly's shoulders drooped. She could read the chief's mind as if the words flashed in a bubble over his head. *You're asking too many questions again. You're putting yourself at risk.*

"To answer your question," Holloway said, "that call was made from a disposable phone. The caller paid cash for the phone, and for a month of service. That was the one, and the only, call made from that phone. And no, it hasn't turned up yet," he added quietly.

"So, you can buy a disposable phone without showing an ID?" she asked.

"Some retailers require an ID, but many don't. In this case, it seems our caller did his, or her, research before buying it. Either that or bought it from a not so legitimate source."

She pointed a playful finger at him. "You said *his* first."

He gave her a tight smile. "Force of habit. Why don't we talk about something else? Val tells me Ari's sister and her niece have been visiting you."

That brought a smile to Carly's lips. "They have, and I've been enjoying them both so much. The little girl, Quinne, is a total darling. She's bright and inquisitive and she adores Havarti. I swear, they've become glued at the hip."

Holloway laughed. "I hope I get to meet them."

"You will. They're coming to the wedding." She opened her door. "Let me get that picture for you. If we sit here much longer, you'll run out of gas."

Carly retrieved the photo of the two sad-looking kids. She slid halfway onto the chief's passenger seat and gave it to him. "As I mentioned, something might've been written on the back, but if it was, it was erased. You can keep this. I already have a copy."

"I figured," he quipped.

Something else had been rolling around in Carly's mind. "Chief, don't think I'm crazy when I ask this, but . . . is it possible Phil Keaton is actually Brice?"

At first, he looked startled at the question. Then he shifted his eyes to gaze through the windshield. "You're not crazy, Carly. And it's not impossible, except for one thing. This past winter, Brice was in an accident. He sprained his arm and sustained a fracture in his wrist."

The accident. Of course.

According to Victor Silverio—and the news article she'd read—Brice had been deemed by the police to be a good Samaritan. He'd ignored his own painful injuries to check on the other driver.

Holloway lifted his chin in the direction of the funeral parlor. "A postmortem X-ray of his body confirmed his identity. The man heading to New Hampshire in that hearse is Brice Keaton."

CHAPTER 22

BY THE TIME CARLY PULLED INTO HER PARKING SPACE BEHIND THE EATERY Friday morning, it was nearly time to open. Suzanne was sprucing up the tables, which included replacing the faux daisies in the vintage soup cans with lifelike marigolds. At the end of each month, Carly looked forward to changing the flowers. It lent a fresh appearance to the restaurant, and customers often commented on it.

Suzanne hummed a happy, off-key tune as she tucked a bouquet of red and yellow marigolds into an old tomato soup can.

Carly grinned at her. "Someone's looking forward to vacation."

"You betcha." She did a little dance. "A week of fresh mountain air and camping with my two dudes? What more could a woman ask for?"

The fresh mountain air, Carly could get on board with. Camping in the woods? Not so much. A quaint bed-and-breakfast would be more to her liking. Preferably with a morning buffet of pastries and fresh fruit.

Suzanne set down her bag of flowers and propped a hand on her hip. "So, what was the service like?"

Carly fetched a mug of coffee from behind the counter. "It was short, thankfully. The chief was there. We had a little chat in the parking lot afterward."

"Oh?" Suzanne's voice rose. "Did he have any news?"

Mug in hand, Carly went around and sat at the counter. "I'm afraid not. My mom is still a suspect, but supposedly they're looking into others."

"I'm sorry." Suzanne slung her arm around Carly's shoulders. "Chief Holloway would probably kill me for saying this, but I have total faith you'll figure it out."

"Thanks," Carly said with a wry smile. "But if the police figure it out first, I will personally do a happy dance."

She carried her tote and coffee into the kitchen. Grant was slicing ham, while Val stood at the stove stirring a pan. Nina was peeking over Valerie's shoulder, her expression one of pure delight.

"Hey, what's cooking?" Carly asked. "Do I detect a hint of béchamel sauce?"

Grant looked up from his slicing and grinned. "Yes, you do. Today's the day, Carly."

"The day?"

"After the lunch crunch," Nina warbled, "we're testing our first croque monsieur." She said it with an exaggerated French accent and a dramatic roll of her hand.

Valerie turned off the burner and gave the pan one final stir.

Carly laughed and plunked her tote on a chair. "Will I be allowed to steal a smidge?"

"Hey, this is your restaurant," Grant said. "That entitles you to be the first taster."

A pang swept through Carly. It *was* her restaurant. The one she'd dreamed of opening since she'd left college over a decade ago. She sometimes missed those early days. Standing over a hot grill, flipping grilled cheese sandwiches. It brought a kind of joy into her life that'd been lacking in her former job.

And then there was Ari. She'd met him when he installed the pendant lighting that lent the restaurant its "cow barn chic," as Suzanne had dubbed it. After that, he stopped in frequently for lunch. Their attraction to one another had morphed into so much more. And now, here they were—preparing to tie the knot.

"Earth to Carly." Grant touched her shoulder.

She shook her head and laughed. "Sorry, I was daydreaming. Can you tell?"

He looked at her with concern. "Is everything okay? I mean, other than your mom's situation. I know that's weighing on you."

It was more like a boulder on her chest, crushing the breath out of her, she thought.

She reassured Grant that everything was under control, but deep down she felt stretched in all directions.

Over the past week, she'd been distracted by Leslie and Quinne's unexpected visit, as well as by her upcoming wedding. Both were important, but maybe it was time she refocused. Nothing would ever be right again if her mom wasn't vindicated. And that meant finding the real killer.

The chief admitted that the police had other "persons of interest," Yvette Carter being among them. Carly hadn't heard from her since she bolted out of the funeral home. Would Yvette try to contact her again?

Who else? Theo Sullivan had been ruled out. Given his confirmed alibi, he was pretty much a dead end, for lack of a better description.

Victor Silverio was an enigma. Had he truly been overwhelmed by guilt, or had he been putting on a show for everyone at the memorial service? He admitted he'd been angry that Brice had stolen from him. He also claimed they'd worked it out between them. One thing was for certain: he knew Brice would be at the high school that day. And yet, why kill him? What would he stand to gain? From what Carly could glean, Brice had been respected at his workplace and by the people at the animal shelter.

And then there was Phil Keaton, Brice's identical twin. Not only had he produced a rock-solid alibi, but the X-ray of Brice's body had proven the identity of the deceased.

Valerie covered the pan and set it aside, then she and Nina left the kitchen. Carly drained her coffee mug and followed behind them.

"Time to get to work," Carly announced to Grant as she headed into the dining room.

It was just eleven. Nina was unlocking the front door when Don Frasco stepped inside. He said "Hey" to everyone, then fetched his usual root beer from the refrigerated case.

After he settled at the counter, Nina and Carly exchanged looks. Nina sat on one side of Don and Carly on the other.

"Hey, guys," he said warily. "What's . . . going on?"

"It has come to our attention," Carly said in a mock serious tone, "that at one time, you were a staunch aficionado of grilled cheese sandwiches. Do you admit or deny these charges?" She tapped the counter with her forefinger like a stern teacher.

Don's freckles turned pink. "Clearly there's been a spy in my midst."

Nina bit her lip. "I'm sorry, Don. I couldn't resist telling Carly about the picture."

After a lengthy silence, he said, "Okay, yes. I confess! I once ate a grilled cheese, and . . . God forgive me, but I enjoyed it!"

His faux histrionics sent the women into giggles. It reminded Carly of a line from a movie, but she couldn't remember which one.

"There, are you happy?" he said, trying hard not to smile.

"Not quite," Carly said. "We want to know why you stopped eating them."

Don's smile faded. "Like I already told Nina, my tastes have matured." He lifted his nose into the air.

"Are you buying this?" Carly asked Nina.

"Nope. Not for a second."

Don folded his hands and stared down at the counter. "When I was a young kid, I used to eat grilled cheese till they came out of my ears. One day, when I was stuffing my face, my dad came over to me and said, 'Better cut back on the grilled cheese, kid, before you turn into one. You already look like a cheese wheel.'"

Nina's jaw dropped. "But . . . that was so mean."

Don's head lowered. "He said things like that all the time. Anyway, that was the same day he bailed on us. Walked out and disappeared like Mom and I never existed. I thought it was my fault. I always associated his leaving with my eating that grilled cheese. Even when I got older and knew that didn't make sense, I still couldn't stomach a grilled cheese."

Nina squeezed her eyes shut, tears leaking out.

Carly touched Don's shoulder. She felt sick, and angry at herself. She'd never have teased him if she'd known that. "I'm so sorry, Don. I apologize for making light of it. I never would have done that—"

"Hey, it's okay. Honestly." He smiled at them both. "A lot of kids are fussy eaters. You had no way of knowing."

Nina squeezed him in a hug just as three women dressed in tennis gear walked into the restaurant. Suzanne quickly grabbed menus and rushed over to seat them.

"Sorry," Nina said, blotting her eyes with her fingertips. "I just . . . got emotional."

"Listen," Don said, "I don't want either of you to feel bad. That experience taught me a valuable lesson. It's something I always keep in mind when I'm writing. Want to know what it is?"

They both nodded.

"Words matter. And now I'd like to place my lunch order. Please tell Val I'd like a grilled cheese with extra chips and pickles. Hold the soup."

Nina's jaw nearly hit the floor, and Carly let out a gasp. She grasped the counter. "Did we stumble into a different dimension? Because I thought I heard Don order a grilled cheese."

Don rolled his eyes. "Very funny, you two. This is only a trial run, so it better be good. If it's not, I'm going back to my regular."

Valerie looked at his order slip, her eyes rounding to the size of truck tires. She pumped her fist. "Praise be to the saints! This is the day we've all been waiting for."

Suzanne came over and clipped her customers' orders to the wheel next to the grill. Then she went over and leaned close to Don. "Hey, I overheard what you said about your father before." She raised a clenched fist. "If he ever shows up again, I'd like to meet him. I have a little present for him." With a smug look, she strode off to seat a group of teenagers who'd just ambled in.

"That's our mama bear," Nina remarked.

Carly laughed. "More like a mama lion."

133

CHAPTER 23

LUCK WAS ON THEIR SIDE. AFTER FINISHING HIS LUNCH, DON PRONOUNCED the grilled cheese to be "better than expected." He promised to try one again with a different cheese.

By twelve thirty the eatery was well into the lunchtime rush. Carly was seating customers when she saw Tillie Lloyd come in behind three chattering teenaged girls. Smiling broadly, she waved at Carly and held up a large plastic container.

After seating the girls, Carly went over to greet Tillie. "Hey, you're back. Nice to see you again."

Tillie's blue eyes danced. "I brought you a present. Here, hold this while I take off the top."

Carly held the container and Tillie snapped open the lid. Inside was a deep-dish pie, its golden crust oozing purple juice through perfectly even slits. Carly inhaled the sweet aroma. "Blueberry?"

"Yup. A seasonal favorite. I was hoping that if you liked it, you might place a few orders for your restaurant." She tilted her head and gave a hopeful shrug. "Maybe a weekly special?"

Tillie's timing was terrible, but the pie smelled delicious. Carly led her into the kitchen, where they set the pie on the pine table.

Grant was working on a batch of salad. Recognizing Tillie from the fundraiser, he came over for a peek. "Hey, nice to see you again. Oh, man, blueberry pie. One of my faves."

"If it's okay with you," Carly told Tillie, "I'll share your pie with my staff. I know it's going to be delicious. But as for adding it to our menu, it's not something I can decide right away. My mom's still considered a suspect, and I have visitors from out of state. On top of that, my wedding is next month. I'm juggling so much right now."

"I understand," Tillie said, her voice laced with sympathy. "I should have checked with you before coming over. And I'm sorry the police still haven't cleared Rhonda. The poor thing—is she going crazy with worry?"

"She's hanging in there," Carly said. "She has a lawyer ready to go to bat for her, but we're hoping it won't be necessary."

Tillie took Carly's hands into her own. "Please let her know I'm thinking of her. Tell her when this is all over, I'm going to treat her to a celebratory glass of wine."

Carly smiled. "She'll like that. Can we make you a grilled cheese to thank you for the pie?"

"Thanks, but I have to scoot back to work. Let me know if everyone likes it!" Tillie hugged Carly and said goodbye to Grant, then left through the swinging door into the dining room.

"She wants to sell her pies here?" Grant said after she left.

"Yeah, she does." Carly tapped a finger to her lips. "I'd like to help her, but I'm not sure how it would work." She threw up her hands. "Anyway, I won't decide anything till Ari and I are back from our honeymoon."

Grant went back to adding crumbled goat cheese to the huge container of salad he was preparing. "It's coming up fast, isn't it? Are you excited?"

Carly laughed, but inside her nerves were jumping like kids on a trampoline. Every day that passed without Brice's killer being arrested meant that her mom was still under suspicion.

"I am, if I can get everything done by then. That's the part that scares me." She looked down at the pie. She hadn't eaten since breakfast, and her stomach was starting to rumble. "Want to try a piece of this with me?"

Grant wiped his hands on a towel. "Sure, I'll try a slice. But don't forget we're testing the croque monsieur today."

"Then we'll only cut thin slivers."

Carly fetched plates and forks and cut two slender pieces from the pie. Grant gobbled his down in three bites. "Oh, boy, this is a keeper," he announced. "This is even better than the one the inn serves. The crust is spectacular."

Carly ate hers slowly, savoring the blend of fresh blueberries baked into a buttery crust. The amount of sugar was perfect. She pointed her fork at the plate. "You're right. This could rival my mom's blueberry pie. Oops! Don't tell her I said that."

"Don't worry." Grant winked at her. "Your secret is safe with me."

Carly swallowed her last bite. "After tasting this, I'm seriously thinking of making a deal with Tillie to sell us her pies. Just think how many customers would love a slice of homemade pie after a lunch of grilled cheese and tomato soup!"

Grant laughed. "I know I would."

"As soon as I'm back from my honeymoon," Carly said, "I'm going to call her and work something out."

For the next hour or so, Carly alternated between helping out in the dining room and cleaning up dishes in the kitchen. Around quarter of two, Valerie came into the kitchen, leaving Nina and Suzanne to cover the dining room.

Grant had set out the necessary ingredients for the croque monsieur. The béchamel sauce was simmering on the stove. On a parchment-lined baking tray, he'd lined up three slices of artisan white bread.

"Croque monsieur is typically made with Gruyere cheese," Grant began, "but I chose Edam for its low melting point and mild, slightly nutty flavor. It's also easy to grate. Today we're going to make three sandwiches. They're very filling, so we'll split them among us. Also, it should be eaten with a knife and fork. Otherwise, you'll have a gooey mess trying to pick it up." He smiled at Valerie and held out a hand. "I now turn the demonstration over to chef Valerie."

Valerie nodded. Using a spoon, she coated the bread slices with béchamel sauce. Over that she layered the ham slices, the grated Edam, and a sprinkling of Parmesan cheese. She topped each sandwich with another bread slice, a layer of the béchamel, and a final helping of the Edam and Parmesan.

She gave Grant a worried look "Does this look okay?"

"It's perfect," Grant assured her. "I've preheated the oven to four twenty-five. We're going to bake it for about five minutes, then broil it for three. It will be ready to serve when the top is golden brown and the cheese is melted."

Ten minutes later, the croque monsieur experiment was deemed a success.

"Scrumptious," Carly gushed.

"Fabulous," Valerie pronounced.

"Perfection," Grant praised. "Valerie, you've created a monster. We're going to want this every day."

"A monster in a good way," Carly mumbled over her last mouthful. "Nina and Suzanne need to try this."

She went into the dining room and sent Nina and Suzanne into the kitchen. Two customers came in. Carly seated them and delivered their drinks, then started their orders. Both chose the daily special—the Party Havarti.

It was a treat, working the grill again. She layered Havarti cheese and tomato between slices of sourdough bread, then buttered both sides and set them on the grill. She was flipping them over when a sole customer strutted in. Through mirrored sunglasses, he tossed his glance around as if he owned the place, then stroked his dark beard.

Carly's heart jolted. Her hand trembled on the spatula. She'd seen him only a few times, and not close up. But she knew instantly who he was. His hard scowl and defiant expression were burned into her brain.

Theo Sullivan.

At that moment, Valerie returned to the dining room and took Carly's place behind the grill. That left Carly the task of seating the newcomer.

Menu in hand, she forced her feet to carry her over to him. "Would you like a booth, sir?" She attempted a smile, but her lips refused to cooperate.

He stood stock-still, and for a moment Carly thought her legs would fold. Those sunglasses were unnerving. "No, I don't want a booth," he mocked. "I wanna know why you took my picture at the coffee shop yesterday in Shaftsbury."

Cold fear surged through Carly, numbing every limb in her body. This man was dangerous. How could the police not see it?

She clutched the menu to her chest. "Why would you think that?"

He jabbed a finger at her. "Because I saw you do it, and then I followed you here. I saw you park that old green Corolla behind this building and walk in through the back door. Try denying that, lady." A drop of spittle formed on his lips. Carly forced herself not to gag.

She moved backward a step. The thought that he'd followed her yesterday made her legs feel liquid. "I took a photo because I thought I saw a bald eagle in the tree next to the parking lot," she lied. "I wanted to show it to my husband."

"Oh, yeah?" He gave her a menacing smile. "Show it to me. Show me the eagle."

"It didn't come out good, so I deleted it. And I'm afraid I'll have to ask you to—"

Valerie shot around from behind the counter and stood within inches of Sullivan, confronting him with fire in her eyes. "Sir, my husband is the chief of police, and I just texted him. He's on his way over, so I'd leave if I were you. I also just took a picture of you threatening my boss."

"You're a liar."

"No, she's not." Grant, who'd emerged from the kitchen, sidled up quietly behind them. He held out his cell phone. "I texted him, too—*and* I took your picture. I'd do what she says, if I were you."

Sullivan's eyes were unreadable behind his mirrored glasses, but his mouth twitched.

Out of the corner of her eye, Carly saw a patrol car pull up in front of the eatery. The young officer driving the vehicle double-parked and made it into the restaurant with only a few quick strides.

Tall, tanned, and muscular, he wore a badge that identified him as Officer Jaden Wykowski. He sized up the situation in an instant, then turned his granite gaze on Theo Sullivan.

"I understand there's been a disturbance," Wykowski said, hands on his hips.

Sullivan shrank a little, then thrust out his chest. "Yeah, there's been a disturbance, all right, Officer." He snarled at Carly. "She's the one who's been spying on me, taking pictures of me. Why don't you arrest her?"

In a voice as calm as she could manage, Carly gave the officer her explanation. She stuck to the bald eagle story, knowing she'd explain the truth later to the chief. She didn't mention Yvette. She worried it would only rile Sullivan more and possibly put Yvette at risk.

"Liar!" Sullivan shrieked, taking a step toward Carly.

In one swift move, Wykowski grabbed Sullivan's arms and cuffed his hands behind his back. "Sir, you're under arrest for disorderly conduct. You have the right to remain silent . . ."

The rest of the warning faded as the officer marched his prisoner into the back of the patrol car.

Carly sagged with relief, her heart still drumming in her chest. Grant took her arm. "Are you okay?"

She nodded, then glanced around. Only a few customers were in the restaurant, including the pair waiting for their Party Havarti specials.

Suzanne and Nina reappeared, both wearing worried expressions. Grant assured them everything was okay and led Carly into the kitchen.

"Sit," Grant said. "I'll get you some iced coffee. Your face is as pale as a ghost."

She dropped onto a chair at the pine table. Grant delivered the iced coffee and sat down adjacent to her. "Okay, now tell me," he said gently. "What was that all about?"

In between sips, she explained what happened at the coffee shop the day before.

Worry lines formed on Grant's brow. "Everything you just told me scares the heck out of me. Carly, what if he's the killer?"

She shook her head. "The police already ruled him out. A bunch of witnesses confirmed his alibi for the time of the murder." She rubbed her fingers over her forehead, which was beginning to throb like Poe's telltale heart. "Look at it this way. Now that he's been arrested, he won't be able to bother me, or Yvette, right?"

Grant folded his arms over the table. "For now, yeah, but he could be out within twenty-four hours. He might even be released today. Then what?"

Carly didn't know whether to cry or scream. She wanted to do both.

The door swung open. They turned to see Chief Holloway ambling toward them.

The chief smiled at Grant. "Good to see you again, Grant. I bet your folks love having you home for the summer."

"Yeah, they're pretty pumped." Grant slid off his chair. "Have a seat. I was just leaving. Want some iced coffee?"

"Nah. I'm good." Holloway lowered himself onto Grant's vacated chair and removed his hat. His thick gray hair was getting a touch of white at the temples, Carly noticed.

"Sullivan's in custody," he said.

"Thank heaven." Carly heaved a sigh.

"We'll hold him overnight, but he'll probably be sprung in the morning. Tell me about the picture he claims you took. You didn't mention it this morning."

"It was yesterday, when Yvette and I stopped at the coffee shop after we left Brice's house."

She explained seeing the black sedan with a hood ornament idling in the parking lot. "I took the picture because Yvette thought Sullivan had been following her. I thought it might come in handy in case she wanted to file for a protective order."

"May I see it?"

Carly reached into her tote and pulled out her phone. After a few taps, she showed him the photo.

Holloway enlarged it with his fingers. "Can you text this to me?"

Carly took the phone and tapped it again. "Done," she said.

"Thanks." Holloway's expression was grim. "You need to be careful, Carly. Way more careful than you've been so far. As I said before, communicating with Yvette Carter is out of the question. I don't mean to beat it up, but I want to emphasize that."

Normally, Carly would rebuff such an edict from the chief. This time, though, she had to admit that his concern was justified. Deep in her bones, she suspected Theo Sullivan wasn't the type to go away quietly.

She gave Holloway a feeble nod. "I understand."

"I know this is getting to you, Carly, but please, listen to me." Holloway pressed his palms together in a praying motion. "The police are going to solve this. That's a promise. But right now, you have a wedding to prepare for, and you have family and friends who need you and care about you and love you."

Carly couldn't resist a smile. "Great job laying a guilt trip on me."

"Did it work?"

"Sort of," she admitted.

"Good." He put his hat on. "Oh, one more thing."

"Yes, Columbo?"

He chuckled. "That photo you gave me yesterday? Another dead end. It's impossible to tell where it was taken, but we examined the back under a better light. It looks as if someone wrote *M plus D* in pencil, then erased it. That's M, then a plus sign, then D. Those kids could be anyone, anywhere, anytime."

Carly mulled that information. M plus D. Neither of the letters meant anything that she could glean.

"Thanks for letting me know, Chief. Like you said, another dead end."

CHAPTER 24

THE REMAINDER OF THE DAY WAS BLESSEDLY BUSY BUT UNEVENTFUL. Though the croque monsieur had been a success, it was labor-intensive enough that Carly didn't know how it would fit into the menu.

Because its preparation required an oven, the best option would be to buy a portable one—maybe an air fryer?—for the kitchen. The question was, would it be worth the cost and the effort?

She couldn't decide now. More pressing issues were riding its tail.

The blueberry pie was still in the kitchen. She asked her staff to please help themselves to a slice, since Tillie had gone out of her way to deliver it.

Grant had left at three to begin his shift at the Balsam Dell Inn. She thanked him again for helping out at the eatery, but he waved it off. "It's what I love to do," he reminded her.

Late in the afternoon, Carly had called her mom to check on her. She'd been relieved to hear that Rhonda was preparing chicken shish kebobs for her and Gary's dinner. She sounded better, more perky than she'd been the past few days. At least she wasn't slumped on the sofa watching old movies.

"By the way," Rhonda said before they ended the call, "you don't have to give a thought to supper tonight. Gary's on his way over to your house with a huge bowl of your favorite taco salad and some fresh corn bread."

Taco salad! Carly could already taste it. It was one of her favorite summer meals. Her mom only made it during the warmer months, as it was meant to be eaten cold. She hoped it was a dish Leslie and Quinne would enjoy.

She texted Ari. *Mom's sending over taco salad and corn bread for supper!*

His response came instantly. *Yesss! Love you to pieces.*

Her heart gave a little flutter. Even on her worst days, Ari made her smile. She texted back a response followed by a string of heart emojis.

Shortly before six, Nina and Valerie pushed Carly out the door. "Go home," Valerie insisted in a firm voice. "Nina and I can close up."

Carly put up a mild protest, but in truth she was grateful. Leslie, Quinne, and Havarti were in the backyard when she arrived home. Ari wasn't home yet, so she assumed he was out doing errands.

The moment Carly opened the back door to the yard, Quinne and her canine companion rushed at her. Carly wrapped Quinne in a hug, then lifted Havarti for a smooch. Leslie waved to her from the base of the maple tree, where she was kneeling next to a cardboard box overflowing with pink impatiens.

"Hey, whatcha doing?" Carly asked her, shading her eyes from the sun.

Leslie brushed dirt off her hands and stood. She looked summery in a flowered halter top and purple shorts. "I hope it's okay, Carly. I wanted to plant some impatiens around the tree to thank you and Ari for being so good to us. Quinne and I went to the local nursery—she helped pick out the color."

Carly was touched by her thoughtfulness. "Les, these are beautiful. Impatiens don't like full sun, so that's a perfect spot for them."

"Anyway," Leslie continued, "let's have some lemonade first." Her eyes had a sparkle Carly had never seen before.

They sat at the umbrella table, while Quinne and Havarti went back to bouncing around in the yard. Leslie poured them each a glass of lemonade from the pitcher. "By the way, did you know your stepdad brought supper over for us?"

"Mom told me. Wait till you taste her taco salad!"

"I can't wait. Sounds like something Quinne will like, too."

Carly took a sip of her lemonade. "If she doesn't, I can always whip up a grilled cheese for her."

Leslie stared at her. "You would do that?"

"Of course I would. Why do you ask?"

Leslie rubbed the back of her hand over one eye. "It's just . . . you're going to make a fantastic mom someday. Ari is so lucky." She looked toward the house and smiled. "And speaking of whom . . ."

"Ladies," Ari greeted, striding toward them. He kissed Carly soundly, then squeezed her shoulder. "I remembered we were low on ice cream, so I stopped and picked up a few quarts."

He waved at Quinne, who was rolling around on the grass with Havarti. "Anyone mind if we head inside and eat? I'm totally starving."

"I'm for that." Leslie beckoned Quinne inside, and they all trooped into the kitchen. Ari filled Havarti's kibble bowl. After washing up, everyone sat down to eat.

Leslie needn't have worried. Quinne loved the taco salad. She started with a small serving, then asked for a second helping.

Once they were finished, Leslie pulled in a deep breath and smiled over at Quinne. "Quinne and I have more good news to share. This afternoon, the DCYF officially approved the adoption. Well, with contingencies."

Carly started to leap off her chair when Leslie held up a finger. "Two things first. They need to do one final home visit, which will happen on Wednesday. And I need to be gainfully employed within thirty days. But I'm not worried about either."

They all squealed at once. Quinne slid off her chair and crawled onto Leslie's lap. She hugged her tightly enough to cut off her breath. "Mommy," she said in a sweet voice.

Tears running down her cheeks, Carly jumped up and wrapped Leslie and Quinne in a bearlike hug. Even Havarti joined in by springing off Leslie's legs.

"Bunch of crybabies," Ari teased, wiping at his own leaky eyes.

Carly felt her heart overflow with gratitude. Leslie and Quinne were a forever family. There'd been no doubt before, but having a seal of approval made it official.

Nonetheless, a tiny twinge of sadness tugged at her. She was hoping they'd find a way to move to Vermont after the adoption. It was selfish, she knew, and she scolded herself for the thought.

Ari spooned ice cream into dessert dishes, and they all ate until they were stuffed. He cleaned up the kitchen while everyone else went into the living room.

"I practiced some new French words today," Quinne said proudly. She sat on the floor with her back propped against the sofa, her thin legs stretched out in front of her.

"You did, huh?" Carly smiled at her, then dropped into one of the overstuffed chairs. She stretched her limbs, hoping to invigorate them, but it only made her more tired. For sure, it had been a day. Mental fatigue tugged at her, pulling her eyes closed. She'd never had a chance to tell Ari about the memorial service, or about Theo Sullivan being arrested in her restaurant. For the past several days, their private time had been at a minimum. Later, when they were alone, she'd tell him everything.

"Auntie Carly?" Quinne was on her knees in front of Carly, holding up her prized French book. "Do you want to hear my new words?"

"I would love to," Carly enthused.

"These are all things that are outside," Quinne said, in the tone of a schoolteacher. "I'll say it in French, and you tell me what they are."

Carly didn't remember much of her high school French, but she was willing to play along for Quinne's sake.

"Okay," Quinne chirped, "the first word is *fleur*." She pronounced it *flurrh*.

"Um, is it a flower?" Carly guessed.

"You got it right! Okay, now this one's harder. What does *shanh* mean?"

Carly racked her brain. "Um . . ."

"It means field! It's spelled c-h-a-m-p." Quinne looked pleased with herself. "What about *bwah*?"

Carly scrunched her face. "Can you spell it?"

"B-o-i-s," Quinne said.

"Mmm, I think that means wood. Or woods."

Leslie went over and smoothed Quinne's hair. "Honey, Auntie Carly is probably tired from working all day. Can you save the other French words for tomorrow?"

Quinne shrugged. "Okay. I'll mark where we left off."

Leslie winked at Carly. "You look exhausted. You should make an early night of it."

"I plan to. Believe me." Carly sat up straighter. "Quinne, I almost forgot to tell you. At my restaurant today, my grill cook made a French grilled cheese." She described the croque monsieur, and how yummy it was. "If you come in tomorrow, we'll make you one. It's very filling, so it's okay if you only want to eat a small portion."

Quinne's hazel eyes grew large, and she jumped into the air. "Yay! Can we, Mommy?"

Leslie looked at her with so much love it made Carly's heart swell. "You bet we can," she told Quinne. "I can't wait to taste it myself."

Carly excused herself and headed into the kitchen. Emotions were swirling inside her, threatening to turn her into a pile of mush. She needed a break.

Ari had stepped outside, and she went out to join him. He was sitting at the umbrella table perusing the *Balsam Dell Weekly*.

"Getting some fresh air?" She sat beside Ari and looped her arm through his.

"Yeah, just a little private time. Which you and I have been sorely lacking this week."

"I know. I love having them here, and I think Quinne's benefited from getting to know her family. But it will be nice when it's just us again." She kissed his cheek and glanced at the paper. It was open to the centerfold, where photos from the fundraiser filled two entire pages.

"Ditto," he said, wrapping an arm around her. "I can tell you've had a rough day. Wanna talk about it?"

With that, Carly blurted everything. The memorial service, her conversations with the chief, and the frightening confrontation with Theo Sullivan.

"Ah, honey, I was afraid of this," Ari said soberly. "I understand why this one's so personal for you, but your safety has to come first, right? This Sullivan guy sounds like a bad character."

"I know." She let out a frustrated breath. "I keep thinking I'm missing something, Ari. Whenever I ask the chief about the video footage from that day, he gets evasive. Says they're still working on it. I asked if I could view it myself and got a big fat *no*."

She glanced down at the paper. Carly realized she hadn't even read it herself. Don usually brought a copy into the eatery every Thursday, the day it came out, but he'd been distracted over the past week.

The photos were the same ones Don had texted her. She'd studied them before, but nothing had jumped out at her. Perusing them again, she still saw nothing worthy of catching her eye.

And then, in the bottom right photo, a familiar face made her pulse do a high jump. A man, strolling through the crowd as if looking for something. She'd met the man only that morning, but she recognized him right away.

Victor Silverio.

CHAPTER 25

CARLY PUNCHED IN THE CHIEF'S NUMBER ON HER CELL. SHE HATED CALLING him this late, but she'd jump out of her skin if she had to wait till morning.

"Yes, Carly?" He sounded tired.

She told him what she'd noticed in the paper, elaborating on what Silverio's former employees had told her at the memorial service. Holloway promised to check it out, but claimed it was probably another dead end. The police had already interviewed Silverio and dismissed him as a possible suspect.

Dead end. Carly was getting tired of those words.

Ari was in the bathroom. She heard the water running in the shower. Carly opened her laptop on the bed, fully intending to google Victor Silverio. But something else tapped at her brain. She'd meant to check it out earlier, but with all the distractions it got pushed to the back of her mind.

She had to know about the fire that killed that couple, the one Brice had been involved in as a teenager. Why hadn't she checked it out sooner? It was so long ago—would it even come up in a google search?

Phil Eaton had given sparse details, horrific as they were. It hadn't come up when Don did a google search of Brice. But at the time of the fire, Brice was fifteen, a juvenile. His record was probably sealed. His name and the other boy's name would not have been released.

The town was in northern Vermont, but Phil had never named it. The only clue he'd given was that the victims had a French name.

Carly googled it different ways, but nothing useful popped up. Finally, after several minutes of searching, she landed on it.

Tragic fire claims lives of local couple.

The fire happened twenty-two years earlier. A photo of the burned-out garage accompanied the article. Beneath that was a picture of the victims— Cecile Deschamps and her husband, Henri—who'd succumbed to extensive burns sustained in the fire. In the photo they looked about thirty years old. Their smiles as they posed for the camera seemed genuine, not faked. *A truly happy couple,* Carly thought sadly.

The woman's features looked familiar, but Carly couldn't put her finger on why. Enlarging it on the screen didn't help. It only made it grainier.

She read through the article, hoping it would mention survivors. The only clues were a vague reference to "two young children," along with one sister of Cecile. Carly googled the sister's name but found nothing.

She was about to search further when the shower stopped running. Carly quickly closed her laptop. She wasn't trying to hide her research from Ari—at least she told herself that. But why worry him more than he already was?

With the kids out of school, Balsam Dell's "Saturdays on the green" tomorrow would be in high gear. Vendors would be peddling everything from cotton candy—Carly's weakness—to handmade toys, crafts, and hot dogs. In one corner, beyond the Revolutionary War statue, music students from the local college would be providing entertainment. Carly still remembered the day she discovered that Grant was a gifted cellist. Gina had taken a video of him playing classical music with two other students.

Was that only a few summers ago? It seemed like eons had passed since then. So much had changed in Carly's life. *But for the better,* she reminded herself.

Except for the occasional murder. Those she would happily do without.

After she and Ari finally shut off the light, sleep didn't come easily. Something Quinne had said was tickling her senses, like an annoying feather. Maybe if she hadn't been so tired, she could've grasped it.

Carly rearranged her pillow at least a dozen times before drifting into a fitful, dream-filled night.

• • •

The temperature on Saturday morning couldn't have been more perfect. Low seventies, with a high of eighty-two predicted for the remainder of the day. It would be a relief from the muggy heat they'd been enduring most of the week.

Quinne was more than excited about her upcoming visit to the town green. After gobbling down an early breakfast, she was practically leaping out of her pink sneakers. As a treat, Leslie had increased her eight-dollar weekly allowance to twenty, but just for that one time. Quinne wanted to use it to buy gifts for everyone.

"And don't forget about the croque monsieur," Carly reminded her before heading to the eatery.

"We won't!" Quinne hugged Carly, then dashed outside to romp with Havarti.

Nina had already arrived when Carly let herself in through the back door. By the time she reached the front of the restaurant, her mug of coffee was waiting for her.

"You look peachy today," Carly said with a grin.

Nina batted her eyelashes playfully, then turned her head from side to side to show off her new earrings—gigantic plastic peaches. "Don bought them for me. Aren't they adorbs?"

"Totally," Carly said after taking a sip from her mug.

Nina blushed. "He's really become a good friend," she said shyly. "I'm very lucky."

"I was surprised he opened up to us yesterday about his dad leaving," Carly said. "He never talked about that before. You've been a positive influence on him, Nina."

Nina's blush deepened. "Thank you. That's a nice thing to say."

"And when he asked for a grilled cheese," Carly said with a laugh, "I nearly fainted."

"Yeah, me too." Nina glanced across the street through the front window. On the town green, vendors were starting to set up their booths or tables. Before long the area would be bustling with people and music and noise.

Valerie arrived next. "Hey, everyone."

"Hey, Val. What's cookin'?" Nina poured her coffee for her.

Valerie scooped up the mug and took a long sip. "Not much. Same old, same old." She slid a look at Carly. "You doing okay?"

"I'm fine," Carly replied, then grimaced. "Val, was the chief annoyed that I called him last night?"

Valerie set her mug down. "No, not at all. It's just—" She hesitated.

"Just what?" Carly pressed, feeling her nerves jangle.

Valerie sighed. "He feels bad that you think the investigation is at a standstill."

"I can't help it, Val, and I'm not blaming the chief. I know the state police are leading the investigation. I just wish they'd move a little faster."

With a kind expression, Valerie went over and cupped Carly's shoulders. "I understand, but you have to remember something. The public doesn't always see the progress being made. Things happen behind the scenes that they're not privy to."

"I know," Carly admitted, though she didn't like being lumped in with "the public." In the past she'd proven to be much more to the police.

"By the way," Carly said, "Leslie and Quinne will be stopping by later for a croque monsieur. Quinne is so excited."

"Yes!" Valerie pumped her fist. "Shall we make it together? You and me?"

"Sounds like a plan." Carly drained her mug and smiled. "Something else I almost forgot. Leslie found out yesterday that Quinne's adoption has been approved, as long as Leslie gets a job within the next month. With Norah helping her, she's confident that won't be a problem. In fact, she already has one interview set up."

Nina threw up her arms. "Then this is a day for great news. Let's hope it ends on the same note."

CHAPTER 26

B<small>Y THE TIME THE EATERY OPENED, ACTIVITY ON THE TOWN GREEN WAS IN</small> full swing. Kids were tromping around with their folks, tugging them toward their favorite food stands. People moseyed about carrying satchels for their purchases. Near the statue, two musicians were warming up. From the distinctive twang of their guitars, Carly guessed they'd be playing some country songs.

Leslie and Quinne planned to arrive there around noon. That would give them time to peruse the various booths and buy some things before crossing the street to have lunch at the eatery.

Earlier that morning, Carly had called her mom to check on her. Rhonda was having one of those days. She was feeling antsy, frustrated that she was still a suspect. Carly had listened to her rant for a few minutes, then promised to check on her later.

"It was fun having Grant helping out this week," Valerie said wistfully. She flipped over two Sweddar Weathers—Swiss and cheddar cheeses grilled between slices of coarse artisan bread.

"It's always a treat to have him here," Carly agreed, adding chips and pickles to the platters. "But he'd already promised to put in a double shift at the inn today. I guess they're having a fancy wedding there."

"Which reminds me," Valerie trilled, "yours will be coming up soon. Still keeping your honeymoon plans a secret?"

"Only half a secret," Carly teased.

She and Ari had chosen a gorgeous coastal resort in southern Maine for the first four days of their honeymoon. Their suite was going to have a fireplace, an ocean view, and a private hot tub. The resort's restaurant was rated one of the best in New England. Ari was already salivating at the seafood offerings on the menu. They'd even signed up for a whale watch.

Carly reminded Valerie of this.

"Yeah, we know that already," Valerie whined. "But what's the other part of the honeymoon?"

Suzanne trotted over with three more order slips and stuck them on the wheel. "Tell me you're not doing something crazy like diving off a cliff," she barked.

"Or bungee jumping off a bridge," Nina piped in.

Carly rolled her eyes. "Of course not! Where do you gals come up with these things?"

She and Ari had been having a bit of fun keeping everyone guessing. When they were planning their honeymoon, it occurred to them that they'd both been blessed with so much in their lives. Family who adored them, friends they could count on, jobs they loved. Because life had given them so much, they wanted to give something in return.

"Be patient," she said with an air of mystery. "You'll all know soon enough."

With that she scurried into the kitchen to prepare for the croque monsieur.

• • •

Leslie came in with Quinne at a little after one. Carly spotted them from one of the booths at the back, where she was busy cleaning off a table. She waved and summoned the two into the kitchen with her.

The smile on Quinne's sweet face went from ear to ear. "Give it to her, Mommy. She's probably starving!"

Laughing, Leslie reached into her bag. "I asked them to put it in a container for you." She handed Carly a paper cup filled with pink cotton candy.

"Oh, you read my mind. Thank you, sweetie."

"I bought it with my own money," the little girl announced proudly. "And I got you something else." She opened her Eiffel Tower tote, pulled out a small envelope, and handed it to Carly.

"Oh my, what's this?" Carly tilted the envelope into her hand. Out fell a key ring imprinted with a picture of a dog. "It looks exactly like Havarti! Thank you so much!" She reached down and hugged Quinne, then winked at Leslie. "As soon as I get a break, I'm going to switch my keys to this." She slipped it back into the envelope and tucked it into the pocket of her capris.

Leslie shoved a stray lock of hair behind her ear. "We had such a great time. I hadn't been to that in years. I'd forgotten how much fun it is. And you can buy some really cool stuff."

"If I get a few free minutes," Carly said, "I might pop over and browse." She rubbed her hands together and grinned. "Now, are we ready for a croque monsieur?"

At that moment, Valerie came in holding two bottles of pink lemonade with paper straws inserted. She gave them to Leslie and Quinne.

"Either you're a mind reader or you were eavesdropping," Carly remarked.

"Both." Valerie wrinkled her nose playfully. "Auntie Carly and I are going to make the croque monsieur together. If you come over to the worktable you can watch."

The process took about twelve minutes, as the béchamel had to be reheated. Carly and Valerie worked in tandem, explaining each step as if they were on a cooking show. Once the sandwich was in the oven, Valerie excused herself to head back to the dining room.

When the sandwich came out from under the broiler, Carly sliced it into four quarters and divided them between two plates.

Leslie sat at the pine table with Quinne. "This is unbelievable," she gushed, slicing off another piece of the sandwich.

Quinne loved eating it with a knife and fork. Watching them, Carly felt herself choking up again. She was amazed at how seamlessly Quinne had gone from "Auntie Leslie" to "Mommy."

After they finished eating, Carly noticed that Quinne had left a small sliver on her plate.

"Auntie Carly," Quinne pleaded, "can I bring this piece home to Havarti? It's only a *teeny tiny* piece."

Gazing into those adorable hazel eyes, Carly would have given her the earth if she could. "Sure, as long as it's just a small piece." She wrapped it up and Quinne tucked it into her tote.

"Well," Leslie said brightly, "it's time we let Auntie Carly get back to work."

Hugs made the rounds.

"See you both later," Carly said, watching them leave.

"Don't forget to eat your cotton candy!" Quinne reminded Carly as she went through the swinging door.

Carly was still smiling when she removed the key ring from her pocket. She went into the closet for her tote so she could switch her keys onto the new one.

She hadn't given a thought to supper. There was plenty of taco salad left over, so they could probably nibble on that. After sharing the croque monsieur, Leslie and Quinne might not be terribly hungry. Carly would figure out something later.

She was fishing around in her tote for her keys when her fingers landed on something unfamiliar. She pulled it out and gasped. It was the card she'd snitched when she was emptying Brice's drawer a few days earlier. How had she forgotten it?

Not that it mattered. No doubt it was another greeting card with a sappy message inside.

Before pulling out the card, Carly looked at the envelope. It was postmarked only two weeks before.

She extracted the card. On the front was a sketch of two golden-haired dogs curled up together on a cushioned chair. Inside, the printed message read *I want to get cozy with you.* Carly's breath halted in her throat. Yvette's note, scrawled in purple ink, said *I forgive you for standing me up Saturday. Maybe we can try again?*

An oversized purple heart was scribbled beneath that.

I forgive you . . .

The words sounded innocuous enough. So why did they send a chill down Carly's spine?

Something else suddenly popped into her memory. Yvette's last words as they were leaving the coffee shop. *Alone again in the world . . .*

Carly shoved the card back into her tote and returned to the dining room.

She was beginning to feel like a slacker. Over the past week, she'd left her staff in charge of the restaurant more times than she could count.

She decided against going across the street. The activity on the green would be there every Saturday, all summer long. The following Saturday would be soon enough to check it out.

For the remainder of the afternoon, she pitched in wherever she could. Valerie, as always, mastered the grill like a pro. Suzanne left at three, leaving Carly and Nina to take orders, serve food, and clean up the tables.

She hadn't heard from Ari, and she still hadn't called her mom. Something else was sticking into her brain like a red-hot poker.

The video footage from the school.

Was it possible Yvette had gone back to the school after leaving the sub shop that day? Maybe she suspected Brice was meeting another woman there and wanted to catch him in the act?

The more Carly thought about it, the more she decided the chief was holding something back. Why were the police taking so long to review the video footage?

If she had to wait any longer, she'd end up tearing her hair out. Then something occurred to her, a way she could see the footage. It might take a bit of persuasion, but she had to give it a try.

She'd left her cell phone in her tote, so she dashed into the kitchen to retrieve it. She was grateful she'd saved his number from when she first signed up for the fundraiser.

Andy Fields answered after two rings.

"Well hello, Carly," he said in a subdued voice. "How nice to hear from you. How're you doing?"

She heaved a world-weary sigh. "Frankly, not great. Andy, I know you gave the video footage from the school that day to the police. I don't know why they're taking so long to review it, but it's making me crazy. I was wondering . . . is there a chance you could play it for me?"

Andy Fields groaned. "Carly, I'd love to accommodate you. Honestly, I would. The thing is, I could get into big trouble if I got caught. The school has rules about—"

"I know, I know," she said, struggling not to sound impatient. She issued a long sigh, as if the weight of the earth was on her shoulders. "I'm just trying to help my mom."

After a long silence, he finally spoke. "All right, tell you what I'll do. The school is all locked up. But if you can meet me there around, say, five thirty today, I'll take you to my office and play the footage for you. Not all of it, though. That would take forever."

Better than nothing, Carly thought somberly.

"That's okay, Andy. Just the part around the time Brice was . . . you know."

She swallowed.

"I hear you," he said wearily. "Truth be told, I feel terrible about Rhonda. If I can help in any way . . ." He left the rest to dangle.

After they ended the call, Carly made another one. Her heart was thudding in her chest at about a thousand beats per minute. When Ari's voicemail came on, she breathed a sigh of relief.

"Hi, honey, I'm heading to the high school around five thirty to do an errand. If you guys get hungry before I get home, there's cold taco salad from last night." She made her usual kissy noises and disconnected.

Carly returned to the dining room. Nina was wiping down tables, and Valerie was working on a large take-out order.

To be at the school by five thirty, she'd have to leave in twenty minutes or so. She apologized to Valerie and Nina when she told them that, once again, she needed to beg off early. She was terrified they'd ask her the reason, grateful to the tips of her toes when they didn't.

"We're totally here for you," Nina assured her.

"Absolutely," Val said. "Nina and I will close up. No problem."

A shard of guilt shot through Carly. If they knew the reason she was leaving early, they'd try to talk her out of it.

She'd promised Ari she wouldn't go anywhere without letting someone know. The message she'd just left him should suffice. She wasn't concerned about meeting Andy at the high school. If he could narrow down the parts of the footage she needed to watch, it shouldn't take too long. And if luck was with her, she might spot something the police had missed. Didn't the chief always say she had an eye for detail?

After thanking Valerie and Nina once again, she jumped into her car and headed to the high school.

One way or the other, she was going to see what was on that footage.

CHAPTER 27

THE PARKING LOT WAS DESERTED WHEN CARLY ARRIVED AT THE HIGH school. As Andy had instructed, she drove around to the back, opposite the deserted football field.

The building itself was a sprawling one-story affair with corridors that seemed to stretch for a mile. Past the football field and behind the bleachers, a chain-link fence ran along a densely wooded buffer. Beyond the woods was a subdivision of homes that were built in the nineteen sixties. Carly always thought the kids who lived there were lucky to have such a short walk to school.

At the back of the building, a lone car—a newish silver sedan—hunkered near a steel door. Carly knew the door led to the boys' locker rooms, although she'd never been in them. It had been a while, but she remembered the school's general layout. During the fundraiser, only the girls' locker rooms were made available to the vendors.

Carly pulled in next to the sedan and killed her engine. She texted Andy, and only a few seconds later the steel door opened.

He smiled and beckoned her over. "Come on in," he said as she got out of her car. "I've set up everything in my cubicle so we can watch it together."

"Thanks, Andy. I really appreciate your going out of your way to do this."

Looking summery in a knitted yellow shirt and plaid Bermuda shorts, he waved a hand. "No worries. I was watching the Red Sox game, and it was *not* going well."

Carly smiled. She wondered if Ari was watching the game.

Andy shot a wide glance around the football field, then ushered her inside. "Right this way," he said.

She followed him down a series of corridors, past rooms that looked unfamiliar. It was obvious that much had changed since she was a student there.

Finally, they came to a large room in which eight or ten cubicles were lined up. Their gray fabric walls gave them a sedate, colorless ambiance. Shallow windows just below the ceiling permitted a modicum of natural light.

"Cubicles?" Carly said. "I don't remember these when I went to school here."

Andy shook his head. "Ugly, aren't they? About five years ago, the town realized that the school needed additional classrooms. They could either build out—a hugely expensive undertaking—or have shared classrooms. They obviously chose the cheaper route," he said with a roll of his blue eyes. "I now have to share a classroom with one of the math teachers."

"Then what are the cubicles for?"

"Well, this room used to be a storage room." He waved his arm over the rows of cubicles. "They turned it into this glorious cube farm for teachers. If a teacher was lucky, they were assigned a cubicle they could use as a private workspace. Not every teacher got one. I lucked out because I'm an assistant coach as well as a teacher. I use mine mostly to grade papers, work on lesson plans, sometimes meet with a parent."

Carly trailed behind him to his own cubicle, which was at the far end. Larger than the inner cubicles, it boasted a full computer setup. Photos of school basketball games had been tacked up willy-nilly on the fabric walls.

He wheeled over a chair from an adjacent cubicle. "Have a seat."

"Thanks." She set her tote on the carpeted floor.

Andy dropped onto the chair beside her. He spent a minute or so tapping away at keys. "I've already set up the video from the front parking lot. Let me just make some adjustments." He moved the mouse around and clicked it a few times. Fuzzy black-and-white images emerged on the screen.

"Here we go." He paused and examined the picture, then froze it. "This is when I saw Rhonda getting out of her car. Remember I told you?"

Carly nodded. "You said you ran out and told her not to come in."

"That's right."

They watched together as the scene unfolded. Still wearing her 1950s getup—the dress with the flared skirt—Rhonda got out of her car. Moments later, Andy could be seen running across the parking lot toward her. He'd gone outside to intercept her before she could get near the school. They spoke briefly, then Rhonda got back into her car and drove out of the lot.

It was exactly as her mom had described it to her.

"I'm sorry, Andy, but can you show me that again? Maybe start when Mom was dropped off at her car? Her friend Lorraine drove her there in her Lincoln."

"Oh, of course." Andy wiggled the mouse and went back to the same scene, this time going further back.

They watched as Lorraine's Lincoln pulled into the parking lot. It slowed down and then idled next to Rhonda's car. After a minute or so, Rhonda got out and into her own car. The Lincoln then drove away.

After another minute or so, Rhonda's door opened and she hurried out, making a beeline for the school. She didn't get far before Andy rushed out from the building and stopped her. They spoke briefly. Then Rhonda got back into her car and bolted. In Carly's mind, it completely exonerated her.

"Is that what you wanted to see?" Andy said.

"Partly, yes." She still wanted to know when Brice went back to the school, after he'd gotten the mystery phone call.

"Andy, Brice was seen leaving the fundraiser before it was over. Which means that after he left, he had to have gone back. Is there a way to see when he went back into the building? Like maybe which door he went in, or if anyone was waiting for him?"

Andy mulled that. "Hmmm, I see your point. I'll have to switch to a different camera." He wiggled the mouse and then froze the screen. "Hey, would you like a coffee? I could use one myself. We have one of those doohickey machines with the pods."

Carly was anxious to watch the next video, but she didn't want to sound ungrateful. He'd gone out of his way to help her. "You know, that would hit the spot. I feel like I've been running on empty since morning."

Andy held up a finger. "Be back in a minute. Regular, not decaf, right?"

"Perfect."

As she waited for him, she shot another glance at the tacked-up photos. Andy appeared in a few of the pics, cheering his team on at some of the games.

She was rising from her chair to get a closer look at one of the photos when she spotted something tucked behind the monitor. It was a small gold picture frame, resting facedown.

Andy still hadn't returned. She quickly picked up the frame and turned it over, then sucked in a sharp breath. It was a photo of a lovely young woman with dark hair and a warm smile. But that wasn't what took Carly aback.

The woman in the photo was nearly a dead ringer for her mom. Not now, but in Rhonda's younger days.

She returned the photo to where she'd found it and sat down again. Who was that woman? Did her mom have a long-lost twin?

No, that was silly, she told herself. She had twins on the brain, that was all.

"Here we go," Andy said, delivering two steaming cups to the table. "Cream, no sugar, right?"

Carly was startled that he knew that, until she remembered she'd had coffee the day they sat together in the eatery. She took a sip. "Thanks. This is good."

It was mediocre but she didn't care. She was more anxious than ever to see the video.

Andy sat down again and wiggled the mouse. It took a few minutes, but then more images came up. "Okay, this angle is from the back of the school. The vendors went in this way to get to the gym. Well, you know that—you were one of them. I never saw Brice when he returned that day, but you're right. At some point he must have gone back inside the building."

"Can we go back to around two forty-five?" Carly asked him.

Andy jiggled the mouse again and tapped at the keys. Black-and-white images moved backward at a fast pace, reminding Carly of the old silent movies. When he stopped the video, the time read 2:47.

"I'll move it forward now, but I'll speed it up a bit," he said with a flat smile. "Otherwise, we'll be here all night."

Carly sensed he was getting irritated spending so much time with her. Especially since he'd risked getting into hot water by doing her a favor.

"I won't take up much more of your time, Andy. Just this last thing."

He nodded, and she leaned in for a closer look. The images moved forward in a herky-jerky fashion. People came and went, some wheeling dollies. Most of the vendors had left that day by two forty-five or so. Brice was murdered sometime between three thirty and four.

Nothing was jumping out at Carly. She'd wasted Andy's time for nothing.

Frustrated, she was about to tell him to shut it down when an alarming image popped into her vision.

A woman, wearing the same wig her mom had worn, ran into the building. The scarf, instead of being tied around the wig, hung in a loose knot around her neck. The flared dress was gone, replaced by white leggings and a short-sleeved blouse. Despite the footage being black-and-white, Carly knew exactly where that wig came from.

The woman, who wore sunglasses, was looking downward, her facial features hidden. She was scurrying into the building as if her feet were on fire. The time in the lower corner read 3:22.

Andy noticed it, too, and his face drained of color. "Saints preserve us, is that Rhonda?"

Carly's fingers felt like ice. She gripped her cup to warm them and took a long sip. "No, definitely not. That is not my mom. Andy, is there a way to freeze that frame?"

He nodded and did as she asked.

"Can you enlarge it?"

"I can, but it won't be as clear." He enlarged the frame to three hundred percent.

"Darn," Carly said. "That makes it worse. Except—"

She edged closer to the screen. Something about the woman was familiar. Something about her shape, her posture . . .

Was this the glitch the chief had mentioned? Did the police think this was Rhonda? If so, why hadn't they taken her in for more questioning?

Fatigue was beginning to tug at Carly. A bone-weary tiredness that made her limbs feel like tree logs.

"Andy, if you can print that image for me, I promise I'll get out of your hair. I just want to show it to Chief Holloway."

"Sure thing." He clicked the Print button. A printer whirred to life in a corner of the cubicle. Andy didn't move.

Another sound reached Carly's ears. The loud click of a door closing.

"That'll be my sister," he said. "I just texted her and asked her to meet me here."

"Your—who?"

"I know you peeked at my picture frame," he said in a monotone. "Did you think I didn't notice you putting it back?"

The photo. The woman who looked like her mom.

155

He swallowed. "That beautiful lady was my mother. The sweetest, kindest woman who ever lived." His voice cracked. "Except that she didn't live. She was taken from us a long time ago. Ripped from our hearts, leaving us alone."

His pain was almost palpable, but it explained so much. "Is that why you wanted to treat my mom to lunch?" she asked softly. "She reminded you of your mother?"

He nodded. "Rhonda looks so much like my mom did, and she was so kind. I . . . just wanted to feel like I was with Mom again for a few hours. It was totally innocent." He cast his eyes downward. "I think Rhonda took it the wrong way."

She sure did, Carly thought. Big-time.

"Do you know my mom never called me Andy?" he went on. He smiled at the memory, his eyes misty. "My real name is Andrew, but Mom always called me Drew. She thought it sounded more refined."

A vicious headache, like an approaching storm, was gathering momentum in Carly's brain. Something was poking at it, urging her to remember.

The woman in the photo, Andy's mom. She'd seen her before. But where?

"We lost her twenty-two years ago," Andy said, blinking hard. "Her and my dad. Some punk kids set a fire in our garage. Dad tried to save Mom. They both died a horrible death. My little sister and me, we had to go live with our mom's sister. She never wanted us. She was an awful woman, nothing like our mom." His damp eyes hardened into blue marbles.

Oh, no. No, no, no . . .

And then it all came crashing down. Andy was the young boy in the picture. The one with the sad face, clutching his sister's hand.

M and D.

D was Drew. The M was his sister. Yvette's given name was Mabel, a name she despised.

Mabel and Drew. Yvette and Andy. They were the same people.

The chief was right when he warned Carly to steer clear of Yvette. She'd been part of it all along. She'd stolen the wig and the scarf. Andy must have been the mysterious caller who lured Brice back to the school. So, which one killed him? Maybe both.

"Did . . . you kill Brice?" Carly pushed out the words.

He glared at her. "Stop pretending, Carly. It's obvious you've already figured it out. As soon as you saw my sister in that video, you knew, didn't you? I'd hoped you'd think it was Rhonda, but you were too smart to be fooled."

"Before . . . you killed him, did he know why?"

"Oh, yes," Andy said with a satisfied twist of his lips. "We made sure of that. Our original plan was that I would stab him. But after all the planning, all the years of waiting, at the last moment I lost my nerve. I'm not a violent person, Carly. Can you believe that punk tried to say he was sorry? He begged for his life. But then my sister used the scarf . . ." He covered his face with his hand.

"You . . . changed your names." Carly forced the words from her lips, but they sounded far away, as if they were floating on a distant cloud.

"No, not really," Andy said. "I didn't change mine at all. I simply anglicized it. Our name is Deschamps, which is French for 'of the fields.' Ergo, Drew Deschamps became Andy Fields. No one ever questioned it. If they did, it was easily explained."

That was it! When Quinne was teaching Carly her French words, she said that *champ* in French meant "field." If only she'd connected the dots sooner . . .

So, Drew became Andy, and Mabel became Yvette. A lot of women used their middle name as their first. But where did the "Carter" come from?

The questions rattled around in Carly's head, but she couldn't manage to form them into words.

"My sister was so desperate to get away from our selfish, chain-smoking aunt that she got married way too young," Andy droned on. "The guy was a lowlife with a capital L. She ditched his sorry butt soon afterward, but she kept his name. It was easier for people to spell than Deschamps." He pronounced the surname with a flair, then his voice hardened. "If our folks had been alive, she could've gone to college, married a decent man who deserved her."

Wait a minute. Yvette had once been married?

From inside her tote, Carly heard the ping of a text. Ari was probably looking for her. She tried to reach for it, but her fingers felt disconnected from her body.

"Shoot," Andy growled. "I should've figured you'd have a phone." He shoved his hand roughly into Carly's tote and extracted her cell phone. He powered it down and stuck it in the pocket of his shorts. "I'll get rid of this later."

Ari knows where I am, she tried to say, but it came out garbled, like letters floating in a bowl of alphabet soup.

Andy looked piteously at her. "I wish you hadn't come here, Carly. This didn't have to happen. Justice was served when that punk Brice finally paid for what he did. His accomplice, another piece of garbage, died in a crash not long after he got out of juvie. Now *that* was a fitting end," he said, his voice a low cackle. "But Keaton did a disappearing act. For a long time, what seemed like forever, we couldn't find him. I googled him constantly. Then an article showed up online about him being in an accident."

And then you planned his murder, she wanted to say, but the words got tangled on her tongue.

"Andy?" a woman called out from the hallway.

He raised his voice. "I'm in here."

Carly's head started to droop. She wanted to raise it higher to face the villains, but her chin dropped to her chest. She might as well have tried to lift a watermelon with a finger.

She'd been drugged. With what, she had no clue. She only hoped it wasn't poison. Although . . . maybe it didn't matter. If she fell asleep, it might be for the last time.

No! I will not let that happen. I have my life ahead of me. Ari needs me. My family needs me . . .

Using every ounce of her will, she forced her eyes open. She blinked furiously, trying to force them into focus.

"My sister is here," Andy told her. "I'd introduce you, but I think you already know her."

"Okay, so what's the plan?" Andy's sister said, when she peeked around the corner of the cubicle.

That voice. Carly knew it.

But it wasn't Yvette.

"Hello, Carly. Long time no see."

CHAPTER 28

THERE WAS NO WARMTH IN THE VOICE. ONLY THE ICY CHILL OF A COLD-blooded killer.

Tillie, the cheery pie lady. What was Tillie short for? Matilda?

"So now what're we going to do?" Tillie snapped at her brother. "You shouldn't have let her come here."

"I know, I *know*. I wasn't thinking straight. She begged me, and I caved. I couldn't help it. I've been a bundle of nerves all week!" Andy moaned. "I couldn't stop thinking about Rhonda, about how much we've hurt her. She didn't deserve this, Til."

"I know she didn't," Tillie soothed. "She's so much like our mom was, isn't she? But Brice deserved what we gave him. I don't regret that at all. If we act fast, we can fix this. Otherwise, it's all over. By now someone's probably looking for her. We'll put her in her car, and I'll drive it somewhere. You can follow me. I'll wear the wig. I brought it with me."

The wig. All this time, Tillie had it.

Tillie's voice softened. "At least you thought to bring your anxiety pills," she told her brother. "I'm proud of you for that."

Anxiety pills. So that's what she was drugged with.

Carly wiggled her fingers. She could move them, but only slightly. She inched her wrist slowly across the desk.

"Okay then, let's do this." Andy slapped his knees. "I'll take her arms. You take her legs."

"For glory's sake, Andy, she's already in a chair. Wouldn't it be easier to wheel her to the door?"

Andy held up his hands. "You're right. I'm sorry, Til. I'm just—"

"Come on, pull yourself together." Tillie reached for Carly's tote and hung it over the back of the chair. Andy had just started to yank the chair out of the cubicle when Carly's fingers reached the coffee cup. Summoning every ounce of her remaining strength, she curled her hand around it. She tossed the coffee at his face, but it landed lower, splattering his plaid shorts.

"Hey, that was still hot!" Andy shrieked. He spewed out a string of nasty epithets, then swiped his hands frantically over his shorts. "I need a towel."

"Never mind that," Tillie said, urgency in her tone. "We'll clean this all up later."

"Oh, all right," Andy huffed.

The chair stuttered backward. Andy swerved it around and rolled it over the carpeting toward the door.

A torrent of terror surged through Carly, threatening to drown her. Her head felt ready to explode.

Linda Reilly

Deep breaths, she told herself. Oxygen will give me strength.

The chair jerked as it went over the lip of the doorway. Carly's head lolled backward. In one of the shallow windows below the ceiling, a faint light flashed in her fading vision. Not a white light. A red light that swirled and throbbed, making her stomach revolt.

The chair turned down the last corridor, the one that led to the steel door. She had to think of something. Something drastic. Otherwise, she was toast.

She began wriggling her body from side to side. The motion made her nausea worse, but it stopped Andy in his tracks.

"Stop it," he ordered, letting out another chain of curses.

"Just keep going," Tillie told him. "If she falls off the chair we'll drag her."

When they finally reached the door to where their cars were parked outside, Tillie said, "Wait. I need her keys."

She reached into Carly's tote and rummaged all around. "Got 'em," she said, holding up the key ring with the dog on it.

Quinne's key ring! Noooo . . .

Tillie bent toward Carly and dangled the keys in her face. "You and I are going for a little ride," she taunted. "That's what you get for not leaving well enough alone."

Rage surged through Carly, boosting her adrenaline. She reached up and grabbed for the keys. Unable to grasp them, she pushed them into Tillie's face instead, then scraped them down her captor's cheek. The keys dropped to the floor.

Tillie yelped in pain. "You'll pay for that," she spat out.

Moments later, the steel door opened abruptly. Chief Holloway rushed inside, but he was pushed aside by Ari.

"Carly!" Ari shoved Andy backward so hard that he hit the floor with a thud.

Ari lifted Carly's shoulders into his arms and shook her lightly. "Honey, are you okay? Talk to me!"

Carly tried to tell him she was okay, but the words wouldn't come.

Two EMTs wheeled a stretcher in. "We'll take it from here," one of them said gently. "You can ride in the ambulance."

Carly felt herself being lowered onto the stretcher and covered with a blanket. All around her, chaos was erupting. Holloway barked orders. Officers scrambled to restrain Andy and Tillie.

Her lips beginning to function again, Carly smiled up at Ari. His face was a little fuzzy, but the love in his eyes was crystal clear. "I . . . am . . . okay."

"You'd better be," he said, tears streaming down his face. He lifted her left hand and pressed it to his cheek. "You need to be ready to roll when I put a wedding ring on this finger."

The commotion faded as the ambulance doors closed.

"Ari," Carly whispered, as an EMT took her vitals. "I . . . need . . . my keys."

CHAPTER 29

"IF I'D HAD TO STAY IN THAT HOSPITAL ROOM ONE MORE MINUTE," CARLY grumbled, "I was going to go nuts." She took a bite of her cream cheese Danish, savoring the sweet blend of cheese and pastry.

After being rushed to the ER the night before, she'd been transferred to a hospital room. They wanted to be sure she was stable and that her system was flushed out before sending her home. She'd consumed enough lorazepam to make her seriously drowsy, but not enough to cause her death.

"You're lucky they let you go when they did," Ari said in a mock stern voice. "The nurse told me they don't usually release patients until afternoon. You were complaining so much they asked the doctor to speed up the discharge."

From the moment they'd arrived home, Ari had been fussing over her and pampering her like an overly attentive nurse. He'd insisted she sit on the sofa, where he tucked pillows behind her and placed a crocheted throw over her legs. Perched beside her on the arm of the sofa, he smoothed back a strand of her hair.

Carly smiled sheepishly. "I'm sorry. I guess I *was* being a pain." She took Ari's hand. "Listen, I know everyone's thinking I shouldn't have gone to the school alone. But I did keep my promise when I called ahead to let you know."

"And thank goodness I played your message when I did," Ari said, blowing out a breath. "But honey, you came way too close this time. I knew something was wrong when you didn't answer my texts or my phone calls."

"I know," she said softly. "And I'm so sorry for what I put everyone through. What's weird is that Andy Fields wasn't even on my radar. I was so sure Yvette Carter had something to do with the murder."

"Don't you dare be sorry," Rhonda lectured, squeezing her daughter for the hundredth time since she and Gary had arrived. She'd plopped herself on the sofa next to Carly, so close she was almost in her lap. "After what those horrid killers put you through . . ."

"It's okay, Mom," Carly said, covering her mother's hand with her own. "It's all over now, and I'm fine."

Carly gazed around the living room, her heart feeling more buoyant than it had all week. Her favorite people in the world were here, well . . . most of them. A few others were on their way.

Yes, she *was* lucky. More so than she ever imagined.

After everyone learned what'd happened, they showed up in droves. The driveway was jam-packed with cars. Quinne was outside playing with Havarti. Leslie worried about leaving her with the adults, since she knew they'd all be talking about Carly's ordeal. That was something an eight-year-old didn't need to hear.

The moment Nate and Norah found out what had happened, they rushed over with enough pastries and fresh berries to open their own farm stand. The chief and Valerie also showed up, as did Don and Nina. Gina and Zach were on their way. They needed to make a few stops first.

Ari brought in extra chairs from the kitchen so everyone could sit. Leslie was in the kitchen making extra coffee, and iced tea for those who wanted it.

Rhonda was still wringing her hands, blaming herself for everything. Her mood swung between bouts of guilt and threats of retribution. "Ooh, I'd like to get my hands on that creep," she sputtered, holding up a closed fist. "Fred, is there any chance I can have a few minutes alone with him?"

Chief Holloway laughed and shook his head. "I'm afraid not, Rhonda. But don't worry. You'll have your day in court. Andy Fields and his conniving sister will not be seeing the light of day for a very long time."

"Are you sure, Fred?" Valerie perched on the edge of her husband's overstuffed chair, her hand on his shoulder. "Didn't you say Andy Fields hired Rhonda's ex-attorney?"

Rhonda gawked at her. "He hired Burt Oakley?"

Fred squeezed his wife's knee affectionately. "I was going to wait to tell you, Rhonda, but yes, he did. Oakley will probably try to play the sympathy card. Personally, I don't think it'll get him very far."

Nina, who'd been unusually quiet, finally spoke up. "What he and his sister did was unforgivable, for sure," she murmured. "But in a way I can understand their anger—losing their parents that way? And then having to live with a mean aunt who didn't want them? So, so sad." She dropped her gaze to her plate of fruit, as if worried she'd said the wrong thing.

Carly was among the few who knew Nina had grown up in a foster home. Although she'd been well cared for, she'd never felt loved.

"I can, too," Carly agreed, recalling Phil Keaton's description of Brice's crime. "But from what I'm hearing, it sounds as if Brice was trying to do better with his life. The volunteers at the animal shelter had nothing but positive things to say about him. As did his coworkers." She turned to the chief. "That reminds me, Chief, did the detectives show that photograph to Andy?"

"Yes, they did. He confirmed it was him and his sister. A neighbor took the photo and gave it to their aunt. He said the aunt cared so little for them that she couldn't even be bothered to write their names on the back—only M and D."

Matilda and Drew.

"Fields mailed it to Brice anonymously at his place of business," the chief continued, "since he didn't know where he lived. Andy said he did it to taunt him, to let him know they hadn't forgotten."

"Chief, one thing I still don't get," Carly said. "Why did you have an ambulance follow you to the school yesterday?"

Holloway gave out a wry chuckle. "Given my past experience with your crime-solving ventures, I wanted to be prepared."

Carly felt her cheeks burn. "Well, thank you. It sure came in handy."

At that moment, Leslie came in carrying a large tray. On it she'd placed a coffee carafe and an iced tea pitcher, along with cups and napkins. In one corner was a sole bottle of root beer.

Leslie smiled and rested the tray on a side table next to the sofa. "Help yourselves, everyone," she announced. "There's another root beer, Don, if you want it."

Don's face brightened and he gave her a nod.

"Thanks, Les," Ari said. "You still planning to leave this afternoon?"

"Yeah, we really have to get back," she said wistfully. "We have a lot to get ready for." She turned to everyone. "The social worker is doing one final home visit this week. And I still need to find a job."

Everyone shouted their congratulations. Norah jumped up and hugged her. "You have job interviews this week, right?"

"I now have two, but there's something else I want to talk to you about. Later, after everyone enjoys their visit." She sat down with a glass of iced tea, while others helped themselves to beverages.

"Fred, I'm curious about something," Nate said to the chief. "It sounds like the brother and sister spent a lot of time planning their revenge, but in the end the whole thing went awry. Did they tell the police what happened?" He took a huge bite of his apple Danish.

"They were questioned separately for hours last night," the chief said grimly. "For starters, Andy and his sister never found out where Keaton lived, only where he worked. He shunned social media and never joined any groups or clubs. He also cut off contact with his brother a long time ago. Phil Keaton knew his brother's cell phone number but had no idea where to find him. At one point Brice changed his number, leaving Phil with no contact info at all."

"He could've hired a private detective to find him," Don pointed out.

"We asked Phil that," Holloway said, "but he felt that if Brice didn't want any contact, then why spend the money. To him, Brice was a lost cause."

"For what it's worth," Carly added, "Phil told me he and his brother were never close. Growing up, Brice had been extremely jealous of him."

"Sounds to me like Brice wanted zero connection with his past," Norah put in. "The reminders were probably too painful."

"Nate, to answer your question," the chief said, "the original plan, once Andy made the call to lure Brice back to the school, was to get him alone in the boys' locker room and stab him. By then most everyone had left." He paused to insert a chunk of cherry pastry into his mouth.

"And?" Ari prompted.

The chief swallowed. "Turns out Andy Fields was too squeamish to go through with it. He had the knife ready, but when push came to shove, he just couldn't stab him, despite his sister screaming at him to hurry up and do it. So instead, Andy slammed Brice's head against a locker. It incapacitated him long enough for Tillie—Matilda—to wrap the scarf around his neck. Between the two of them, they managed to strangle him. Despite their clumsy moves, they were, unfortunately, successful at killing him."

Nina clamped her fingers over her mouth and closed her eyes. Without saying a word, Don reached over and wrapped his hand around her free one.

One thing still puzzled Carly. "But why did she steal Mom's wig and scarf in the first place?"

"Tillie decided, last minute," the chief explained, "it would make a good disguise for when she went back to the school to help her brother. After she left the fundraiser, she went home to change, then returned looking quite different."

Carly licked cream cheese filling off her thumb. "Was that the glitch in the video you talked about?"

"Actually, no. The glitch was that four minutes of the footage was missing from the video. The deletion was cleverly done, but a sharp investigator caught it. Fields was questioned about it, but he claimed he had no idea how it happened."

"Is it possible to restore the lost four minutes?" Ari asked.

"It is, if you know what you're doing. Now that we know who was responsible, it shouldn't take long. Fields has already agreed to cooperate."

"What do you think is on those missing minutes?" Norah asked.

Holloway wiped a napkin over his mouth. "We suspect they'll show Tillie leaving the building and running back to her car. It'll help seal the case against her, if we can get a decent image of her face. Although it's pretty much moot, since we recovered the wig from her trunk."

Rhonda plucked another Danish from the tray and set it on her plate. "I can't believe I was nice to that witch," she griped. Then her shoulders sagged, and she turned to Carly. "Did . . . their mom really look like me in that picture you saw?"

"It was uncanny, Mom. It reminded me of the photo you showed me of when you and Dad got engaged. Right then, Andy's obsession with you began to make sense. In a super-creepy sort of way." She gave a slight shiver.

Rhonda took Carly's hand and smiled. "Speaking of your dad, on the way over here his favorite song came on the radio. I hadn't heard it in a long time."

Carly blinked. "'And I Love Her' by the Beatles, right?"

"That's right. To me it was a sign that he's watching over all of us, especially the amazing daughters he was so proud of."

With an embarrassed look at Rhonda, the chief said, "Rhonda, I apologize profusely for everything the police put you through. I knew darn well you didn't kill Keaton, but my personal feelings didn't count. In a murder investigation, everything has to be done by the book. The state police are sticklers for protocol."

Rhonda blew out a noisy breath. "I understand, Fred. No hard feelings."

Valerie reached over and tapped Don's hand. "You'll have a lot to write about in your paper this week."

"That reminds me," Holloway said to Don. "The lead investigator said he'd be glad to talk to you, if you'd like to interview him tomorrow. I can give you his name and contact info."

Don's eyes widened. "He will? That's . . . I mean, thanks, Chief! That'll be awesome." He looked as if he'd just hit the jackpot in Vegas.

"Chief, I meant to ask you something else," Carly said. "Did Victor Silverio ever explain why he was spotted at the school fundraiser?"

The chief chuckled. "Yeah, he did. He felt so bad about making Don miss his event with the animal shelter that he wanted to show up in person and apologize to him. He got there too late, though. Brice had already left."

A loud knock at the door startled everyone. Ari jumped up to answer it. "Hey, you finally made it," he joked.

Grasping a covered metal baking pan, Grant followed him into the living room. "Hey, everyone."

A chorus of "hellos" and "heys" rose from the group.

"I planned to get here sooner," he told them, "but I promised my folks I'd make snacks for their Sunday afternoon music ensemble. When they heard what happened to Carly, they insisted I bring these here instead."

"Yay! We scored," Valerie said with a laugh. "But what are your folks going to do?"

"No worries. They'll stop at the bakery and pick up some goodies." Grant looked all around. "Someone's missing. Where's Suzanne?"

"She and her 'dudes' left early this morning for their camping trip," Valerie told him. "She talked to Carly before she left, though. So, when are you gonna show us what's in the pan?"

"Oh. Yeah. This pan keeps stuff warm, so I won't have to reheat them." He made a show of slowly removing the cover.

Nate pulled in a deep breath. "Do I detect a hint of bleu cheese?"

"More than a hint. They're appetizers made with bleu cheese, apple, onion, and walnuts, stuffed into baked phyllo shells. I'll pass them around."

For the next few minutes, everyone gorged on the treats.

"The variety of contrasting flavors is inspired," Nate praised, adding a few more to his plate.

Even Don tried one and pronounced it "not bad."

"If Carly and Ari are okay with it, I'd like to make these for the pre-wedding party."

The sound of the front door opening was accompanied by a jaunty voice.

"Sorry we're so late," Gina warbled, marching into the living room. "We didn't really have errands, but Zach had something to finish up."

With a wide smile on his face, Zach went over to Carly and handed her a gift bag. Concern in his eyes, he bent toward her. "Hey, you feeling okay?"

"I sure am," Carly assured him. "Better than ever, Zach." She looked into the bag. "What's this?"

Ari peeked over as Carly lifted out a picture frame encased in tissue. But it wasn't a picture. It was their beautifully crafted wedding invitation in a handmade wooden frame.

"It's so gorgeous!" Carly exclaimed.

Ari squeezed her shoulder. "A perfect keepsake. We'll have to decide the perfect place to hang it."

"Zach made the frame," Gina said, grinning at her boyfriend. "It was almost done, but after we heard what happened, he got up early to finish it."

Rhonda took one look at it and burst into sobs. "My little girl is getting married," she blubbered, digging out a tissue from her pocket.

Norah rolled her eyes. "So why are you crying, Mom? Isn't that a good thing?"

Rhonda sniffled and waved a hand at her, then pressed the tissue to her eyes. Gary rushed over with another pack of tissues.

Zach nudged Ari with his elbow. "By the way, did you give her the um, you know, the *thing* yet?"

Ari's face froze. "Not . . . yet," he said slowly.

"Ah, geez, I'm sorry." Zach winced. "Did I mess up the surprise?"

"What surprise?" Carly bounced her gaze from Zach to Ari.

Ari clapped his friend's shoulder. "No problem. Actually, this is a good time to show her, since everyone's here." He excused himself and dashed into the kitchen.

Carly's insides were dancing a jitterbug. She couldn't imagine what Ari's surprise was.

A few minutes later, Ari returned and presented her with the secret project he'd been working on.

She held it up, then gasped with delight. It was a large wooden clock shaped exactly like a grilled cheese sandwich. Even the edges were painted to resemble cheese oozing out the sides.

"Oh, Ari, this is fantastic. You made this yourself?"

"With a lot of help from Zach," he said humbly. "He's the expert woodworker. My work is barely passable."

"Don't believe him, Carly," Zach put in. "He did nearly all of it himself. I only gave him a few pointers."

"Ari, this is amazing," she breathed. "It's for the restaurant, isn't it?" She turned it and held it up for everyone to see.

He shrugged and held up his hands. "Well, we can't have your customers thinking it's perpetually two forty-five, right?"

She laughed and leaned into him. "Right."

As the framed wedding invitation and the clock were passed around for everyone to admire, Carly felt her heart spill over with gratitude. She sent up a silent thank-you to the universe for all she'd been blessed with. It didn't get much better than this.

Leslie rose and headed for the kitchen. "I'm going to bring Quinne and Havarti inside. She's feeling a little down that we have to leave today."

I am, too, Carly thought. She'd grown so accustomed to having that little girl around that the house was going to seem empty without her.

A minute or so later, Quinne shuffled into the living room with Havarti at her heels. Though her usual sweet smile was absent, she greeted everyone politely.

Leslie pulled her close and smoothed her braided red hair. "Just think, sweetie. Next month we'll be coming back for Auntie Carly and Uncle Ari's wedding!"

Quinne leaned into Leslie. "I know," she said in a tiny voice.

Carly rose from the sofa and went over to Quinne, taking the little girl's hands into her own. "Hey, Quinne, Uncle Ari and I need a favor. We don't have anyone to carry our wedding rings during our marriage ceremony. Would you be willing to help us out?"

Quinne's expression went from glum to elated. "Yes! I can do that." She wrapped her arms around Carly's waist. Havarti barked his approval.

Her eyes shimmering, Leslie mouthed *thank you* to Carly.

Valerie folded her arms over her chest. "Hey, you two, it's about time you told us the rest of your honeymoon plans."

"Yeah, we've been patient long enough," Gina agreed, snagging another one of Grant's appetizers.

Carly and Ari exchanged sly glances.

"Okay," Carly said, "we won't keep you in suspense any longer. We already told you about the resort we'll be staying in. After we leave, we'll be driving to a place about an hour from there called Seniority Rules. It's a home for senior dogs whose owners didn't want to keep them any longer."

"Instead of going to a shelter," Ari explained, "they live out the rest of their days in a beautiful, dog-friendly home where they get all the love and care they deserve."

"For the four days we're there," Carly continued, "we'll be helping to take care of them. We'll feed them, play with them, even do some cleanup. The main thing is to shower them with attention and make them feel adored instead of abandoned."

Everyone fell silent, until Gina said, "You guys, that's—" She rushed over to hug Carly, her dark eyes leaking tears.

"I'm not surprised," Valerie put in. "You're two of the kindest, most generous people I've ever known."

The chief wrapped his arm around his wife. "Ditto," he said with a nod.

Rhonda raised her coffee mug in the air. "To Carly and Ari," she said, a quaver in her voice. "May they—" She sucked in a loud snuffle, and her voice broke. "Oh, never mind, just drink up," she burbled before swallowing a slug of coffee.

Everyone laughed, then followed her lead and joined in the toast.

Ari patted his flat abdomen. "Well, thanks to all the goodies you guys brought over," he said, "I've eaten enough today to last me all week."

"I know one thing I don't ever want to eat again," Carly quipped, "or at least for a very, very long time."

Ari squeezed her hand. "What's that, honey?"

"Pie."

CHAPTER 30

PASTOR PHOEBE JACKSON SMILED AT THE PAIR STANDING BEFORE HER.

"Do you, Carly Joan Hale, take this man, Ari Aaron Mitchell, to be your lawfully wedded husband . . ." The pastor's voice, crisp and well-modulated from decades of practice, resonated over the guests.

Carly barely heard her own voice responding, "I do." She felt as if she were floating about a foot off the ground, that's how happy she was. And when Ari slid the ring over her finger, her joy was complete.

The wedding was taking place on the stone terrace that overlooked the inn's sprawling back lawn. Wildflowers skirted the edge of the terrace. Beyond that was a granite birdbath in which a cherub poured water into an overflowing basin. They couldn't have found a more idyllic backdrop to their special day.

She and Ari had been prepared to hold the ceremony inside, if need be. But Mother Nature cooperated and delivered a sparkling, sunny day. Carly hoped it was a good omen.

After the pastor pronounced them husband and wife, Ari lifted Carly and swept her into his arms, and the two engaged in a passionate kiss. The guests clapped and hooted. Rhonda sobbed and cheered. Their photographer began darting around, snapping photos in rapid succession.

Carly gave her mom a hug, then bent down and gathered Quinne into her arms. "You did a great job presenting the rings, Quinne. Thank you so much for being part of our wedding."

Quinne's hazel eyes beamed. "You're welcome, Auntie Carly."

The little girl looked like an angel in a pale pink chiffon dress with a large white bow at the back. Leslie had styled her red hair in a French braid, securing it with a pink plastic butterfly.

Quinne fingered the delicate gold necklace she was wearing, with its heart-shaped charm engraved with a Q. "And thank you for my necklace. I decided I don't want to change my name. I think Quinne is the perfect name for me."

"I think so, too," Carly said.

Three days earlier, Leslie and Quinne had arrived with fantastic news. Quinne's adoption was official, but that wasn't all. Although Leslie had gotten an offer to work as a full-time hygienist for a busy dental group, she opted instead to take a summer job as a hygienist temp. She had plans she wasn't ready to share yet, but the excitement in her voice told Carly something big was up.

As flutes of bubbly made the rounds, the servers came around with trays of the bleu cheese tarts Grant had made. A week earlier, they'd been such a hit at the pre-wedding party that everyone begged Grant to make them for the wedding. He'd happily obliged.

After everyone sampled the appetizers, they strolled through the double doors that led into the dining room. The Grand Versailles Room, where the reception would take place, had been transformed into a land of enchantment.

Above the gargantuan stone fireplace, a garland of white hydrangeas and summer greenery stretched the length of the mantel. Tiny white lights glimmered among the leaves. Each linen-covered dining table was graced with a bouquet of blue and white hydrangeas nestled in a crystal vase.

For her own bouquet, Carly had chosen clusters of delicate white roses. Later she would do the traditional tossing of the bouquet. She knew Gina was hoping to catch it. Carly promised she'd do her best to aim it in her direction. No guarantees, though.

She and Ari sat at the head table, Rhonda and Gary on one side and Leslie and Quinne on the other. Norah and Nate, along with Gina and Zach, also had seats at the head table. Gazing around the room, Carly's heart filled once again. Everyone she loved had joined her and Ari to celebrate their marriage.

Grant's girlfriend Ellie had driven up from Boston to join him. His folks were there as well, sitting with Pastor Jackson, their longtime friend. They all sat at a table near the raised bandstand, where a trio of musicians would later play.

Suzanne and her hubby, Jake, chatted with Nina and Don. It didn't surprise Carly to see Don so animated. These days he smiled more often than he scowled. The difference Nina's friendship had made in his life was evident in his demeanor. In her quiet way, she encouraged him to be himself, not to sweat the small stuff.

Fred Holloway and Valerie sat with Fred's daughter, Dr. Anne, and her partner, Erika. It was Dr. Anne who'd encouraged Carly to adopt Havarti. These days, Carly couldn't imagine her life without the little dog. Also at their table were Joyce, Carly's former landlady, and Becca, who'd been Joyce's caretaker. After a year in assisted living, Joyce was thriving. She swam daily and read voraciously as the facility's book club president. Becca, who'd soon be a licensed nursing assistant, would be joining her there as a full-time employee. Carly would always be grateful to Joyce for selling her beautiful old home to her and Ari. Though no one could predict the future, the house had room enough for whatever came into their lives.

More dogs? Cats? Kids?

She'd need a crystal ball to know the answer to that.

A few weeks earlier, Carly received a hand-written note from Yvette Carter, thanking her for being so supportive after Brice's death. Phil Keaton had texted her photos of Moxie, who'd settled nicely into her new digs. It made Yvette realize she needed a kitty of her own, so that was next on her to-do list.

Dinner arrived, and everyone indulged in the inn's well-known featured dishes. When most everyone had finished, the musicians walked onto the bandstand and began warming up.

"Is it too soon to cut the cake?" Carly asked Ari.

He planted a kiss on her cheek. "Hey, it's our wedding. We can cut the cake whenever we want."

Rhonda, who overheard them, said, "I'm on this."

Ten minutes later, a tuxedoed waiter wheeled the wedding cake into the dining room. He rested the glass cart behind the head table.

"It's even more beautiful than I imagined," Carly breathed.

She and Ari rose from their seats and went over for a closer look. Guests began gathering around them.

The three-tiered cake was a masterpiece, adorned with sugary strands of bright yellow frosting buttercups that cascaded around the layers. The cake topper with the bride, groom, and dog had everyone grinning. It reminded Carly that one guest was missing—Havarti. The powers that be at the inn hadn't been keen on violating the health code to allow the dog into the dining room.

Without fanfare, Carly cut the first slice of cake. The guests clapped as she and Ari each ate a forkful. After that, two servers took over and cut enough slices to feed the guests.

Next, trays of cookies were placed on each table. Last Christmas, Nina had promised to bake the cookies for Carly's wedding. With each one shaped like a different flower and intricately frosted, they were even more fabulous than the ones she made for the eatery.

While everyone enjoyed coffee or drinks with their dessert, the band began to play. Ari held out his hand to Carly. Taking the dance floor, they swayed to Lady Gaga's "Always Remember Us This Way."

After that, the music ramped up, and the dance floor turned lively. Rhonda and Gary led the pack, doing their version of a 1970s hustle. After everything her mom had been through, it made Carly nearly weep to see her so happy.

Eventually the band took a break, and everyone ambled back to their tables. All except Grant and his dad, who walked quietly onto the bandstand. Grant's cello and Alvin Robinson's violin had been tucked away in a corner. To Carly's surprise, Nate joined them on the bandstand. Intrigued, she reached over and took Ari's hand.

When the song began to play, Carly knew immediately what it was. His gaze on Carly and Ari, Nate began to croon "And I Love Her" in his silky tenor voice.

The guests fell silent, all except Rhonda, who cried quietly into a tissue. When the song ended, everyone cheered and clapped. "Encore!" someone called out, but Nate only smiled and returned to his table.

"Your dad really is watching over you," Ari whispered in Carly's ear.

"Over us," she murmured, clasping his hand.

Gina stomped over to Carly on her four-inch heels. "Hey, lady, when are you going to throw that bouquet?"

"The band *is* on a break," Ari pointed out.

"Okay, but I'll need a few minutes," Carly said slyly, lifting her bouquet from the table.

Rhonda came up behind Carly and squeezed her daughter's shoulders. "Leave it to me. I'll take it from here."

Carly smiled. Who needed a wedding planner when they had Rhonda Hale Clark for a mom?

"Thanks, Mom. Remember, everyone can join. Not just singles and women."

Rhonda walked over near the bandstand and clapped her hands to get everyone's attention. "The bride is ready to throw the bouquet," she announced. "If you'd like to participate, please gather here." She indicated the area in front of her. "Everyone is welcome. That includes the men and the non-singles."

Murmurs rose from the guests, then several of them, men and women, hopped off their chairs to join in the fun. Leslie guided Quinne to the front of the group.

When Carly was ready, she separated the multiple strands of ribbons streaming from her bouquet. Her back to the group, she tossed it behind her. When she turned around, the sight that greeted her made her heart sing.

The bouquet had separated into a dozen small clusters of white roses, each with a ribbon tied at the stems.

Quinne's face broke into a huge grin, and she raced over to Leslie. "Look, Mommy, I got one!"

Norah had one, too, but Gina did not. So why was Gina grinning like a circus clown?

Carly suddenly realized why. His mini bouquet tucked into the breast pocket of his tux, Zach lifted Gina into his arms and swung her in a circle.

Arm in arm, the pair went over to Carly, their faces alight with elation. "We didn't want to interfere with your wedding by telling you sooner," Gina said in a low voice, "but we got engaged last night, after the rehearsal."

Carly nearly collapsed with the happy news. She felt tears poke at her eyelids as she embraced them both.

"Please don't tell anyone yet," Gina pleaded. "This is your celebration, not ours. After you and Ari get back from your honeymoon, we'll all celebrate together."

Carly promised to keep it under wraps, except to tell Ari. She was so excited over the news she was nearly jumping out of her shoes.

The band resumed playing, and the wedding wound down. Glancing around, Carly noticed that Becca had disappeared. She wouldn't have left without Joyce, so where was she? Carly hoped nothing was wrong.

Carly was weaving her way over to Joyce when a loud squeal erupted from the dance floor. Heart thrumming, she swerved toward the sound. She saw Quinne racing toward the double doors that led outside to the terrace. In the next moment, Quinne dropped to her knees as Havarti, his leash trailing behind him, flew into her arms.

Ari went over to Carly and smiled. "Becca borrowed my key. Your mom spoke to one of the kitchen managers and got permission, but only for a short visit. But they can stay outside on the veranda as long as they want."

Carly laughed. "Mom sure is a miracle worker, isn't she?"

"She must be," Ari said softly. "She made you."

• • •

"I'm glad we decided to head to Maine tomorrow instead of today," Carly said, her head resting on Ari's shoulder.

They sat outside on the terrace on one of the tufted patio sofas. The sun was still high but edging toward the west. Birds chattered in the surrounding trees, and the wildflowers moved gently in the light breeze.

"Yeah, me too," Ari agreed, taking her hand. "We'll start out fresh tomorrow. That'll still give us time for a relaxing afternoon at the beach."

Other than Carly and Ari, only Leslie, Quinne, and Havarti remained at the inn. Leslie had asked for a few minutes of private time with the newlyweds before they all left.

Quinne was sitting on the lawn with Havarti, her pink dress rumpled beneath her. She looked a bit tired, no doubt from the day's activities. Starting the following day, Leslie and Quinne would be moving into Carly and Ari's house for the week as live-in dogsitters.

A glass of ice water in hand, Leslie strolled over and pulled up a chair beside the couple. Her dark eyes shimmering, she looked so much like Ari that it made Carly's heart wrench.

"I wanted to give you our news before you left for Maine," Leslie began. "I finished taking the exams in Vermont that I needed to pass to be licensed here. Last week I had two lengthy Zoom interviews with a dentist in Bennington. She was impressed with my résumé, and with my work history. Her longtime hygienist is retiring at the end of August. She wants someone experienced to take her place. I'm going to meet her in person this week at her office."

Carly sat up straight. "Les, does that mean . . . you'll be moving to Vermont?"

Leslie's smile nearly outshone the sun. "It does, if the job pans out. If it doesn't, I'll keep temping until I find a job, but we really want to make Vermont our home."

His eyes full of emotion, Ari went over and wrapped his sister in a hug. "My God, Les, this is such good news. We can go back to being a family again, even better this time." He went back to sitting with Carly, who was trying unsuccessfully to hold back tears.

Carly blinked. "I can't imagine a better sendoff for our honeymoon than this," she said, a tremor in her voice.

Leslie went on. "Quinne and I will be checking out apartments this week. For now, I'm hoping to rent with an option to buy. There's a condo village in Bennington that looks perfect for us." She signaled to Quinne to join them.

The little girl came over and squished herself onto Leslie's chair. She stuck out her lower lip. "I got grass stain on my dress, Mommy. I'm sorry."

Leslie kissed the little girl's hair. "Well, I spilled coffee on my dress," she said lightly. "Don't worry, honey. The dry cleaner will get all the stains out."

Quinne smiled and snuggled even closer to Leslie. Havarti plopped his furry body onto Quinne's lap, making it a threesome.

Ari pulled his bride close. "Well, you're stuck with me now," he murmured in her ear. "Any second thoughts?"

Carly shook her head, unable to speak. She didn't need to. Every cell in her body was singing out loud, rejoicing for a life overflowing with love.

RECIPES

Valerie's Croque Monsieur

Carly was delighted when Valerie offered to create a French grilled cheese. While this recipe is fussier than making a typical grilled cheese, the result is a decadent myriad of butter, tangy cheese, and smoky ham—so rich you might think it has a bank account!

This recipe is for two sandwiches, but the ingredients can easily be doubled to make four.

Ingredients for béchamel sauce

2 tablespoons unsalted butter
⅛ cup all-purpose flour
¾ cup whole milk
Salt and pepper to taste
⅛ teaspoon Dijon mustard
Dash of ground nutmeg (about ¼ teaspoon)

Ingredients for the sandwiches

4 slices of white bread (sourdough works well; avoid using a soft, delicate bread or thick slices)
4 slices of high-quality smoky ham (or any good-quality ham), sliced thin
½ cup grated Edam (you may substitute Gruyere or Swiss cheese, if desired)
⅛ cup grated Parmesan cheese

To make the béchamel sauce

Melt the butter in saucepan over medium heat.

Whisk in the flour and cook it for about 2 minutes, or until lightly golden (don't overcook).

Gradually add the milk, stirring well until the mixture is smooth.

Continue stirring and cooking until the sauce is thickened.

Add salt and pepper to taste (don't oversalt).

Remove the pan from the heat and whisk in the mustard and nutmeg.

Set aside the pan.

To make the sandwiches

Preheat oven to 425 degrees F.

Line a baking tray with parchment paper.

Spread the béchamel on four slices of bread, going all the way to the edges; place two of those slices on the prepared tray (sauce side up).

Top each of the first two slices with two slices of ham and half the grated Edam.

Sprinkle sandwiches with half the Parmesan cheese.

Place the remaining two slices of bread atop the first two, béchamel side up.

Top sandwiches with the remaining Edam and the remaining Parmesan.

Bake in the oven for about 5 minutes, or until the cheese is melted. Turn the oven to Broil and broil until the top is bubbly and golden, approximately 3 minutes. For best results, eat immediately.

Serve with your favorite salad and a cup of tomato soup. You'll have a meal fit for royalty.

Because of its consistency, you'll need to eat your croque monsieur with a knife and fork. Otherwise, you'll end up with a gooey mess on your hands!

There are many recipes for a croque monsieur, some more complex than others. With Grant's guidance, Valerie designed this one for ease of preparation in a busy, fast-moving eatery.

Grant's Bleu Cheese Tarts

In keeping with the traditional wedding motif of "Something borrowed, something blue," Grant wanted to prepare an exceptional treat for Carly and Ari's pre-wedding party, and for the wedding reception. Using bleu cheese as the primary ingredient, he created these tantalizingly delicious appetizers that got rave reviews from the guests. If the blend of apple and onion seems odd, don't worry—you'll find that it's a marriage made in culinary heaven.

Although Grant makes his own phyllo dough, he knows that it's a labor-intensive task that takes some practice. To save time, he suggests using the miniature phyllo shells available in the freezer section at your supermarket (a 1.9-ounce package yields 15 tart shells). If you're a talented baker, or adventurous enough to make your own phyllo dough, some great recipes can be found online.

Once you serve these gourmet treats, your guests will be clamoring for you to make them often!

2 teaspoons butter, preferably unsalted
1 large Granny Smith apple
1 medium onion, finely chopped
1 cup of crumbled bleu cheese
4 tablespoons finely chopped roasted walnuts
½ teaspoon salt
1 package (1.9 ounces) of frozen miniature phyllo tart shells
Dried basil

Preheat oven to 350 degrees F.

Melt butter in a nonstick skillet over medium heat.

Add apple and onion; cook and stir until tender (3 to 5 minutes) and remove from heat.

Stir in bleu cheese, *three* tablespoons of the walnuts, and salt.

Spoon a rounded tablespoon of the mixture into each phyllo shell, and place them on an ungreased baking sheet; bake for 5 minutes.

Remove from oven and sprinkle with the remaining walnuts and a light touch of dried basil; bake another 2 to 3 minutes or until lightly browned.

Serve warm out of the oven. After they're cooled, they can also be frozen in a freezer container, separating layers with wax paper.

About the Author

As a child, Linda Reilly practically existed on grilled cheese sandwiches, and today they remain her comfort food of choice. Raised in a sleepy town in the Berkshires of Massachusetts, she retired from the world of real estate closings and title examinations to spend more time writing mysteries. Linda is a member of Sisters in Crime, Mystery Writers of America, and Cat Writers' Association. She lives in southern New Hampshire with her two feline assistants, both of whom enjoy prancing over her laptop to assist with editing. Visit her on the web at lindareillyauthor.com or on Facebook at facebook.com/Lindasreillyauthor. She loves hearing from readers.

Made in the USA
Thornton, CO
07/13/25 19:49:48

259e3f54-7ae1-4c1c-b3c3-26c3555c5bdbR01